Bolan sprinted across the roof, heading for the fire escape.

A pistol cracked, and he heard the whisper of a bullet as it streaked past his cheek. One shooter was behind him when he turned, and Bolan saw another peeking from the rooftop access doorway. He sent the shooter spinning away with a 3-round burst, his white shirt spouting scarlet, then sent three more rounds to make the doorway peeper duck back out of sight.

With ammunition running low, he glanced over the parapet, saw no shooters prepared to pick him off as he descended and swung out onto the fire escape. Gripping the side rails with his hands and bracing the insteps of his shoes against them, Bolan slid down until he landed in a crouch fifty feet below.

Gunshots echoed above him, a reminder that he had no time to waste. Raising the MP5K's muzzle, Bolan fired a burst and saw a face fly back.

His rented wheels waited for him half a block away.

Bolan ran.

DON PENDLETON'S MACK BOLAN®

NINJA ASSAULT

A GOLD EAGLE BOOK FROM
W☉RLDWIDE®

TORONTO • NEW YORK • LONDON
AMSTERDAM • PARIS • SYDNEY • HAMBURG
STOCKHOLM • ATHENS • TOKYO • MILAN
MADRID • WARSAW • BUDAPEST • AUCKLAND

Recycling programs
for this product may
not exist in your area.

First edition July 2015

ISBN-13: 978-0-373-61578-0

Special thanks and acknowledgment to
Mike Newton for his contribution to this work.

Ninja Assault

Only the dead have seen the end of war.
—Plato

Human predators will never be eradicated. A new crop pops up when the old one is cut down. There is no cure for the plague of evil and avarice, but I can fight the symptoms when they surface, wherever they surface.
—Mack Bolan

For Captain William D. Swenson,
1st Battalion, 32nd Infantry Regiment

PROLOGUE

Atlantic City, New Jersey

Tommy Wolff leaned closer to the window, peering at his face and raising one manicured hand to prod the pouches underneath his ice-blue eyes. He'd chosen Kisdon lighting for the penthouse bathroom, fixtures planned with flattery in mind, but lights could only do so much.

Time for a touch-up there, he thought, and made a mental note to fit it in.

Not that the ladies waiting for him in the bedroom would object to pouchy eyes. They'd been well paid to service him, with cash and with cocaine. They'd do whatever Wolff required, as he required it, and they'd damn well like it.

Hell, why not? They hadn't seen his *schmeckel* yet, and they were bound to be impressed.

The ladies always were. No work required in that department.

Wolff retreated from the mirror, taking in the long view of himself from neck to knees. His time spent in the private gym had paid off handsomely. At fifty-five, he now looked better than he had in twenty years, his stamina was better, and he rarely needed a Viagra boost to keep the ladies happy.

Almost never.

Tommy Wolff preferred his women young, and—he

had a guy who double-checked IDs in order to protect him from a statutory rape charge. Wolff had enough to think about on any given day, with IRS leeches and spies from the state Casino Control Commission crawling up his ass. The very last thing that he needed was to wind up on TV, doing the perp walk over some sweet thing who'd lied about her age to get a little taste of power.

Okay, not a *little* taste. But, still.

Wolff took his new robe off its hook behind the bathroom door. *Kimono* was the proper term, he understood, a black silk number, knee-length, with those baggy sleeves that stopped short of his wrists and made him feel like he should trade it for a larger size. Across the shoulders, looping down around his right hip, an embroidered wolf was snapping at a frightened lamb.

He liked that image. Liked it very much indeed.

The robe—kimono—was a gift from one of Wolff's new partners in Japan. They'd pooled resources to erect a new resort in Tokyo, where current law prohibited casino gambling, but with nudges in the right direction and strategic contributions to the major players, rules could always change. Meanwhile, there was pachinko, mahjong, and *kōei kyōgi*, betting on a list of "public sports" that covered racing horses, bicycles, speedboats and cars.

Wolff slipped on the kimono, nothing underneath except his tanned, taut flesh, and broke eye contact with the mirror. Too much self-examination could be bad for anyone.

He thought about the young women in his bedroom, high atop Nero's Hotel-Casino, with its sweeping panorama of the boardwalk. "Caesar's" had been taken, but he'd found a Roman emperor who suited him, regardless. Nucky Johnson never dreamed of anything like Nero's when he ran Atlantic City for the syndicate, and it was all completely legal now.

Well, close enough.

The girls—one blonde, one redhead, one brunette—had suddenly gone quiet in the bedroom. Frowning, Wolff considered whether he had left them too much coke to play with in his absence, but he doubted it. Besides, if one of them had OD'd, he'd expect the others to be panicking.

"You little bitches better not be dozing off," he muttered to himself. "You've got a long, hard night ahead of you."

Longer than any of the three expected. Harder, too.

The *schmeckel* humor always made Wolff smile.

He lost the smile as he stepped through the bathroom doorway, turning toward the bed. It was the emperor size, imported from Ireland, forty-two square feet of padded playground on a hand-carved wooden frame, with satin sheets that had been white when Wolff went to the bathroom.

Why were they red now, and dripping on the carpet?

Wolff blinked, found two of the girls stretched out across the bed diagonally, side by side. It looked as if they'd been engaging in a little foreplay, but it hadn't lasted long. The redhead, lying on her back, had one arm raised as if to shield her face. The other arm was... where, again?

Wolff felt the Lobster Thermidor and Provençal asparagus he'd eaten half an hour earlier trying to come back on him, but he kept it down with effort, taking in the gash below the redhead's chin and shifting toward the nubile body sprawled beside her.

Someone had been more efficient with the brunette, taking off her head completely, propping it atop two pillows, wide blank eyes turned toward the bathroom doorway where Wolff stood. As far as he could tell, that was the only wound she'd suffered, but it had obviously done the job.

A mewling from his left brought Wolff around to face the blonde. She stood before him, naked as the day she'd come into the world but far from innocent, flanked by two men no taller than herself—say five foot six, if that—all dressed in black from head to toe.

Not black *suits*, mind you. These were some kind of commando costumes, maybe one piece, though Wolff couldn't really tell. They both wore snug, formfitting hoods like ski masks, only thinner, that hid everything except their glinting eyes. And there was something odd about their shoes that took a second glance to recognize: split toes, of all things, which was new in Wolff's experience.

But what he really focused on was the long sword each man held in his right hand. *Katana* they were called, as if it mattered now. Americans normally called them samurai swords.

"Jesus Christ."

It came out as a whisper, barely audible even to Wolff as he spoke. The picture set before him clarified itself immediately, even if he still had trouble grasping its reality. He had a shitload of security downstairs to stop this kind of thing from happening, yet here he stood, confronting death times two.

Negotiation wouldn't work. He knew that much instinctively. They'd come too far for that. Blood had been spilled, and only more blood could erase the problem.

Now, the only question: Was he fast enough?

Wolff kept a Glock 31 in the top nightstand drawer, to the right of his bed. It was chambered for .357 SIG rounds, loaded with Triton Quik-Shok bullets, and Wolff had practiced using it. There was no safety switch to fumble with in an emergency, just fifteen rounds in the magazine and one up the spout.

If he could reach the piece before one of the swordsmen got to him, Wolff thought he had a fighting chance.

Big *if*.

And standing there, considering it, only wasted precious time.

He bolted for the nightstand, heard a squeal behind him, from the blonde, and didn't turn to watch her dying. Bimbos were a dime a dozen in AC, but Tommy Wolff was one in a million.

An endangered species, at the moment.

There was no time to circle the emperor bed, so Wolff clambered across it, mattress springing underneath his feet, trying to topple him. The dead girls lolled and rocked, the redhead's one arm flopping as if reaching out to grab him by the ankle. Bloody satin squelched beneath his bare soles, slippery and treacherous. Wolff heard one of the men in black behind him, rushing toward him, and he vaulted toward the nightstand, stumbling on a bare, firm thigh and plunging headlong toward the finish line.

His forehead struck the nightstand's edge, received a stunning gash that added Wolff's blood to the mix, but he pushed past the pain and sudden dizziness, ripped at the drawer and pulled it free as he went down on to the floor. It banged against his chest, more pain, and Wolff upended it, dumping its contents on his torso, littering the black kimono.

Condoms. Moist towelettes. A vibrator.

The Glock.

Wolff grasped it, flung the empty nightstand drawer away from him, and raised the pistol as one of the black-clad swordsmen loomed above him. Finger on the trigger with its built-in safety, he was just about to fire when steel flashed, and a bolt of icy pain shot through his upraised arm.

Wolff saw his right hand flying, still clutching the Glock, and barked with startled laughter as his index finger clenched the trigger, firing one shot toward a limited edition of Picasso's *Buste de Femme au Chapeau Bleu*, drilling the woman's offset nose. All things considered, not a bad shot overall.

Wolff saw the sleek *katana* rising, flinging drops of crimson toward the ceiling, while his wrist pumped gouts and torrents of it. In the microseconds he had left to think about it, Tommy saw the story of his life written in blood.

For one last time, he'd gambled and he'd lost.

CHAPTER ONE

Atlantic City, Two Days Later

The boardwalk simmered, thronged with tourists on this summer afternoon. Mack Bolan didn't mind the crowd, divided between gamblers seeking action and the families a person saw in any tourist town when school was out and vacation rolled around. Young couples held hands, sharing ice cream cones as if they were a promise of more intimate activities to come, while aged seniors passed with cans and shopping bags, regarding youth with envy.

Bolan, for his part, was wary.

Nothing special there, since he was always wary, anywhere he went.

That was the price of waking up each day in a hostile world.

Before Hurricane Sandy, the Atlantic City boardwalk had extended from Absecon Inlet in the north to Ventnor City, six and a half miles southward. Rampant nature had wiped out the promenade's northern end, but the rest—built in 1870 and billed as the "Showplace of America"—had managed to survive unscathed. The vast casinos facing the North Atlantic had ignored that storm, as they'd ignored all other challenges from God and man since they were legalized, back in the 1970s.

AC had been the new Las Vegas in those days, and while the new had quickly faded, tourism declining with renovations in Las Vegas and erection of new gambling palaces in Connecticut, the boardwalk and its temples of mammon remained the city's backbone and its throbbing, greedy heart. The flood of cash and service jobs had done little for the middle class, much less the residents of ghettos where resentment smoldered, ever ready to ignite.

Back in 2005, *Forbes* magazine had called Atlantic City "dangerous and depraved," boasting a crime rate triple that of any other US city, double on the murder rate. While gross gambling revenue increased each year, the number of casino jobs declined.

AC had bet its future on the gaming tables. Some would say the town had lost its soul.

Of course, it hadn't started in the seventies, by any means. That was the era when casinos had been legalized—controlled, in theory, by the guardians of civilized society. Supporters of the scheme had looked at Vegas, saw the neon and the bottom line without considering the downside, and had rushed ahead to claim their places at the trough. But vice had put down deep, abiding roots decades before a modern crop of architects had dreamed the Taj Mahal or the Borgata, run by men who settled scores with lead, instead of million-dollar lawsuits.

Atlantic City was the midwife to America's crime syndicate, born on that very boardwalk, Bolan knew, during May of 1929, when every hood who mattered in the eastern half of the United States had come to hammer out their plans for the remaining years of Prohibition. Those who weren't invited had been killed within a year or so, clearing the dead wood as a younger generation rose to claim its due.

Bolan was standing outside Nero's when another tall man stopped beside him, frowning from the shadow of a gray fedora. "Penny for them," said the new arrival.

"I keep watching out for Nucky Johnson."

"Thompson."

"Johnson," Bolan said again. "They changed it for the TV series."

"Ah. Wrong century, regardless," Hal Brognola said.

They shook hands, old friends and combatants in a struggle that would outlast both of them. They knew the rules, expected no heavenly trumpets to declare their final victory and took it one day at a time.

"So, this is where it all went down," Brognola said, tilting his head back, squinting at the sharp metallic gleam of penthouse windows high above, where seagulls wheeled and screamed.

"The Wolff thing," Bolan said.

"None other. Four dead in the penthouse, three more from security before the hit team made it all the way upstairs."

"Messy."

"But quiet," Brognola replied. "They knew what they were doing. Never fired a shot."

"On CNN, they're talking stab wounds."

"Make that *sword* wounds, and you've got it right."

Bolan had no response to that. He waited, knowing the big Fed would get around to it in his own time.

"You know much about Tommy Wolff?" Brognola asked.

"A younger version of The Donald or Steve Wynn. More cash than he could spend in twenty lifetimes."

"And he didn't even manage one."

"I'm guessing that the Bureau and the state police are on it."

"Absolutely," Brognola agreed. "And getting nowhere."

"Why's that?"

"Well, for starters, Wolff and all the rest of them were killed by ninjas."

"The real deal."

"Looks like. Black tights and balaclavas, swords and split-toe shoes. It's all on video."

"So, no ID on any of the perps."

"Not even close. They've got ICE working on it, too, the passport angle."

"ICE" was Immigration and Customs Enforcement, part of the Homeland Security umbrella that had theoretically shielded America from foreign attacks since September 2011. In practice, Bolan knew, safety required much more than uniformed guards and a roster of alphabet agencies.

"They're thinking Japanese, then?" Bolan asked. "Ninja originals?"

"Why not? We know they're out there."

Right. Bolan had faced some personally, once upon a time, and lived to tell about it. If he was allowed to tell. If anybody would believe it.

"So?"

"I sent a coded file to your smartphone, when you get a chance to take a look," Brognola informed him. "Same password as usual."

"You want to run the basics past me?"

"Abridged version, Wolff had been negotiating with a company in Tokyo to build a Nero's Far East, matching this one, the joint he's got—well, *had*—in Vegas, and the Nero's San Juan, down in Puerto Rico."

"There's no legit casino gambling in Japan," Bolan stated.

"Say he was hopeful, betting on a sea change."

"Or he had some other kind of action in the works."

"Or that."

"Which was it?"

"All I hear, so far, is that he'd stepped on certain toes in Tokyo. The Sumiyoshi-kai, for starters."

"Big toes, then."

"And highly sensitive."

The Sumiyoshi-kai was Japan's second-largest Yakuza family, claiming some twenty thousand oath-bound members and at least that many hangers-on. As number two, they tried harder, chasing the larger, stronger Yamaguchi-gumi, while the Inagawa-kai snapped at their heels.

"Still, taking out a guy Wolff's size, with his high profile…"

"Sends a very public message," Brognola filled in for him.

"Why do I get the feeling this isn't a one-off?" Bolan asked.

"Because you know your way around. Six months ago, out in LA, Merv Mendelbaum dropped out of sight. He hasn't surfaced yet. The family's been sitting on it, but they're lawyered up and getting out the carving knives."

"That's Mendelbaum of Goldstone Entertainment?"

Brognola nodded. "Owner of casinos in Las Vegas, Reno, one up in New London and another in Biloxi."

"So, coincidence?"

"Goldstone was also putting feelers out to Tokyo, feeling its way around the National Diet, schmoozing with the prime minister and leaders of his party."

"More toes bruised," Bolan surmised.

"The Yakuza likes things the way they are, most forms of gambling banned but readily available through outlets they control. They stand to lose a fortune—not a small one—from another US occupation."

"What about their operations stateside?"

"They'd love to have a stake in gambling where it's

legal, if they don't lose anything at home. Right now, they mostly smuggle methamphetamine and heroin into the States, and take guns home."

Bolan knew that Japan's gun control laws ranked among the world's strictest. Police estimated there were 710,000 firearms in civilian hands, scattered among 128 million citizens—or one gun for every 180 Japanese. America, by contrast, had at least 270 million guns floating around the civilian population, one for every 1.2 men, women and children. The upshot was 32,000 gun deaths per year in the States, versus eleven annually in Japan.

Coincidence?

Unlikely.

Bolan brought his mind back to the topic on the table. "So, the Sumiyoshi-kai could benefit from taking out a few top men," he said. "Keep US gaming corporations out of Tokyo and cause a power vacuum over here."

"It cuts both ways," Brognola said. "Just like a sword."

"Suspects?"

"They're listed in the file I sent you, but we don't have any solid evidence. The Sumiyoshi-kai had *kyodai*—'big brothers,' similar to capos in the Mafia—both here and in Las Vegas. If the family killed Wolff and Mendelbaum, they'll be the place to start."

Brognola didn't have to say the rest, but Bolan looked downrange. "What about carrying the fight back home?" he asked.

"It's not my place to second-guess a soldier on the ground," the big Fed said. "But obviously, if we have a chance to make the problem go away, at least for now…"

He let the sentence trail off, staring up at the casino. There was no need to explain what both of them already knew from long experience.

The predators would never be eradicated. Some defect

within humankind itself produced a new crop every time the old one was cut down. Evil could be beaten down and held at bay, but it could never be extracted from the human genome. There was no cure, no inoculation, for the plague of avarice and cruelty that lurked behind the thin facade of "civilized" society.

No cure, perhaps, but he could fight the symptoms when and where they surfaced.

Starting now.

The file was waiting for him, just as Brognola had said.

Roughly two hundred years older than Sicily's Mafia, Japan's homegrown version of organized crime had arisen from a merger of two criminal classes: the *bakuto*, itinerant gamblers, and the *tekiya*, peddlers who furnished goods and services proscribed by feudal law. After resisting for a time, the Edo Dynasty had bowed to the realities of daily life, legitimized the syndicates and granted their leaders—known as *oyabun*, "fathers, or godfathers"—the right to carry short *wakizashi* swords, while the larger *katanas* were reserved for full-fledged samurai. The overall syndicate's name, *ya-ku-za*, translated as "8-9-3," a losing hand in *Oicho-Kabu*, the Japanese version of blackjack.

This day, the Yakuza consisted of some seventy-odd rival clans, fighting for turf in the shadow of Japan's top three families. Only the Sumiyoshi-kai concerned Bolan as he began to scan Brognola's file.

The outfit's *oyabun* was Kazuo Takumi, based in Tokyo, which kept him near the seat of government and all the major economic action. Sixty-one years old, he'd earned his reputation the old-fashioned way, by wading in the blood of rivals, and had risen to the status of a recognized philanthropist whose generosity to charity was known throughout Japan. He held shares in a score of thriving companies and sat on several of their boards, ensuring that the firms he graced were never short of cheap materials or healthy profit margins.

The *oyabun*'s only son and heir apparent was Toi Takumi, something of a cipher in the file Brognola had provided. He had earned a playboy's reputation in his early twenties, but now, approaching thirty, he had dropped out of the social scene and rarely showed his face in public.

Growing into his position as the next boss of the Sumiyoshi-kai, perhaps.

Or was it something else?

Atlantic City's "big brother" was Noboru Machii, thirty-one, an ex-con who'd done time for smuggling methamphetamine before a key witness recanted and committed suicide—*seppuku* in the native tongue. That had blown the prosecution's case, freed Machii on appeal and helped restore the honor of the dead man's family—along with a substantial contribution to their bank account, supposedly the payoff from a life insurance policy that didn't quibble over self-destruction in a righteous cause.

Now, Machii had a foothold on the boardwalk and was bound for bigger things, it seemed. If he could hand a piece of Tommy Wolff's casino empire to the Sumiyoshi-kai, he would be well positioned for a top spot in the syndicate. Who could predict what might transpire when old Takumi finally cashed in his chips?

It was a gamble, right, and Machii had one strike against him, going in.

He didn't know Bolan had dealt himself into the game.

CHAPTER TWO

Sunrise Enterprises, Atlantic City

The office complex wasn't much to look at in comparison to the casinos standing tall along the boardwalk, one block closer to the ocean. Just four stories high, a drab rectangle painted beige, it gave no hint that anyone inside was tinkering with local history or planning to tap a vein of gold from the exalted gaming industry that kept Atlantic City on the map.

To spot those signs, a person had to look behind the stucco, maybe close one eye and make believe there was no weedy vacant lot next door, where homeless people had been known to light a bonfire on a winter's night. A person had to know about Sunrise, and it was helpful if there was a team on tap like Hal Brognola's crew at Stony Man, hidden within the Blue Ridge Mountains of Virginia, picking secrets from the cloud, thin air, wherever, and reviewing them until they all made sense.

In this case Sunrise Enterprises was a paper company, incorporated like so many others of its kind in Delaware, existing for the sole purpose of purchasing and selling stock in other companies. On paper, it was all strictly routine, aboveboard, and the company filed tax returns on time, paying its debts without complaint.

Look deeper, though, and Sunrise was an offshoot of another company, the G.E.A. Consortium, whose initials stood for Greater East Asia. It was just a fluke, perhaps, that during the 1930s and '40s, Japan's imperial masters had called their captured territory in the Far East and South Pacific the Greater East Asia Co-Prosperity Sphere.

Maybe.

Look deeper yet, and G.E.A. was owned by three middle-aged members of the Sumiyoshi-kai, including the family's administrative officer, its legal adviser and its top accountant. Needless to say, they served at Kazuo Takumi's pleasure and could be replaced at any time they ceased to please him.

Break it down. The drab four-story box was Takumi's nerve center in Atlantic City. Strings were pulled inside those offices that ended human lives and had potential to disrupt the city's—and, perhaps, the state's—economy.

Bolan saw two approaches to the viper's nest. He could obliterate it, salt the earth and scatter any stray survivors, or he could attempt a soft probe, look for opportunities to gain further intelligence and plan his final killing stroke accordingly.

On second thought, why not combine the two ideas?

One item in his bag of tricks was an infinity transmitter, designed to monitor conversations within a room through its telephone line, whether or not the phone itself was in use. Its name derived from the fact that phone line transmissions could be received at an infinite distance, unlike other bugs with a finite physical range.

But it still required that Bolan get inside to plant the bug.

And for that, he needed a diversion.

The internet provided a schematic drawing of the office block, showing him where and how to cut the building's juice. There were battery-powered emergency lights on all floors, but severing the trunk line would deactivate security cameras found on all floors, while leaving the fire alarms live. If he could generate sufficient smoke to rout the office occupants, it all came down to a matter of time and nerve.

Sorting through his mobile arsenal Bolan selected weapons first. He wasn't planning an attack, per se, but meant to be prepared for any unforeseen eventuality. An MP-5 K submachine gun fit the bill ideally—"K" for *kurz*, or "short," in German, easily concealable even with a suppressor screwed on to its threaded muzzle. He would wear it on a shoulder sling, beneath a lightweight jacket, backed up by a Glock 17 that was lighter, easier to handle and loaded a higher-capacity magazine than the Beretta he had carried into countless other skirmishes.

For the diversion proper, Bolan chose four AN-M8 smoke grenades, each filled with nineteen ounces of Type C hexachloroethane—HC. Each cylindrical canister would emit thick white smoke for 105 to 150 seconds following ignition, enough to choke a four-story building's ventilation ducts and keep any occupants scurrying for the nearest exit once fire alarms set them in motion.

Getting in and out before firefighters reached the scene was Bolan's problem.

Make that getting in and out *alive.*

NOBORU MACHII FELT like celebrating. He had carried out the order from his *oyabun* without a hitch, had seen the two imported killers off, beginning their long flight back to Japan, and felt he had the local situation well under control. It was too early yet, of course, for a direct approach to Tommy Wolff's estate, but Machii had his battery of lawyers hovering, gauging the time and monitoring every move by Wolff's board of directors since the penthouse massacre, the night before last. As expected, there was posturing and jockeying for power, but Machii held the winning hand.

He'd spent the past eight months uncovering the secret sins of every member on the board at Wolff Consolidated. There were seven of them, and Machii knew them well, although they'd never met. In fact, he knew them better than their partners, wives and children did.

Machii knew that one of them collected child pornography and traveled once a year to Bangkok, where his indiscretions had been filmed. Another had been stealing from the company, a third selling insider knowledge to the firm's competitors for half again his yearly salary. A fourth was what Americans presumed to call a "high-functioning" alcoholic, though he had not functioned well enough the night he struck and killed a homeless African-American with his Mercedes-Benz in Newark. No suspicion had attached to him so far, but that could change within an instant.

So it went, on down the line, with six of seven board members. The seventh was above reproach—a miracle, of sorts—but he could not prevail once Machii had secured a majority of the directors to support his takeover of Wolff Consolidated. In addition to the preservation of their guilty secrets, he would promise them secure positions and the standard golden parachutes in place.

As if a written contract could protect them when Machii tired of having them around.

He would have another kind of contract waiting for them then, and nothing any lawyer said would rescue adversaries of the Sumiyoshi-kai. Machii had taught Tommy Wolff that lesson, and if the dead man's underlings refused to learn from his example, their deaths would be tantamount to suicide.

As far as celebrating went, however, it was premature. The prize was now within his grasp, but he had not secured it yet. Until the transfer of authority was finalized, Machii could not rightfully claim victory.

"How long shall we wait for the approach?" Tetsuya Watanabe asked.

Machii's lieutenant was younger, still learning the art of patience. Left unchecked, he might have overplayed their hand, but he inevitably followed orders from his boss.

"After the funeral is soon enough," Machii said. "A few more days will do no harm. If we approach them prematurely, they might panic and do something foolish."

"I understand."

Of course, Watanabe understood. The order had been simple and required no verbal answer, but he still observed the standard courtesy.

Noboru had another thought. "We should send flowers, yes? Preserve proper appearances, and—"

Suddenly, the lights went out. The air-conditioning gave a little gasp and died.

Machii swiveled toward his office window, with its view of the boardwalk casinos. Lights were blazing in the massive pleasure palaces, along the piers and on Atlantic Boulevard below. Rising from his chair, he told Watanabe, "It's our building only. Find out what is wrong."

"Yes, sir!" Watanabe was halfway to the office door when he acknowledged the command, already reaching for the knob. Beyond the door, the hallway's emergency lights had kicked on, illuminating escape routes from the building in case of disaster.

A simple power failure that affected only Sunrise Enterprises?

It was possible, of course. And yet...

Machii reached into his desk's top right-hand drawer, removed the SIG Sauer P250 pistol he kept ready there, and held it at his side. There was no need for him to check the weapon. It was fully loaded and ready to fire as soon as he depressed its double-action trigger. Its magazine held ten .45-caliber rounds, with one more in the chamber, enough to keep any prowlers at bay until his security team reached the office.

Machii was moving toward the panoramic office window when the fire alarm went off, making him flinch. The action was involuntary, barely noticeable even if he had not been alone, but it embarrassed him, regardless.

Fire?

It seemed unlikely, but it might explain the power cut. Instead of waiting in his office, he should—

Even as the thought took form, Machii smelled it: smoke. The scent was unmistakable.

Coming from where, exactly?

"Jesus!"

There was no one in the room to hear him curse or note his momentary loss of calm. With pistol still in hand, Machii went to find out what was happening and right the situation.

BOLAN HAD PARKED his rented car on Atlantic Avenue and locked it. As it was getting on toward closing time, he'd crossed through spotty traffic in the middle of the block and made his way along an alleyway behind Atlantic Avenue, past long ranks of commercial garbage Dumpsters bearing names of their respective pickup companies. He'd met no one along the way, except a stray cat that examined him in passing and decided that he wouldn't make a meal.

At the rear of Sunrise Enterprises, Bolan found a fire

escape. The lower portion of the ladder operated on a counterbalance system, wisely using nylon bushings and stainless-steel cables to ward off corrosion. When he jumped to grasp the lowest rung, that section of the ladder dropped to meet him, making no more noise than Bolan would expect from a bicycle passing through the alley.

Scrambling up the fire escape, bolt cutters dangling from his belt, the MP-5 K swinging underneath his right arm, Bolan checked each window that he passed. Some of the offices were empty, others occupied, but no one noticed him, bent to their work as if clock-watching at day's end had been decreed a mortal sin.

Atop the roof, he found the junction box and used the bolt cutters to clip the padlock's shackle. Once the small gray door was open, he could see the trunk line pumping power through the building, keeping it alive.

The bolt cutters had rubber grips, so there was no need for insulated gloves as Bolan spread the jaws to clasp the thick trunk line. One flex of his arms and shoulders, one brief shower of sparks, and twenty feet beyond the junction box, the building's air conditioner shut down.

So far, so good.

Wasting no time, he crossed to stand over the air-conditioning unit, opened it and slit the silver wrapping on a large duct set into the roof. When that was open, Bolan took his smoke grenades in turn, removed their pins and dropped each of the four smoke bombs into the vent he had created with his blade. The unit wasn't running to propel the smoke through lower ducts and vents, but each grenade contained enough HC to spread fumes through the topmost floor, at least.

And that was all that Bolan needed.

He approached the rooftop access door—no padlock on the outside there—and tried it. Locked, of course.

With numbers running in his head, he stepped back from the door and raised his stubby SMG, firing a muffled 3-round burst into the steel door's dead-bolt lock. Another moment and he was inside, descending steep stairs dimly illuminated by pale ceiling-mounted emergency lights.

Halfway there, Bolan removed a lightweight balaclava from his pocket, pulled it on and made a quick adjustment to permit clear, unobstructed vision. He had borrowed the idea from Tommy Wolff's assassins, caught on video, and saw no reason why it shouldn't work for him, if he was seen by anyone he wasn't forced to kill.

Just plant the bug, he thought, but knew it might not be that simple. Nothing ever was, once battle had been joined.

Voices below made Bolan hesitate, but they were all retreating from the service stairs. No one would think of heading for the roof when they lost power. Down and out would be the drill, assisted by floor plans posted in offices and corridors, reminding people where to go in the event of an emergency.

He reached the bottom, peered around the corner and immediately saw the fire alarm wall unit to his left, within arm's reach. Unseen, he grasped the unit's pull-down handle, yanked it sharply, and was instantly rewarded with a clamor echoing throughout the building.

Sixty seconds, give or take, cleared out the fourth-floor hallway, even as the smoke from his grenades began to filter down through ceiling vents. Downrange, the last two visible employees reached a stairwell leading to the street below, pushed through its heavy door and disappeared.

Noboru Machii had a corner office at the far end of the hall, to Bolan's right. Turning in that direction, Bolan double-timed to reach his destination, submachine gun gripped in one hand, while the other delved in a pocket and extracted the infinity device.

The clock was running now. Bolan could hear it in his head, louder than the insistent fire alarm.

The *kyodai*'s office, reeking of smoke, was vacant when Bolan got there, and a white haze was seeping from the ceiling vents. He left the door to the reception area wide open, as he'd found it, and moved on to penetrate Machii's private sanctuary.

Empty.

Bolan went directly to the spacious desk, set down the bug he'd taken from his pocket and retrieved a small screwdriver. Within ten long seconds he'd removed the base plate from the telephone, surveyed the wiring and began the installation.

When he'd cut the trunk line on the building's roof, it had no impact on phone service to the floors below. Landlines were powered by another system altogether, usable in blackouts, and he hadn't touched their power conduit when he was turning off the lights at Sunrise Enterprises. He scanned the phone's guts, finally wedging the infinity transmitter in beside the set's digital answering machine. A simple clip job finished it, with no need to strip any wires and risk short-circuits sometime in the future. A few keystrokes on Bolan's cell phone, and the bug went live, the arming signal cut before the desk set had a chance to ring.

He was finished, except for putting back the base plate. He had three screws set, was working on the fourth, when he heard voices coming down the corridor in his direction, speaking Japanese.

Unhappy voices, which was natural enough, and now he had to scoot.

Bolan tightened the fourth screw down as far as it would go and pocketed his screwdriver. He replaced the phone as he had found it, nothing out of place as he surveyed the desktop, making sure no traces of himself remained.

Now, out.

Machii's office had a private washroom, and the washroom had its own connecting door to yet another room beyond, labeled as Storage on the floor plan he had memorized. That room, in turn, had its own exit to the corridor from which he'd entered the office. If his luck held, he could slip around behind whomever was approaching in a heated rush, and slip back to the roof while they were fuming in the office.

And if not, at least he might come out behind them. Give them a surprise.

Meeting opposition was a risk on any soft probe, always kept in mind, no matter how much preparation went into avoiding contact. With his work done, the transmitter live and waiting to broadcast whatever words were spoken in Machii's office from now on, it wasn't absolutely critical for Bolan to escape unseen.

But it was vital for him to escape *alive*.

The washroom door was shut when Bolan reached it, and he closed it tight behind him once he was inside. No dawdling in the john to eavesdrop on the Yakuza returning to the office. He was out the other door in seconds flat, and found that Storage meant a bedroom where Machii could sleep or party privately, with someone who had caught his fancy. There was no one in the boudoir, smoky now and ripe with HC's tangy odor, and he crossed directly to the other door. Bolan paused there, ear pressed against the panel, listening.

And heard nothing.

Behind him, in the Machii's private office, two men conversed, their words incomprehensible to Bolan. Taking full advantage of their evident preoccupation, he stepped out into the corridor—and found two young men gaping at him in surprise.

"Hakujin!" one declared.

"Supai!" the other snapped, as both reached for their holstered pistols.

Bolan didn't need to speak the language to know that they had pegged him as an intruder. He had them beaten, going in. The MP-5 K sneezed two muted 3-round bursts from less than twenty feet, stitching the young men's chests with 9 mm Parabellum hollow-point rounds, mangling their hearts and lungs, stopping those hearts before the guards knew they were dead. They fell together, but he didn't stick around to see it, sprinting for the service staircase that would take him to the roof.

It was a judgment call. To reach the street without retracing his original approach meant running back the full length of the corridor and rushing down eight flights of stairs—two zigzag flights per floor—among Sunrise employees exiting in answer to the fire alarm. If he got past them all, that route would put him on Atlantic Avenue, busy with traffic and pedestrians. If someone brought him under fire out there, it could become a massacre.

Better to do the unexpected thing, descend via the fire escape and exit through the alley. Cornered there, if he ran out of luck, at least Bolan could fight without much fear of injuring civilians.

He was on the roof and sprinting for the fire escape when someone shouted from behind him. Next, a pistol cracked, and Bolan heard the whisper of the bullet as it flew past his cheek.

One shooter was behind him when he turned, and

Bolan saw another peeking from the rooftop access doorway, clearly not as bold as the front-runner. Bolan sent
the shooter spinning with a 3-round Parabellum burst, his
white shirt spouting scarlet, then sent three more rounds
to make the doorway peeper duck back out of sight.

Eighteen rounds remained in the MP-5 K's magazine,
and Bolan didn't plan on using any more of them topside
than he could help.

He still had no idea what might be waiting for him in
the alley below.

He glanced over the parapet, saw no shooters prepared
to pick him off as he descended, and swung out onto the
fire escape. Taking the metal ladder rung by rung was
slow. Instead, he gripped the side rails with his hands
and braced the insteps of his shoes against them, sliding down until he struck the asphalt fifty feet below and
landed in a crouch.

Above him, gunshots echoed. One round struck a
commercial garbage bin to his right and spanged into
the heaped-up garbage it contained. Another slapped
into the pavement, closer, a reminder that he had no
time to waste.

Raising the MP-5 K's muzzle, Bolan chipped the concrete parapet above him with a parting burst and saw a
face fly back, out of frame. He couldn't rate that as a
hit and didn't care. His rented wheels, a Honda Civic,
waited for him on Atlantic Avenue, no more than half a
block away.

He ran.

The rooftop shooters would need time to reach the
alley. As for soldiers on the inside, he'd already dealt
with two and given any more something to think about.
Assuming they had walkie-talkies for communicating,
someone from the lobby could be on his case by now and

waiting for him when he reached the sidewalk, but it was a chance he'd have to take.

The alley was a trap now; staying where he was meant death.

A brief pause at the alley's mouth, tucking the MP-5 K out of sight beneath his jacket, hand still on its pistol grip through a slit pocket on his right, and Bolan cleared the sidewalk, glancing right and left as if it was a normal day, nothing to be concerned about. When no one called him out or gunned him down, he stepped off from the curb, jaywalking as if he did it every day, angling through traffic that, with any luck, would slow his pursuers.

Twenty feet from the Honda, Bolan palmed the keyless entry fob and released the driver's door lock, instantly rewarded by a flash of taillights and a perky blipping sound. A moment later, he was at the wheel and gunning it, letting the taxi on his tail brake sharply, driver leaning on his horn and offering a one-finger salute, as Bolan pulled away from Sunrise Enterprises.

He could listen to the office bug right now, in theory, but he had more pressing matters on his mind—survival being foremost on the list—and Bolan figured that Noboru Machii wouldn't spend the next few minutes in his office, strategizing with his men. There would be firefighters to deal with, and police, the problem of eliminating corpses in a hurry.

Something else he'd thought about, while planning his incursion: when Machii *did* begin to talk, the odds were good that he'd be speaking Japanese. While Bolan's talents were diverse, he'd never had the opportunity to learn more than a smattering of Japanese. And that would have been a problem, if the superteam at Stony Man Farm hadn't devised a program for his smartphone, offering real-time translated readouts from a list of major languages. The readout wasn't perfect—something on the order of closed captioning on normal television—but he'd get the gist of what Machii said and go from there.

First, though, he had to get away. Find somewhere it was safe to sit and eavesdrop once his adversaries chilled a bit and had a chance to think.

Bolan checked his rearview, frowning as he saw a car behind him, weaving in and out of traffic, closing fast. Three shapes were inside the vehicle, maybe four, and while they might be office workers in a rush to get to happy hour, Bolan wasn't taking anything for granted.

What he needed was a place to take the shooters, if they *were* shooters, and dispose of them without civilians getting in the way. The Ventnor City wetlands were behind him, too much trouble to reverse directions, and O'Donnell Memorial Park, five blocks ahead, would probably have too much foot traffic for him to risk a firefight.

What was left?

He thought of Chelsea Harbor, on Atlantic City's other waterfront, three-quarters of a mile inland from the Atlantic and the boardwalk. There would be civilians, naturally—workmen, people going in and out of restaurants, whatever—but it sounded better than the obvious alternatives.

He reached South Dover Avenue, turned left against the lights and traffic, hoping there were no cops at the intersection to observe him. If the chase car *wasn't* chasing him, he'd lose it there.

The matter was decided when the vehicle turned in Bolan's rearview, clipped a motorcyclist and came charging after him.

CHAPTER THREE

Sunrise Enterprises

Noboru Machii watched his soldiers zipping bodies into heavy plastic bags and cursed them for their awkwardness.

Red-faced with exertion and humiliation, they worked faster, well aware that the police and firefighters would soon be pouring through the doors downstairs, searching the premises for any trace of fire. In fact, Machii understood, the smoke had been a ruse, but he could not tell that to the authorities. It raised too many questions that he did not wish to answer—most particularly with two corpses in the place and one up on the roof.

What would he do with those?

There was a garbage chute on each floor of the building he had rented as his local headquarters. Rubbish went down the chute, into a basement garbage bin, where he had another pair of soldiers waiting to receive their lifeless comrades. From the bins, they would be consigned to basement lockers while the search went on—no reason anyone should think the lockers harbored flammable materials—then from lockers into car trunks and away, when it was clear for transport.

While he waited for the law, Machii mulled the news he'd heard from one of his survivors on the roof. Someone—their prowler, who had killed three of his men—

had cut the building's trunk line, killing power, and had cut his way into the building's main air-conditioning vent, inserting some kind of device to generate smoke. From there, he'd blasted through the rooftop access door, set off the fire alarm and gone about his bloody work.

But what was that?

Two dead men in the corridor outside his office, with his bedroom door wide open, let the crime boss piece together what had happened. Halfway to the street, descending on the service stairs, he had smelled something fishy, as the *gaijin* liked to say, and he'd begun the climb back to the top floor, taking soldiers with him. Standing in his empty, smoky office, he'd felt slightly foolish for a moment—until all hell had broken loose.

Now he was certain someone *had* been in his office, standing at his desk perhaps, or riffling through his files. A glance had shown no sign of any locks picked on the filing cabinets, but Machii wouldn't know until he had more time and privacy.

And, naturally, he would have to tell his *oyabun* about the raid.

But not just yet.

Before he broke bad news to Tokyo, Machii hoped to mitigate the damage. When his soldiers caught the man responsible, Machii would have answers. If they took the man alive, he would inevitably spill his motives and the names of his employers. If they had to kill him…well, in spite of the old saying, sometimes dead men *did* tell tales.

Both corpses were inside their bags now, and his men were hoisting them, scuttling like peasants toward the garbage chute. Above, the soldier cut down on the rooftop had already slithered to the basement in his own rubber cocoon and should be safe inside a locker now. As for the bloodstains on the runner outside his office…

"Kenji!"

"Yes, sir!" his soldier answered.

"We require an explanation for these stains that will deceive the police. Do you understand?"

Young Kenji nodded, but his blank expression made it clear he understood nothing.

"You came to check on me," Machii said, coaching him. "As you approached the office, you collided with another member of the staff. Sadly, your nose was broken by the impact and you bled on to the carpet."

"Sir?"

Before the puzzled frown had time to clear, Machii slammed a fist into the soldier's nose, felt cartilage give way and caught him as he staggered, doubling Kenji over at the waist and holding him in place while bright blood drained from his nose, soaking into the older stains.

"Good man. That should be adequate. You serve the family with honor. Now, remember what we talked about."

"Yes, sir!"

It would be an hour, likely more, before Machii finished with the investigators, then more time to get an electrician on the job, restoring power to the office block. By then, he hoped to have the prowler in his hands and know exactly what in hell was happening.

South Dover Avenue

THE FIRST CROSS street in Bolan's way was Ventnor Avenue, with traffic lights and people crossing at the corner. Checking out the chase car in his rearview one more time—it was a black sedan, of course, the model indeterminate—he slowed enough to judge the two-way traffic pattern up ahead, and let a couple of pedestrians get closer to the curbs on either side, then floored his gas pedal and blasted through the intersection. He was mindful of stores to the right, then houses, as he braced himself for sudden impact if he had miscalculated.

More horns blared at him, tires squealed, but nothing slammed into the Civic as he cleared Ventnor and shot across to North Dover. No deviation in the street's beeline toward water, but a slightly altered name for the convenience of police or postal workers. Bolan flicked another glance behind him, through the rearview, and was disappointed when the chase car made it through the intersection as he had, all in one piece.

What were the odds that someone passing by on Ventnor, having been surprised or frightened, would take time to phone the cops? Bolan pegged it at fifty-fifty, if he and the Yakuza pursuing him had pissed off somebody enough to make it worth the time and effort.

The response time, if they did call?

Bolan had done his homework, memorized the basic layout of Atlantic City and the landmarks that were meaningful to him. Police department headquarters was on Atlantic Avenue, at Marshall Street, three-quarters of a mile to the northeast. There would be cruisers closer to the waterfront, of course, but any calls would still be routed through the cop shop, and back to the street via dispatchers.

Say five minutes until the word came through on some patrolman's radio or one of those computer terminals that could be found in most prowl cars today. From there, the hypothetical responding officers would need another five minutes, at least, to reach the scene of the disturbance, now two hundred feet behind Bolan as he approached the next stoplights, at Sussex Avenue.

He caught the green this time, a lucky fluke, and ran with it, spotting a gap in southbound traffic as he cleared the intersection, passing one slow driver on the left and slipping back into the proper lane before the startled stranger saw him coming. Bolan's trackers tried the same thing, but a bus got in their way and slowed them.

He used that interruption to his own advantage, putting on more speed, continuing past stores on either side to Norsex Avenue, the next-to-last cross street before he reached the waterfront. He'd have a choice to make at Winchester, go left or right, decide which part of Chelsea Harbor he would turn into a battleground.

It was another guessing game. He knew the area from an online mapping service, its detailed maps and zoom-in aerials that let him count the cars in any given parking lot, but only real-time passage on the streets would let him choose a kill zone. Bolan knew what to avoid: popular restaurants, a shopping mall or multiplex. Beyond that, it was all decided in a heartbeat, as he judged a scene in person, from the ground.

Traffic was light on Norsex, and he cleared it on the yellow light, leaving the hunters on his tail to jump the red. They made it, with a near-miss from a Pepsi truck, and came on strong.

Winchester Avenue was dead ahead.

Beyond it, in a few more moments, someone would be dead and gone.

"MOVE IT!" ENDO EISHIN SNAPPED.

"I'm hurrying, goddamn it!" Ken Tadayoshi answered from the driver's seat.

In back, Aoshi Yoshikage asked, "Where the hell is he going?"

"I don't *know*," Tadayoshi spit. "Shut up and let me drive!"

Eishin knew that was good advice, but he still couldn't let it go. "We're losing him!"

"He's right there!" Tadayoshi told him, lifting one hand off the steering wheel to point, his index finger jabbing at the windshield. "See?"

Eishin could see, all right. He saw the car speeding ahead of them, and he could also see the future, if they let the gunman slip away. Noboru Machii would be furious, demanding restitution for their failure. If he let them live, a sacrifice would be required.

Eishin's left hand, clutching the Ithaca Model 37 Stakeout shotgun in his lap, looked oddly lopsided at first glance. A closer look revealed the first two segments of the little finger to be missing, severed by his own hand in the ritual of *yubitsume*—"finger shortening"—and solemnly presented to the bosses he'd offended by his failure to perform as they required.

Two relatively minor errors. Two small sacrifices to the family.

What would Noboru Machii order if they let the man who'd killed their brothers get away? Perhaps a hand in recompense? Or possibly a life?

The better way was to complete the job they'd been assigned, capture the gunman and bring him back alive if that was possible. From what he'd seen at Sunrise Enterprises, Eishin did not like their chances of succeeding on that score, but if they killed the rotten son of a bitch, that would be the next best thing.

Some satisfaction for their boss, at least, and they would not have failed.

He swiveled in his seat, peering at Yoshikage and Kanehira next to him, both holding short assault rifles. And smiling, as if this were just one of the damned video games they loved to play at any given opportunity. They looked like morons, sitting there.

"Listen to me," he cautioned them. "This guy is good. Professional. He took our brothers down like they were nothing. Take no chances with him. If we cannot capture him alive—"

"We waste his ass!" Kanehira chimed in, grinning like a monkey with a fresh banana in his hand.

"Smoke him!" Yoshikage said, smiling from ear to ear.

Eishin despaired of his men, sometimes. The young ones coming up these days were rash and often reckless, straining at their leashes until something stopped them short. In his day, not so long ago, the discipline was paramount and rigidly enforced. There'd been no second chances, as attested by his own truncated flesh.

"Just follow orders," he advised the backseat soldiers, glowering. "This isn't one of your video games." They blinked at that, as he pressed on. "If you get shot out here, there are no do-overs. You don't jump up and start again. Understand?"

Both nodded their understanding, looking chastened, but Eishin had a sense that they would smirk at him, the moment that his back was turned. Dismissing them from his mind, he turned back toward the chase and saw their quarry crossing Winchester, continuing toward Phyllis Avenue.

It was to be the eastern side of Chelsea Harbor, then, where they would run him down and take him, one way or another.

"Faster!" Eishin ordered, and ignored the growl from the driver, focused on his prey.

THE ONLY CHOICE was turning right on Phyllis Avenue. Dover did not go on from there, but in a short block Bolan had another chance to turn left, on to Chelsea Court, which led him closer to the waterfront. Ahead of him, along the curving street that circled back toward town if he went far enough, stood offices and shops, all closed for the night. To Bolan's right was some kind of gym or recreation center with a swimming pool out back, no one outside to be a random target at the moment. Bolan knew he wouldn't find a better killing ground nearby, and circling Chelsea until it turned into North Harrisburg and started back toward town would only make things worse.

So it was here or nowhere. Do or die.

Now, all he had to do was make it work—and make his adversaries die.

First thing, he needed room enough to turn and face the carload of pursuers who were now a block behind him, closing rapidly. The road was clear ahead, and Bolan wasted no time taking full advantage of it, standing on the Civic's brake, cranking its steering wheel hard left, whipping the rear end through a power slide on screeching rubber. It was nothing that they taught in driver's ed, but if you handled it correctly it could be a lifesaver.

Like now, perhaps.

Before the Honda came to rest, with Bolan facing back the way he'd come on Chelsea Court, he had the MP-5 K's shoulder rig unsnapped, the submachine gun resting in his lap. He put the Civic in Reverse, checking his rearview to make sure the coast was clear, and started running backward toward the curve where it changed street signs to become North Harrisburg. A row of townhouses obscured his view around the curve, but that was fine. He didn't plan on going that far, anyway.

In front of him, the chase car had slowed, still following, but waiting now to see what Bolan had in mind. A window powered down behind the driver's seat, and

Bolan saw an Asian shooter lean out with a weapon in his hands, maybe an Arsenal AR-SF or a Micro Galil. Either way, it was deadly and had to be countered at once.

Bolan raised the MP-5 K in his left hand, angling out the Civic's open driver's window. Aiming wasn't possible, per se, but with a steady hand and skilled eye he could do the next best thing.

Still set for 3-round bursts, the little SMG could fire six times before he had to switch its magazine, an operation that would mean taking his right hand off the steering wheel. In fact, he did that now, shifting the Honda from Reverse to Drive and bearing down on the accelerator, closing up the gap between himself and his pursuers.

He had a choice of firing at the driver or the shooter, but the gunman was the greater threat. Bolan squeezed off a burst, too low, and saw his bullets slash the chase car's left-rear door. It wasn't likely that hollow-point rounds would penetrate the passenger compartment through sheet steel and insulation, but the triple impact made his target squawk and pull back from the window without firing at the Civic, as they passed each other on the two-lane blacktop.

Now what?

He could take off, fleeing back into the maze of Atlantic City's streets, or stay and finish it. Whichever choice he made, the time for a decision was right now.

Enough running.

Bolan hung on and took the vehicle through another power slide, coming around behind the chase car so that he was in pursuit now, and the hounds were running from the fox. It took only a second for the Yakuza driver in front of him to catch on, but in that time Bolan had his submachine gun leveled and had smashed the black sedan's rear window with another 3-round burst.

Two faces, furious and frightened, gaped at Bolan through the open window frame, before both men raised automatic rifles into view.

"HE'S BEHIND US NOW!" Eishin exclaimed.

"I see that," Tadayoshi answered through clenched teeth.

"Well, do something!"

"What did you have in mind?"

Before Eishin could think of anything, their back window imploded, spraying pebbled safety glass like buckshot through the passenger compartment. Pieces of it stung his scalp and neck. Something more deadly struck the windshield, halfway between him and his driver, knocking a chip out of the glass and rattling on the dashboard.

Eishin ducked and saw a mutilated bullet resting on top of the central heating vent. If it had been diverted ten or twelve inches to the left or right, he might be dead now, or the car could be speeding off course, with a corpse behind the wheel.

Yoshikage and Kanehira sat in the back, chattering like two macaques, preparing to return fire, when another burst struck home. Its bullets marched across the trunk lid, striking with the force of hammer blows, and one spanged off the lower window frame, to ricochet inside the car. The driver cried out this time, slumping, left hand clutching at his shoulder, steering with his wounded right.

Feeling foolish even as he spoke, Eishin asked him, "How bad is it?"

"I'm not a doctor!" Tadayoshi rasped, showing bad form by his tone.

"Well, can you drive?" Eishin demanded.

"Do you *see* me driving?"

Although fuming over the man's insubordination, Eishin knew it might be suicide to chastise him just now. Instead, he turned to see their enemy tailgating them, his two soldiers in the back trying to recover from the last incoming fire, raising their weapons once again.

Instead of waiting for them, Eishin fired his cut-down shotgun at the Honda, making both soldiers in the back yelp and cringe as thunder filled the car, stinging four sets of ears. He saw his buckshot, double 0, take out a portion of the Honda's windshield larger than a dinner plate, but he had missed the driver by at least a foot.

He pumped the Ithaca's slide-action, chambering another 12-gauge round. The cartridge he'd ejected bounced off the driver's cheek and dropped into his lap, provoking a string of curses.

They would have to talk about that later, set things straight between them and cement the clear lines of authority that governed every member of the Yakuza.

Assuming that they lived.

In the backseat, Yoshikage cried, "I've been hit!"

Eishin glanced at his squealing soldier, saw no blood and snapped, "You're not wounded! Shut your whining mouth and do your job!"

Red-faced, the soldier turned away from him and aimed his stubby carbine through the car's rear window, firing as his partner did, their muzzle-flashes visible as dusk descended on the waterfront. Eishin considered firing one more shotgun blast between them, but decided it would only spoil their shaky aim.

And Tadayoshi wasn't helping, in the driver's seat. He swerved the car erratically, cursing under his breath as more slugs from their quarry's automatic weapon struck the vehicle. At least one found its way inside, clipping the rearview mirror from its post and dropping what remained of it at Eishin's feet.

"Stop all this crazy skidding!" Eishin ordered. "How can we hit anything, the way you drive?"

"He's hitting *us*," Tadayoshi replied, shooting a quick glance toward the spot where there had been a mirror seconds earlier, mouthing another curse when he saw nothing but a chip out of the windshield's glass.

"Drive straight!" Eishin repeated. "That's an order!"

Tadayoshi turned to glare at him, then gave a jerky nod and straightened the steering wheel—just as their adversary's bullets found their left-rear tire and shredded it. The car's tail end immediately whipped around, the wheel's rim biting into asphalt, and they went into a skid, the backseat shooters howling like a pair of lunatics.

Eishin clutched the nearest grab handle and hung on for dear life.

BOLAN RECKONED HE had been lucky with the last burst, trying it before his magazine ran dry. He eased off the accelerator as the Yakuzas' car went into its final skid, jumping a curb off to the right, its nose crumpled against a lamppost with a granite base. He drove past, checking as the occupants began to move around inside. The left-rear door sprang open, and a dazed-looking hardman tumbled onto the pavement, still holding his carbine in one hand.

Bolan passed on three or four doors farther down the street, then swung his car around to block both lanes and bailed out on the driver's side, keeping the Civic between himself and his would-be killers. Three of them were EVA as Bolan got his SMG reloaded, the driver seeming to have trouble with unfastening his shoulder harness.

Bolan helped him with it, rattling off a 3-round burst

that turned the wheelman's face into a bloody stir-fry. That brought in return fire, but it wasn't organized as yet, or aimed precisely. Bolan's car had taken hits during the final moments of the chase, and he could hear more bullets striking it along the passenger's side, drilling the bodywork, evaporating window glass.

Somebody else's headache, since he'd bought the full insurance package when he took delivery on the Honda. Not in his own name, of course—Mack Bolan had been "dead" for years—but on a credit card whose bills were promptly paid from Stony Man. As long as it was drivable and he could leave the scene when he was done, Bolan was satisfied.

If not? Plan B, whatever that was.

First, he had to move, close with his enemies and take them down before the racket they were making drew police to swarm the block.

Bolan had only two rules in the field. He would not harm or threaten innocents, and he would not use deadly force against police—even though some of them were far from innocent themselves. It was a short list of restrictions, but he rarely deviated from those basic principles.

And he was not about to do so this day.

He made his move while they were trying to get organized, recovering from having seen their driver killed before their eyes. One of the three surviving Yakuzas saw Bolan moving, shouted something to his comrades and squeezed off an autorifle burst that missed its moving target by at least ten feet.

Bolan returned fire, did a better job of it and saw the shooter drop his rifle as three Parabellum shockers ripped into his gun arm, taking out the shoulder. In the movies, shoulder wounds were treated lightly, on par with paper cuts, but in the real world they were serious, often disabling, sometimes fatal if projectiles nipped the brachial or subclavian arteries.

Whatever, Bolan pegged the odds at two-to-one against him now, and focused on reducing those.

Bolan reached the nearest sidewalk, ducked behind a bulky standing mailbox, then proceeded with his charge. Another Yakuza shooter was firing at him—and he had been right, that *was* an Arsenal AR-SF—until the next burst out of Bolan's SMG nearly beheaded him.

Three down, and now the last Yakuza on his feet sprang out from cover, brandishing a stubby shotgun with a pistol grip. He pumped the slide, ejecting brass and plastic, screaming something Bolan couldn't understand without his smartphone translator. Before the screamer had a chance to loose another buckshot cloud, Bolan zipped him across the chest and slammed him back against the crumpled wreckage of his car's front end.

One left, and he was still alive, sitting in blood, his eyes half-closed, lips moving silently, when Bolan walked around the car. Bolan considered him, knew they were running out of time to talk, even if they possessed a common language, and he fired a single mercy round into the man's forehead.

All done.

He got the Honda started and was rolling out of there, already thinking downrange toward the best and quickest place to find another car.

CHAPTER FOUR

Sunrise Enterprises

"No, Detective. I have no idea who might desire to vandalize our offices. Do you?"

The bald, fat officer stared at Noboru Machii, his suspicion thinly veiled, and said, "No, sir. But I'll be looking into it."

"Perhaps you'll trace the smoke grenades," Machii said. A firefighter had found them in the air-conditioning duct, while seeking a source for the smoke that still hung around them in the lobby.

"I couldn't rule it out," the detective said. Was his name Davis? Dawkins? No matter. All Machii wanted was for him to leave the premises. "These things are mass-produced, you understand."

"Of course."

"Your ordinary public's not supposed to have them, but does that mean anything these days? Between the internet and dealers on the street, forget about it."

"So, it's hopeless then?" Machii asked.

"Oh, nothing's *hopeless*," the detective answered. "But I wouldn't get my hopes *up*, if you follow me."

"I understand. Now, if there's nothing else…"

The plainclothes officer was rummaging inside his rumpled jacket, pulling out a dog-eared business card and offering it to Machii, who accepted it and held it gingerly, between his thumb and index finger, checking it for sweat stains.

"Call me if you think of anything that might be helpful, eh? You got my office number on there, and my cell. *Work* cell, that is. Nobody gets the home number, know what I mean?"

"Indeed," Machii said.

"Okay, then. If I find out anything, I'll be in touch. You'll still be doing business here?"

"I will. Power should be restored within the hour, once your people clear the scene."

The fat detective nodded, turned and waddled toward the exit, glancing at the team of electricians as he passed them, no doubt wondering how much a rush job after hours would be costing.

And the answer, as Americans would say, was *plenty*: triple time for labor, plus materials. Restoring power to the building was about to cost Machii three grand, with another thousand minimum on top of that, to fix and flush the air-conditioning. He had that much and more in petty cash, but he was seething over the audacity of the assault.

And he was worried that no suspects sprang to mind.

Of course, Machii had his share of enemies, but most of those were in Japan. The few he'd made so far, around Atlantic City, had been dealt with swiftly and decisively. Unless he started to believe in zombies, they no longer posed a threat.

But someone clearly did.

He nodded curtly to the electricians and the air-conditioning technicians standing with them. "It is clear now," he informed them. "Get to work."

A couple of them didn't seem to like his tone, but that meant nothing to Machii. When they were as rich as he was, when they'd killed as many men and when they had a family of twenty thousand oath-bound brothers standing at their back, supporting them, he would consider their opinion.

In the meantime, they were nothing more than servants.

Machii climbed the stairs, hating the smoke taint in the air be breathed, and found his office as he'd left it. As expected, the police had asked about the bloodstain on the hallway carpet, and he'd trotted out his underling to lisp the fable of his accident. The fat detective had refrained from asking any questions on that score, being more interested in the smoke bombs from the AC duct.

Thank heaven for small minds.

Back in his office now, Machii started a more thorough search than he'd had time for while he'd waited for emergency responders to arrive. First thing, he checked his desk, found nothing out of place, and then repeated the inspection with his files. Needless to say, he kept nothing at the office that might incriminate him, guarding against situations such as this, but if he found some normal business papers disarranged or missing, it might point him toward enemies behind the raid.

When Machii found nothing to direct him in the filing cabinets, he stood back and surveyed the room, inhaling its polluted scent as if the latent fumes might hold a clue. If not to steal from him or kill him, why would anyone attack Sunrise? No other possibility immediately came to mind, and since the power blackout had deactivated all of the building's security cameras, no answers awaited him on videotape.

What next?

He had two calls to make. The first, to Jiro Shinoda in Las Vegas, would be a deliberately vague inquiry, trying to determine whether he had experienced any disturbances of late, without alerting him to what had happened in Atlantic City. After that—and there was no escaping it—Machii had to report the raid to Tokyo. His *oyabun* had to be informed within the hour, or suspicion might begin to ripen in his mind. And that, above all things, was something that Machii wanted to avoid.

His hand was on the telephone when Tetsuya Watanabe knocked, then entered without waiting for a summons. "Excuse me, sir," he said.

"You are excused. What is it?"

"Endo and his team…"

"They've captured the intruder?" Sudden hope flared in Machii's chest.

"No, sir," Watanabe said. "They're dead."

Tropicana Casino and Resort, Atlantic Avenue

FINDING ANOTHER CAR had not been difficult as night fell on Atlantic City. Bolan had left his shot-up Honda Civic in a multilevel parking garage at AtlantiCare Regional Medical Center, swapping it for a Toyota RAV4 whose owner played it "safe" by hiding a spare key in one of those magnetic holders, tucked under the right-front fender. Bolan switched the license plates, transferred his mobile arsenal and cleared hospital grounds within ten minutes, flat.

The Sunrise Enterprises bug went live as he was driving along Atlantic Avenue, so he'd pulled into the casino's parking lot to listen and to read the captioned messages on his smartphone. He'd missed the number that Machii dialed, but soon worked out from the conversation that the call was placed to Vegas. That meant Jiro Shinoda, since Machii—as a *kyodai*—would not seek input from inferiors.

Staying alert to his surroundings, ready to depart immediately if security rolled up on him, Bolan surveyed the boxed translations on his phone's screen.

"You have surprised me," Shinoda said.

"There is something I must ask you."

"Yes?"

"Please, do not question me."

"Very mysterious." A hint of mirth entered Shinoda's tone. "Proceed."

"Are you experiencing…difficulties, where you are?"

Shinoda thought about that for a moment, then replied, "Aside from the Internal Revenue, nothing to speak of. Why? Are you?"

"Something has happened, but I cannot speak about it now."

"That's even more mysterious," Shinoda said. "Are you suggesting I should be concerned?"

It was Machii's turn to pause and think. At last, he answered, "No. I'm sure it has nothing to do with you. Strictly a local matter, but I must report it to our godfather."

"Ah. In that case, I'm afraid that I cannot advise you further. Do what must be done, of course."

"If you hear anything…"

"I, too, shall do what must be done," Shinoda said.

Sly as a fox, that one. The threat of squealing to their *oyabun* was left unspoken, but Machii had to have known Shinoda would turn any given circumstance to personal advantage, if he could.

All mobsters were alike that way, Bolan knew, regardless of their nationality, skin pigment or the oaths they'd sworn on joining their respective rotten "families." For all the vows of fealty, defense of brothers and the rest of it, the bottom line was always each man for himself. "Honor" was highly touted in the underworld, enforcing codes of silence and the like, but it was stained and tattered like an old dust rag, each rip another captain who had overthrown his boss, or one more witness who had squealed to save himself from prison.

Bolan listened while the two *kyodai* traded pleasantries, Machii clearly anxious to be off the line and on to some more pressing task. Bolan's infinity device would transmit any conversation from Machii's office, not just phone calls, and he hoped there would be more to hear before he had to leave the Tropicana's parking lot.

As if in answer to that wish, a voice he didn't recognize chimed in, asking, "Will you call our godfather now?"

"It cannot be avoided. If I do not, he will learn by other means. Delay might have been possible, if we had caught the prowler, but with four more dead…"

He left it dangling, no response from his companion in the office. Bolan pictured them, the search they had to have executed prior to calling Vegas, their reactions when they had found nothing out of place. Machii knew he had been targeted, but didn't know by whom, or why. Uncertainty would give his nerves a workout and might prod him into reckless action.

"I will leave you to it," said the *kyodai*'s anonymous subordinate.

"Tetsuya, wait. I will be sleeping at the other house tonight," Machii said.

"Yes, sir. I'll make all the arrangements."

"Thank you."

"You're welcome, sir."

A door closed. If Machii had more men inside his office, they stayed silent. He delayed another minute, almost two, before he dialed another number. Bolan read it from his smartphone's screen: "0011" was the international code used for dialing outside the States; "81" was Japan's international code; "3" was Tokyo's area code; and the last ten digits represented someone's private line.

The *oyabun*'s, presumably.

Bolan saved the number to his phone and sat back to listen in.

Sunrise Enterprises

NOBORU MACHII DREADED his next call but could not postpone it. Timing was not a problem, with Tokyo thirteen hours ahead of Atlantic City. It was breakfast time tomorrow in Japan, and the *oyabun* of the Sumiyoshi-kai had always been an early riser. Even in his sixties, fabulously wealthy, he maintained an active schedule, sleeping no more than five or six hours per night.

Kazuo Takumi would be awake, and probably at work, but was he ready for the news Machii had to share?

Quit stalling. Time to get on with it, said the stern voice in Noboru's head. And he *was* stalling, there could be no doubt of it. Whatever happened in the next few minutes could decide his fate.

He sat in his favorite recliner, in the private office bedroom, put his feet up in a futile effort to relax, and dialed his master's number, tapping out seventeen digits, then listening to empty air before a telephone halfway around the world began to ring.

As usual, the first ring passed, then it was answered midway through the second. Machii pictured the *oyabun*'s houseman and chief bodyguard, Kato Ando, scowling as he answered.

"Who is calling, please?"

Machii gave his name and said, "I need to speak with him."

Ando grunted, a disapproving sound, then said, "Just a minute, please."

Machii waited, as instructed, switching hands with the telephone because his palm was sweating, even with the air-conditioning back on and blowing cool, clean air. When Kazuo Takumi took the phone, his voice was deceptively soft.

"Noboru. I've been expecting you."

"You have, sir?"

"Jiro called ahead. He fears you have encountered difficulties."

Rotten sneak! Machii ground his teeth and made a mighty effort to control his tenor.

"It is true, sir. Difficulties have arisen."

"Tell me."

So he did, in outline, leaving out only the price his men had paid in blood. With the scrambler on his own phone, and the *oyabun*'s private security measures in place, Machii had no fear of law enforcement snatching his words from the air. Still, there was no reason to link himself with any killings, just in case. Police already knew about the raid on Sunrise Enterprises. There was nothing to be lost by mentioning the smoke grenades or the prowler's escape.

Takumi heard him out, then told him, "You were fortunate to have no injuries."

Machii bit the bullet, said, "A few employees have departed over the affair."

"Oh, yes? How many?"

"Seven, sir."

"Unhappy news. But you can carry on without them?"

"Certainly. I'm taking measures as we speak."

Measures to run and hide, that was, where he would have better security.

"What of the project?" Takumi asked, all business.

"It's proceeding well, sir. I anticipate a breakthrough later in the week."

"That's excellent. I shall expect another call when all of it is finalized."

Meaning Machii should not call again until he had good news. The *kyodai* nodded, feeling slightly foolish when he realized his master could not see him.

"I shall definitely be in touch, sir."

"I look forward to it with anticipation. Goodbye."

And the line went dead.

Machii was not sure if he should feel relieved or apprehensive, maybe some of each. His boss had not raged at him, but that was not the *oyabun*'s style. If he wanted you dead, he would smile to your face, then make arrangements for your execution when it suited him. A soldier who displeased Kazuo Takumi might be left as an example to his comrades. Other targets of his anger simply disappeared.

Machii knew he was not safe yet. To secure himself and his position in the family, he had to correct the problems that beset him. First and foremost, he had to find out who had dared to move against him and eliminate the threat. When that was done he could proceed with taking over Wolff Consolidated.

Which, of course, included a casino in Las Vegas. That, under the old plan, would have gone to Jiro Shinoda, but Machii had other plans for Shinoda now. He would not forget being stabbed in the back.

And he would not forgive.

Azabu, Tokyo

AZABU WAS THE richest neighborhood in Tokyo, home to celebrities and business moguls, living side by side with foreign embassies. It bordered the Akasaka business district and upscale Aoyama, where fashion was everything. Aside from the Roppongi entertainment district, most of Azabu was relatively quiet, considering its placement in the world's most crowded city. One-bedroom apartments in Azabu started at 700,000 yen—call it $8,500—per month.

That had no impact on a man who owned seven high-rise apartment buildings.

Kazuo Takumi kept large suites in five of those buildings, and smaller bolt-holes in the other two, sometimes spending a month or more at one apartment, other times shifting each night, if he believed that staying in the same place might involve some risk.

Above all else, he took no chances where his safety was concerned.

This day he had awakened at his second-favorite home, on Block 8. City addresses in Japan did not depend on street names, but on numbered blocks. Within each block, buildings were numbered by their age, with "1" assigned to the oldest, and so on to the newest structure. Thus, Takumi's present home, however briefly, sat atop building 12 on Block 8, with a view of traffic gleaming on the Sakurada Dori freeway.

He was troubled by the two calls from America. Jiro Shinoda had been on the line as soon as he had finished speaking with Noboru Machii in Atlantic City, voicing his concern, twisting the knife in a transparent effort to advance himself. That was unfortunate, but nothing unexpected for a relatively young, ambitious big brother.

Bad blood would separate them now, a fact Takumi had been conscious of when he informed Machii of the call from Shinoda.

It was always best to keep subordinates at odds with one another, constantly competing for their master's favor, rather than agreeing to conspire against him while the master's back was turned.

Machii's call had been more troubling. Seven men lost, and police would now be on alert to watch him, if there had been no surveillance previously. An attack was bad for business, all the more so when its source was unidentified. Noboru would be working urgently to solve that problem, knowing that his very life depended on it, but the crime lord wondered now if his Atlantic City *kyodai* was equal to the task.

Machii had disposed of Tommy Wolff, using the agents he'd supplied, but now the takeover of Wolff Consolidated would be stalled until Machii solved the riddle of his latest difficulty. Should that drag on much beyond Wolff's funeral, Takumi was prepared to send more men around the world to lift the burden off his *kyodai*'s shoulders.

And, if necessary, they would lift his head at the same time.

Machii had a short window of opportunity in which to prove himself. And when that window closed, it would descend upon him like the blade of a *katana* in a ninja's hands.

After victory, he thought, quoting a proverb from his youth, tighten your helmet strap.

The moral: premature excitement over great success might cause a careless man to drop his guard before the war was truly won.

Takumi never quit, never let down his guard. As for Machii…

The Yakuza crime boss decided he would send another team, four of his best this time. His private jet was always ready on a moment's notice, and the flight from Tokyo to Atlantic City International Airport was fourteen hours long. If they arrived in time to help Machii, fine. If not, at least they would be on-site to begin the cleanup process.

Put things right before it was too late.

Meanwhile…

Takumi had his own concerns at home, completely unrelated to the situation in America. His son and heir apparent had not grown into the man Takumi hoped would run his empire when the time came for him to depart this life. In youth, Toi had been frivolous and spoiled— his father's fault, of course, as it had to fall on any father. Lately, he had grown more serious, but also more distracted, as if no part of the family business inspired him in the least. The thought that Toi might try to leave the Sumiyoshi-kai appalled Takumi, but he could not rule it out.

Worse than the personal insult, of course, would be the blow Takumi suffered in the eyes of other godfathers when he could not control his only son. It would be viewed as weakness, and he could not argue with that judgment. Toi's abdication, if it happened, was a threat to the whole family. Better if he had not been born, in fact, than to run off pursuing other friends and goals entirely foreign to his upbringing.

That was a problem for another day, however.

Reaching for the intercom beside him, Takumi summoned Kato Ando and greeted him with curt instructions. "Call The Four," he said. "They must be ready to depart within the hour."

"Yes, sir," Kato replied, and left the room without a backward glance.

Atlantic Avenue, Atlantic City

BOLAN'S INFINITY TRANSMITTER was not hampered by the scrambler on Machii's telephone, because it picked up conversation from the office, not the phone line. There were pros and cons to that: he only heard the *kyodai*'s side of the discussion, had to guess what he was hearing from the other end, but Bolan still had contact when Machii cut the link and called out for his flunky.

"Tetsùya!"

A moment later, Bolan heard the second now-familiar voice, reading the captions as his smartphone carried out translation.

"Yes, sir?"

"Are we ready to get out of here?" Machii asked.

"As ordered, sir. The limousine is downstairs, waiting."

Bolan twisted the RAV4's ignition key and pulled out of the Tropicana's parking lot, turned left and drove southwestward, back toward Sunrise Enterprises. There was traffic, sure, but it would slow Machii's getaway as much as it did Bolan's progress, thirteen blocks to cover from the huge casino to the office building where he'd killed three men that evening.

Machii had disposed of their remains, presumably, since he hadn't been carted off for questioning. It didn't pay to underestimate the Yakuza, either in terms of their ferocity or their efficiency. The Yakuza served as the planet's oldest criminal syndicate—older even than the

Chinese triads—and survival spanning some four hundred years meant they had learned a thing or two along the way.

Bolan was approaching Windsor Avenue when he saw a black stretch limo turning into traffic on Atlantic, headed in the same direction he was going. That saved him time and inconvenience, since he didn't have to box the block and come around Machii's crew wagon. All Bolan had to do now was maintain visual contact with the limousine until it dropped the *kyodai* at the "other house" he'd mentioned in his office. Bolan couldn't eavesdrop on the limo's passengers, since they had left his bug behind, but he could follow them all night if necessary, until they found a place to roost.

In fact, it didn't take that long. At Washington, the limo took a right-hand turn and traveled past the Margate City Historical Museum, then hung a left on Ventnor Avenue and followed that until it crossed the JFK Bridge and became Route 152, skirting the Atlantic coast of an unnamed barrier island. It was marshy ground, with serpentine canals or rivers winding through it, trees along the north side of the highway, beaches kissed by breakers to the south.

Bolan trailed his quarry past the Seaview Harbor Marina, then watched the limo turn northward, on to a two-lane access road that disappeared from view around a curve. He dared not follow it too closely, so drove on two hundred yards, until he found a place to turn and double back.

Machii's ride was long gone by the time Bolan returned to where they'd parted company. It was a gamble, trailing him, but still the only way of finding out exactly where he'd gone. Nosing into the two-lane access road, he braked and pulled a pair of night-vision infrared goggles from the bag of tricks beside him on the shotgun seat, and slipped the straps over his head, then killed the RAV4's lights.

The goggles let him see for fifty feet without another light source, but a half moon rode the sky this night, extending Bolan's vision to fifty yards or more. He'd have to take it easy, keep from edging off the road and on to marshy ground, but there'd be ample warning if another car was headed his way, and he'd show no lights of his own unless he stepped on the Toyota's brake pedal.

The drive in seemed to take forever, but the dashboard clock—light dimmed until it was barely visible—told Bolan he was making decent time, all things considered. Stealth took longer than a mad charge toward the firing line, and that was what he needed now.

He spent ten minutes on the looping access road before he spotted lights a quarter or half mile farther on. The vehicle had come to a stop in front of a large, two-story house, not quite a mansion, but the next best thing for its surroundings. Open fields and marsh surrounded it, making a foot approach more dangerous, but that would clearly be the only way to go.

Bolan stopped a quarter mile out from the house, switched off the RAV4's dome light prior to opening the driver's door, and then went EVA. Standing in moonlight, he removed the goggles and surveyed his target through a pair of field glasses that brought the place up close and personal. He saw two gunmen on the front porch, covering a driveway that branched off the access road, and figured there'd be more in back, watching the alternate approach.

Machii doubtless thought that he was safe out here, away from everyone and everything.

The Executioner had plans to prove him wrong.

CHAPTER FIVE

Noboru Machii was not ready to relax. It helped, having some distance from Atlantic City, but uncertainty gnawed at his nerves, making him restless, even after he had downed three cups of *sake* at room temperature. When the sweet rice wine failed to relieve his tension, he had switched to Bushmills twenty-one-year single malt whiskey, hoping its higher alcohol content would do the trick.

So far, no go.

Tetsuya Watanabe knocked and poked his head in through the study's open door. Machii glanced up from the cold fireplace in front of him and nodded his permission to proceed.

"The guards are all in place," Watanabe said. "Six men, positioned as you wished. I think you can sleep safely now."

"You think?"

Watanabe shrugged. "We should be safe here, sir," he replied.

"We *should* have been safe at the office. I assume there's been no progress in the city, finding out who's sent us into hiding?"

"None so far," Watanabe admitted ruefully.

"What of Endo and the others?"

"The police have them, sir. They'll be dissected by the medical examiner, of course."

"Autopsied."

"Gomen'nasai."

"There's no need to apologize. Work on your English."

"Yes, sir. It will be difficult for the authorities to link them with the family. None are on file with immigration, and they have not been arrested in America."

"Suspicion still attaches to us, given the succession of events."

"Suspicion is not proof."

"But it's enough to prompt investigation, if they are not looking into us already."

One more headache, on a night that was replete with them. Machii pushed that prospect out of mind and focused on his unknown enemies. He made it plural, since the man or men behind a raw act of aggression, in Machii's world, would never carry out the act themselves. That left him with a list of possibilities to ponder, none of which stood out above the rest.

New Jersey was awash in crime and government corruption. That had been a fact of life for generations, going back a century and more, beyond the days when simple-minded folk thought they could cure a nation's ills by banning alcohol. These days, the old Italian Mafia was in decline from former glory days, competing for survival in an ethnic stew of Chinese and Koreans, Cubans and Jamaicans, Russians and Albanians, Vietnamese and Japanese. Anytime contending sides brushed shoulders, there was bloodshed. Thanks in large part to Machii's acumen, the Sumiyoshi-kai had managed to stay clear of overt violence so far.

Until this night.

Now, in a few short hours, everything he'd worked for was at risk. His very life was riding on the line, if he could not eliminate the danger to his family.

But so far, he had no idea where to begin the search.

"Is there a chance that Endo's men wounded the person they were chasing?" he inquired.

"Our man on the police force doesn't think so, but it's possible his car was damaged by the shooting. Chips of glass were found, he says. A search is under way for cars damaged by gunfire, but it could be anywhere."

And if they found it, Machii thought, it would probably be stolen, anyway. A competent professional would no more take his own car on a raid than he would dress up in *kabuki* robes.

"Who is most likely to move against us in Atlantic City, then?"

Watanabe thought about it for a moment, then replied, "I think, the Russians. Shestov knows you represent the family, and he's been looking for a foothold in a great casino."

"Shestov's Ukrainian, not Russian."

"What's the difference?" Tetsuya asked. "They're all barbarians."

He had that right, at least. Pavlo Shestov was tough, ruthless and driven by ambition. It was said he watched the movie *Scarface* once a week, at least, and tried to mimic the ferocity of its protagonist. With thirty-five or forty soldiers on his payroll, he was capable of starting trouble, but would he be fool enough to take on the Sumiyoshi-kai?

Perhaps.

It was a starting place, at least.

"Pick up one of his men," Machii ordered. "Try for the lieutenant. What's his name, again?"

"Palatnik."

"Question him. If Shestov is behind this, he should know."

"And when we're finished with him?"

"We can't let him run back home and tattle, can we?" That would start a war with Shestov, if they weren't already in the midst of one.

"No, sir."

"Well, then."

"I shall see to it myself."

Machii raised a hand to stop him. "Let Yoshinori handle it," he said. "I want you here with me."

Watanabe frowned, as if uncertain whether he should take that as an insult or a compliment. Instead of answering, he tipped his head, a token bow, and marched out of the room.

Machii was about to pour another glass of whiskey, wondering if he should have a sandwich first, when an explosion rocked the house.

BOLAN HAD PULLED OUT all the stops for his incursion on Machii's hideaway. He took the silenced MP-5 K, backed up with a Colt M4A1 carbine sporting an Aimpoint CompM4 reflector sight and an M320 grenade launcher mounted under the carbine's barrel, fitted with its own side-mounted day/night sight. To feed the guns, he wore two bandoleers across his chest—one fat with 5.56 mm magazines, the other packing 40 mm high-explosive rounds—and wore a triple belt pouch for the SMG's curved magazines. All together, Glock included, he was packing in 450 rounds of sudden death, hoping it was a great deal more than he would need.

Off road, the ground was treacherous beneath his feet. He had the goggles on again, scanning the turf for streams and ponds, long-stepping over them from one firm hummock to another. On his way, he kept checking the house, confirming that Machii's lookouts were not on the move with a patrol into the marsh. From what

Bolan could see, two hundred yards and closing through the moonlight, they seemed fairly well at ease, smoking and chatting on the porch.

That didn't mean that they weren't dangerous, by any means.

The Yakuza was not a blood in/blood out operation that required each new recruit to take a human life. Some members never got their hands dirty, beyond cooking the books at firms the syndicate controlled. Soldiers, by contrast, were recruited from the *bosozoku* "restless tribe" gangs in Japan, equivalent to outlaw bikers in the States, who grew up fighting for a scrap of urban turf and had their consciences seared out of them before they got to high school. Given any chance to join the big leagues, they jumped at it, seizing any opportunity to prove themselves through terrorism, homicide and torture.

All the best of *manga* entertainment, with real corpses.

Bolan had no doubt the guards would die to save their *oyabun*, and he was ready to accommodate them. First, though, he desired to get in closer, scout the lonely home's perimeter and get a feel for how many defenders he was facing. When he made his move, he wanted it to come as a surprise and catch the soldiers with their guard down.

Stopping at the fifty-yard mark, well beyond the floodlights mounted on each corner of the house, Bolan began to circle clockwise, watching as he went for any traps, alarms or hidden cameras that might betray him to a watcher on the grounds. He found none and continued, counting half a dozen lookouts on his circuit. There were two in front, two more out back, one by himself on each end of the manor, north and south. The darkened patio, in back, offered the best approach, with tall translucent sliding doors fronting some kind of lighted recreation room.

The Executioner closed in, moving slowly in a half

crouch, weighted by the guns and ammunition that he carried. He gripped the silenced MP-5 K, carbine slung across his back where he could reach it readily at need, both the rifle and its under-barrel launcher primed and ready. At a range of thirty yards, he stopped, knelt and checked again for any lurkers whom he might have missed.

The paired-up guards were definitely on their own.

Approaching them would be a needless risk. Bolan lined up the MP-5 K's iron sights with a hooded post in front. He pinned them on the watchman to his left, no special reason, and squeezed off a snuffling 3-round burst that put him down, blood spreading from beneath him on the paving stones.

Before the second lookout could react, Bolan had swiveled toward him, squeezed the trigger once again, and opened up his chest with hollow-point rounds. The dying hardman slumped backward, but his index finger clenched around the trigger of his Micro-Uzi, rattling off a burst like fireworks in the dark, still night.

So much for stealth.

Before more lights came on inside the house, before the home team started cursing, shouting orders, Bolan let the MP-5 K drop and dangle from its sling, hauling the Colt around and bringing it to bear. He peered into the M320 launcher's day/night sight, using its laser range finder, and sent an HE round across the patio, smashing through plate glass on its way and detonating when it struck the rec room's southern wall.

NOBORU MACHII DROPPED his whiskey glass and bolted to his feet, cursing a sudden rush of dizziness he recognized as the effect of too much alcohol. He was not drunk, per se, but heard a buzzing in his ears completely unrelated to the blast of seconds earlier, and wobbled on his legs until he braced one hand against a side table and got his balance back.

He made it halfway to the wall-mounted gun cabinet before Tetsuya Watanabe burst into the study, pistol in his hand, asking, "Are you okay, sir?"

"Yes, I'm fine." Machii almost snarled at him. "What's happening?"

"I'm not sure, yet. I came to check on you. It may be—"

Gunfire crackled from the general direction of the rec room, soldiers crying out.

Machii did snarl, then. "Get out and deal with that! I'll be there in a minute."

At the cabinet, he fumbled with a small brass key to open it and took a shotgun from the rack inside. It was a Benelli M3 Super 90 12-gauge, which allowed a choice of pump-action or semiautomatic fire. Its magazine held seven rounds of triple-0 buckshot, with one more in the chamber, each equivalent to six .36-caliber bullets inside one cartridge. At close range, it was devastating.

And exactly what Machii needed at that moment.

As an afterthought, he snatched a pistol from its hook inside the cabinet, a fully loaded Walther PPQ, which stood for "police pistol quick defense" in German. That would give Machii eighteen extra shots, in case his 12-gauge and the guards stationed to defend him all proved useless.

The whiskey bottle beckoned to Machii as he left the study, but he cursed it and moved on, following sounds of combat toward the east side of the house. A smoky, chemical aroma in the air reminded him of the munitions that had fogged his office earlier, but this was subtly different. He recognized the scent of burnt gunpowder and explosives mixed together, and he had no doubt the house was under siege.

How had his nameless enemies located him? There was no time to think about that now, while they were still alive and doing everything within their power to kill him. Not police, he knew that much, since they always arrived with sirens, flashing lights and warrants. Someone else, then, who was not concerned with legal niceties, but only with the bottom-line result.

Machii's ears rang with the sounds of gunfire now, the softer hiss of liquor working on his brain cells smothered by the battle din. He needed no guide to locate the firing line, but hesitated well short of the rec room, pausing in the hallway as another trio of his men ran past him, heedless of his presence on their way to join the fight.

If he could make it to the car and slip away, while they were busy...

Flushed with shame, Machii cursed himself and started moving toward the action, one foot following the other at a cautious, almost creeping speed. He kept his index finger off the shotgun's trigger, worried that he might shoot one of his own soldiers accidentally, but he was ready to unleash a storm of lead within a split second, if threatened.

Another blast ripped through the house, much closer than the first. A rain of dust and plaster flakes sprinkled Machii as he huddled in the hallway, nearly deafened now. It was disorienting, but he knew where he was headed, only had to keep on walking in the same direction to become part of the action.

If he ran, there'd be no end to running. And no man escaped his private shame.

One of Machii's guards staggered into view, emerging from a side door to the kitchen. He was unarmed, clearly dazed, a flap of scalp dangling above one eye as blood streamed down his face and soaked his white dress shirt. The soldier did not recognize his boss, shuffling toward him like a zombie, one arm out to brace and guide himself along the wall.

Machii stepped in front of him and clutched the wounded man's lapel. "What's happening?" he asked the soldier who stood blinking in his grasp. "Who is attacking us?"

"I do not know, sir," came the reply.

Of course the young man didn't know. How could he? He was stunned, brain scrambled, and the enemy would not have introduced himself. Machii stepped around his useless flunky, finding new courage in his own ability to move with purpose toward the battle.

With his finger on the shotgun's trigger, he was prepared to kill his adversaries or die trying.

BOLAN HAD KILLED five gunners since entering the house, which made it seven altogether from the patio until he reached the modern, institutional-sized kitchen. Three had been together in the rec room when his first HE round detonated there, one more or less beheaded by the blast and shrapnel, while the other two were shaken to the point of immobility and sat there, staring at him, while he put them down for good.

The other two came charging in as he was moving through the smoke and dust from the explosion toward a door connecting to the kitchen. Sighting him, they both gave out kung fu–type shouts and leveled pistols in his general direction, but their zeal did not equate with combat readiness. One bullet hissed past Bolan's ear, a foot or more off target, and the second shooter didn't have a chance to fire as Bolan's M4A1 carbine answered, stuttering short bursts and gutting them with 5.56 mm manglers.

The NATO rounds were made to yaw and fragment at their cannelures, shredding a target's vital organs with a storm of shrapnel while the main part of the slug tumbled through flesh and muscle, carving out a devastating wound channel. The two gunners went down, flailing, out of action in a heartbeat, likely dead before their slayer cleared the kitchen door.

The large room, mostly stainless steel and copper, had three exits. Bolan had one covered, while the others, he supposed, would serve a dining room and, possibly, a hallway running through the house to other rooms. He had the kitchen to himself for ten or fifteen seconds, then his ears picked up the sound of more hardmen closing from the right, beyond a swing door. Bolan crouched behind a serving island in the middle of the kitchen, carbine angling toward the door.

When it flew open, Bolan glimpsed the formal dining room beyond—something from *Better Homes & Gardens*—then three gunners blocked the view, crowding the doorway in their rush to meet the enemy. Two of them carried submachine guns, and he couldn't see the third one's hands.

Instead of wasting bullets on the trio, Bolan let them have a 40 mm HE round, ducking behind the heavy wood-and-granite island as it blew, unleashing thunder in the kitchen with a storm of brick dust, plaster, ventilated pots and pans. When Bolan looked again, two of the attackers were down, the third no longer visible, either propelled back through the doorway by the shock wave or—a slim chance—quick enough to save himself.

Bolan rose from cover and proceeded toward the dining room, uncertain where he'd find Machii in the house, now that his probe had turned into a running firefight. Some commanders, in that circumstance, would lead their soldiers by example; others, a majority, would be content to issue orders, all the while intent on looking out for Number One. The samurai mind-set might help determine how Machii acted, but he couldn't count on that to put the Yakuza boss in his rifle sights.

First thing through the door into the dining room, he saw that the third shooter *had* escaped, leaving a trail of blood across beige carpet and along the nearest wall, likely from trailing fingertips. With no one else in sight, Bolan went after him, the smears and splashes leading to another door six yards in front of him. There was a blood smudge on the doorknob, verifying that his quarry had passed through it in his flight from the explosion.

He hesitated at the door, listened and heard nothing beyond it. Careful to avoid the bloody knob, he eased it open, started to lean through—then jerked back as a sudden movement to his right warned Bolan of a trap in waiting.

He recoiled, crouching, and grimaced as a shotgun blast shattered the door frame, heavy buckshot pellets drilling wood and drywall. Bolan waited for a follow-up that didn't come, while calculating odds of getting nailed if he proceeded through the exit to the corridor beyond.

A shotgun gave his adversary an advantage. Marksmanship was secondary, with a scattergun, to nerve and steady hands. If Bolan rushed the doorway, he could wind up getting peppered, and the gunner was loading double-0, at least. One hit, much less a pellet cluster, could be fatal or debilitating.

On the other hand, if he stayed where he was, it could mean reinforcements coming down the corridor or through the kitchen at his back. They might come *both* ways, trap him in the dining room and finish him, if they had guns and guts enough to pull it off.

Given the choice, Bolan would almost always choose attack, and this was no exception.

But he had a little something different in mind.

He fed the M320 its third helping from his bandoleer of HE rounds, angling it to his right, well past the door, picking a chest-high spot along the wall some ten feet farther on. Sheltered behind a corner of the massive dining table, hand-carved ebony, he triggered the grenade and ducked, shielding from its blowback.

As intended, it blew through the drywall like a wrecking ball, spraying the outer corridor with shrapnel, shattered lumber and a cloud of choking dust.

MACHII BLINKED THROUGH swirling smoke and dust motes, staring at the ceiling, marveling that he was still alive. If he had held his ground after the first blast from his shotgun, rather than retreating to a safer distance, shrapnel might have disemboweled him, maybe shearing off his legs. Instead, he had escaped without a wound of any magnitude, except the sudden deafness that enveloped him and a tremendous headache, throbbing in between his useless ears.

No time to lose, if he intended to survive.

Machii used his shotgun as a walking stick to help him stand, avoiding contact with the trigger as he rose. Having missed death by the narrowest of margins, he did not intend to shoot himself by accident, the ultimate indignity.

The thunderclap after his own Benelli blast informed him that he'd missed his target—or, at least, had not inflicted a disabling wound. If he had waited just a fraction of a second longer, for the raiders to reveal themselves...

Too late to think about that now. His plight demanded focus on reality as it existed at the moment, not lamenting things that might have been.

Machii thought he could survive this, but he had to keep his wits about him, take aggressive action to destroy the raiders who had breached his private sanctuary. If he had the chance to capture one of them alive, so much the better. And if not, extermination in itself would still be satisfying.

Crouching in the corridor, Machii tried to shout for help but could not tell if he was actually making any sound. His throat felt strained from yelling, breathing dust or both, but he was still deaf to all sound of any kind. Raising a hand to his left ear, he felt moisture and saw his fingers slick with blood, suggesting ruptured eardrums.

"Guchi no kuso musuko!"

Even as he mouthed the curse, Noboru could not hear the words.

One final shout for help, if he *was* shouting, and he turned back to the ruptured wall before him. One of his enemies was hiding in the formal dining room—or had he slipped into the kitchen now, hoping to come around Machii and surprise him?

That thought made him whip around, swinging the shotgun's muzzle back the way he'd come, but no one loomed in front of him. There was no threat from that direction—yet.

He spun back toward the ruptured wall, rushed up to shove his shotgun's muzzle through the ragged opening and triggered two quick blasts in semiauto fire. The weapon's stock kicked back against his hip, bruising him, but the Yakuza boss barely noticed. Dropping to one knee, he peered in through the porthole, nostrils flaring at the stench of high explosives, while he tried to scan the dining room beyond.

Machii's view was limited, at best. He saw no movement in the room where he'd enjoyed some fine meals in the past but never would again. The house was ruined for him now, another crime scene that he had to abandon, grateful that it had been purchased through a paper company without his name attached to any phase of the transaction.

Growling like a wounded animal, aware of it only through the vibration of his vocal cords, Machii rose and burst in through the doorway to the dining room. He found no bodies there, then turned to check the kitchen and discovered two of his young soldiers sprawled in blood beyond the shattered threshold. When he couldn't think of either's name offhand, it felt like a betrayal, but he swallowed it, one more addition to his list of sins.

He stepped around the bodies, careful not to slip on blood and fall. The kitchen was a shambles, evidently from the second blast he'd heard while he was seeking out the sounds of combat. Following the shotgun's muzzle like a dowser with his wand, Machii headed for the kitchen's other exit, straining dead ears in a fruitless effort to pick up on sounds that might portend a threat.

Nothing. His world was like a vacuum now, except that he could breathe.

When he had reached the door, the Yakuza boss paused again, raising a hand to touch his right ear this time. When his fingers came back clean of blood, he forced a yawn and simultaneously slapped the right side of his head, rewarded with a small *pop* from his ear canal. His head cleared on that side, enough to hear it when he coughed up dust.

A voice behind him asked, "Looking for me?"

BOLAN HAD CLEARED the formal dining room before Machii started firing buckshot through the blown-out wall. He'd circled through the kitchen, retracing his earlier steps, and reentered the corridor just as the mobster lunged into the dining room, hoping to finish him off. No other Yakuzas had come to intercept him there, so it had been a simple step to trail Machii, slipping back into the dining room behind as the *kyodai* proceeded hunting Bolan.

Checkmate.

At the sound of Bolan's voice, Machii froze, his shoulders slumping just a little as the disappointment of his failure hit him. From the angle of his head, cocked slightly to one side, it figured he was thinking of a move to save himself—or, at the very least, take Bolan down with him.

"It won't work," the Executioner told him. "You're not fast enough."

"You don't know me," Machii said without turning.

"I know enough. It ends here."

"You plan to shoot me in the back?"

"Back, front, it doesn't matter. If you want to turn around, first lose the shotgun."

"If I drop it—"

"Nothing ought to happen. Let's find out."

Machii played it safe, tossing the scattergun away from him, off through the kitchen doorway, where it clattered on a tile floor. "Satisfied?" the *kyodai* inquired, showing his empty hands.

"Almost. No sudden moves."

Any discussion with Machii was a waste of time his soldiers might be using to surround the dining room, but Bolan took the chance. Sometimes, confronting death, a predator was moved to boast or bluster, maybe even plead, disclosing intel that he should have taken with him to the grave.

Machii turned, his face deadpan. "A white man. But you're not a Russian."

"No."

"What, then?"

"Someone who wished you'd been smart enough to stay at home."

"This is the land of opportunity," Machii countered.

"It's supposed to be," Bolan replied. "For those who play it straight."

"Like your industrialists and your politicians? Your police and lawyers? I have simply followed their example."

"Let's just say I'm cleaning up one toxic puddle at a time."

"This will not stop my family," Machii said.

"You're just the first step on a journey," Bolan answered.

And his time was swiftly running out.

"My *burazāzu* will destroy you."

"Sorry. I lost my Rosetta Stone."

"My brothers. They will not forget this, or forgive it."

"I suspect you've got replacements lining up. I'll ask Shinoda when I see him."

"Ah. Then you are truly the walking dead."

"At least I'm walking out of here," Bolan replied, shooting Machii through the forehead as the Yakuza hardman made a sudden, futile play for the Executioner's weapon.

Bolan heard voices in the hallway, not too close as yet, but narrowing the gap by cautious stages. He could not have said how many voices, and he didn't pause to puzzle over it. Feeding the M320 one more round, he also dropped the carbine's nearly empty magazine and snapped a fresh one into place. He confirmed that the fire selector switch was in full-auto mode and made a small adjustment to the carbine's sling, for comfort, as he edged back toward the exit from the dining room.

The plan was to lead with the 40 mm HE round, then hose the Yakuza gunners with 5.56 mm slugs as he retreated toward the rec room, going out the way he'd come in to Machii's home away from home. It was a bold plan, risky, but the only one on tap for Bolan at the moment. He'd achieved all that he'd hoped to, and the time to split was now.

He made one small refinement to the plan before he kicked off. Rather than emerging cold and hoping he could beat them to the punch, Bolan approached the gaping wall breach that his last grenade had opened, which Machii had converted to a gun port without managing to score a hit. Edging around to give himself the proper angle, peering far enough downrange to see a Yakuza scout edging closer, Bolan fired the M320 through that gap and waited for the blast before he charged out of the dining room.

Showtime.

CHAPTER SIX

East St. Louis Avenue, Las Vegas, Nevada

Night Moves was rocking. Sitting in his office on the second floor, Jiro Shinoda heard the music from downstairs and felt it through the floor, through thick carpeting and through the lifts inside his handmade shoes that added two full inches to his height. He lit a cigarette—too late for it to stunt his growth at thirty-one—and tried to focus on the money he was making, just by sitting there, instead of letting stray thoughts wander toward New Jersey.

Night Moves was a thriving gentlemen's club, two blocks east of South Las Vegas Boulevard—one long block beyond the northern limit of the famous Vegas Strip—and just around the corner from an all-night wedding chapel, just in case one of his patrons fell in love while watching Shinoda's dancers do their business on the catwalk. Up and down the side street, fast-food takeout joints eliminated any need for Night Moves to maintain a kitchen. Guests were free to bring their own food with them, which permitted them to smoke under the current law, while they were swilling Shinoda's beer and watered liquor, gaping at the naked talent.

No kitchen on the premises, no rules except the silly hands-off regulation that was honored on the main floor, for the most part, with an eye toward unannounced city inspections. If a rube wanted to play grab-ass, and any given dancer was amenable, Shinoda had half a dozen VIP suites where the private dances would be screened from public view.

And monitored by hidden cameras. Strictly for safety's sake, of course.

Shinoda sipped from a tall glass of whiskey, still uncertain whether he was celebrating or trying to soothe jangled nerves. On one hand, any problem that beset Noboru Machii in Atlantic City was potentially good news for Shinoda, offering him a chance to shine while his competing brother suffered in the estimation of their *oyabun*. Conversely, if the trouble spread and flared out of control, it might turn into Shinoda's problem, and that was the last thing that he needed when he had the rubes in Vegas almost where he wanted them.

Almost.

Merv Mendelbaum was part of that. Eliminating him had been Shinoda's aim from the beginning, as Noboru Machii had been tasked to deal with Tommy Wolff. Of course, Shinoda had shown himself superior at strategy, making his target disappear in lieu of butchering him with a crop of rent-a-cops and hookers in his own hotel. Granted, that had a certain flare, but if the blood trail led back to the Sumiyoshi-kai, it would be bad for business.

On the downside, Mendelbaum's vanishing act meant that he could not be declared dead for a period of years without a body to support that claim. Meanwhile, his widow and the various vice presidents of Goldstone Entertainment were engaged in grappling for control of Mendelbaum's empire, smiling in public, quietly subverting one another anytime they saw an opening.

At heart, Shinoda knew his *oyabun* was disappointed by his choice of tactics, subtler than Machii's, but with a potential long delay in ultimate success. Shinoda had been brooding, worried that he might be forced to sacrifice a pinky in atonement, until he'd received Machii's call sketching the trouble in Atlantic City. Naturally, it had been Shinoda's duty to alert their *oyabun*, soften the blow of hearing it direct from his New Jersey *kyodai*.

What was a brother for, if not to lend a helping hand in time of need?

A phone purred softly but insistently beside him, on his desktop. Glancing at the lighted button on its base, Shinoda discovered that the line engaged was one reserved for sources of significant intelligence. Caller ID and his own memory told him the call originated from New Jersey, within Atlantic City's "609" area code. That narrowed down the field to three potential callers, any one of whom was worth his time.

Shinoda lifted the receiver. *"Hai."*

"Hai, Sensei."

He recognized the voice immediately as belonging to his mole inside Noboru Machii's Jersey crew. The same man had briefed him on the raid at Sunrise Enterprises, earlier that day, and on the loss of life involved.

"What news?" Shinoda inquired, without preamble.

"Noboru Machii is dead."

The unexpected statement shocked Shinoda and excited him at the same time.

"What happened?"

His informant told the story without frills, apologizing three times in the process for his lack of further details. It was plain enough for any child to understand, except for who had done the deed. That troubled the *kyodai*, on his own account, but was of no immediate concern.

"Thank you for keeping me informed," he said at last.

"Should someone call our godfather?" his caller asked.

"Leave that to me," Shinoda replied. "Sad duties should be carried out by one of a more elevated rank."

"Hai, Sensei." And with that, the line went dead.

Two small clocks on his desk told Shinoda the time difference between Las Vegas and Japan, not that the hour mattered in this instance. News this grave—and as potentially prodigious for himself—could not afford to wait.

Pressing a button on the phone's base to engage his scrambled line, he began to dial.

Joint Base McGuire-Dix-Lakehurst, New Jersey

THE GARDEN STATE once claimed three military bases sprawling over 42,000 acres in New Jersey's two largest counties, Ocean and Burlington. The bases had included Fort Dix (US Army), Naval Air Station Lakehurst and McGuire Air Force Base. They had been consolidated in October 2009 and given the cumbersome name that most personnel automatically shortened to JB MDL.

Bolan was expected when he completed the drive from Atlantic City, sixty-six miles southeast of the base. He had explained his plan to Stony Man, emailing from AC, and they had run with it from there, pulling the necessary strings—through Hal Brognola in Washington—to make him welcome briefly, and arrange a flight to Nellis Air Force Base, north of Las Vegas. That meant he'd be spared the hassle of discarding weapons in New Jersey and collecting more upon arrival in Nevada, and it also saved him time on booking a civilian flight, with any stops at "travel hubs" along the way.

It still remained to be seen what kind of "welcome" he'd receive at JB MDL, but Bolan took for granted that the basic military courtesies would be observed, and he did not intend to linger on the base a moment longer than required to catch the next plane headed west.

Two guards—one army MP and one naval SP, shore patrol—checked Bolan's fake ID and verified that he was listed on their clipboard, while an airman from the Air Base Ground Defense watched from a nearby guard shack, ready with a panic button and a range of weapons if the meet-and-greet went sour. It didn't, and within two minutes of arrival, Bolan cleared the gate, hewing to the directions he'd been given to a hangar on McGuire's part of the base.

Two airmen were waiting for him as he pulled up to the hangar. Both wore basic Air Force blues, one with a master sergeant's stripes on short sleeves strained by sculpted biceps, while the other had a captain's double silver bars pinned to his collar, and a name tag that identified him as "G. SHERMAN." Neither showed a smile as Bolan stepped out of the hot RAV4 and stood before them, waiting out the silence to see who would break the ice.

"Good morning, Colonel," Captain Sherman said, using the rank Bolan had received after he'd "died" and was reborn through Stony Man. "I hope you had a safe trip."

"Fine." No one had tried to kill him in the hour-plus that he'd been on the road, which suited Bolan to a tee.

"We understand you won't be staying with us long," Sherman went on.

"Depends on downtime, waiting for my ride," Bolan replied.

"It's ready now, sir. You have gear inside the vehicle?"

"I do," Bolan confirmed, and turned to fetch his three bags from the SUV's backseat.

"I'll help you with those, sir," the master sergeant said.

"Big one's the heaviest."

"No problem, sir." The biceps barely rippled as the master sergeant took the bag containing Bolan's hardware, but the noncom shot a quick glance toward his captain, who received the message loud and clear.

No comment and no questions from the stoic officer. He settled for, "Please, follow me, sir," and Bolan obliged, trailing his escorts through the hangar's open bay. Inside, beneath fluorescent lights, a Boeing C-17 Globemaster III transport plane sat gleaming, while mechanics finished with its preflight checkup.

The C-17 was a certified workhorse. In service since the 1980s, when it was developed from the McDonnell Douglas YC-15, it was designed for moving troops and cargo anywhere the military needed them to arrive on time and in one piece.

Bolan had been expecting something smaller, but he kept that to himself, watching the burly master sergeant lug his bags aboard. The captain seemed to read his mind, saying, "The other troops should be along directly, sir. Feel free to go aboard, or use the waiting room, whichever you prefer."

"Thanks, Captain."

"If there's nothing else, sir?"

"Nothing I can think of," Bolan said. "Dismissed."

Azabu, Tokyo

THE MOMENT HE saw Kato Ando coming, with the cordless telephone in hand, Kazuo Takumi braced himself for more bad news. He'd spent the past few hours pondering the trouble in Atlantic City but had come to no conclusions. He would need reports from his appointed soldiers, once they landed in the States, but they were hours out from touchdown yet, and would not call their *oyabun* for any reason while in transit, barring failure of their aircraft.

Ando reached him, holding out the telephone, and said, "Jiro Shinoda."

Takumi allowed himself a small frown as he took the phone and answered. This time, for variety, he might chastise his *kyodai* if Shinoda started telling tales about Noboru Machii.

Or, he might not.

As it was, after obligatory courtesies, Shinoda immediately spilled his news. There'd been another shooting in New Jersey, this time with the worst conceivable result. Noboru Machii was among the dead, no final figures yet, but it was Shinoda's duty to inform his *oyabun*, and so on. He was still apologizing when Kazuo Takumi cut him off.

"Chinmoku!" The command for silence instantly truncated Shinoda's flow of words.

"You must prepare yourself," Takumi ordered. "Be alert in all respects. Until we know who is responsible, our operation in Nevada also is at risk."

"I am prepared, master," Shinoda replied, too quickly.

"This is not a time for arrogance," Takumi said. "I'm sure Noboru thought he was prepared, as well."

"But—"

"Double-check all of your preparations, then go back and check again. Goodbye."

Takumi cut off the call and placed the phone in Ando's waiting hand.

His old and trusted friend studied his master's face, reading his mood, although he could not guess the details of Jiro Shinoda's call. "What shall we do?" he asked.

"I've done all that I can do, for the moment," Takumi

replied. "But I must take my own advice. Warn everyone within the family to stay alert. No deviation from
our normal business is required, as yet, but anything unusual must be reported back without delay. Understand?"

"Yes!"

"If they desire to speak with me…"

"I'll tell them you are indisposed," Ando suggested.

"Perfect."

Everyone of value in the Sumiyoshi-kai already knew
that Ando was Kazuo Takumi's voice in many varied
circumstances. He would pass his master's order to the
captains, who would pass it on to their subordinates, until
it reached the lowest gambler, dealer and pimp on the
street. Whoever got the word—and that meant twenty-
thousand members of the family, plus all of their asso-
ciates—would know it came from Kazuo Takumi's lips.

And they would do as they were told.

The main thing, now, was not to panic. He had lost
Noboru Machii, and perhaps the whole New Jersey operation, but Takumi had survived worse losses in the past
and still emerged victorious from the last battle.

Ando was about to leave and carry out his orders when
his master stopped him. "Have you seen Toi?"

"Not since Friday," Ando answered, making no attempt to hide his frown.

"Call him. Tell him I want him here. Immediately."

"Hai, Sensei."

Kazuo would not tell his son that he was *needed*, even
through an intermediary. Toi tested his father's will at
every opportunity, and it was time to jerk his leash, remind him of the debt he owed for all the privilege that he
enjoyed and took advantage of, while sometimes feigning bland indifference.

If nothing else, the present crisis might propel Toi one

step closer to becoming a real man. Or, failing that, it could reduce him to the status of a child who knew his place and ventured from it only with permission from his father.

Toi would learn that if it killed him, leaving Kazuo Takumi without a rightful heir.

Airborne, Over West Virginia

THE "OTHER TROOPS" aboard the Boeing Globemaster were fifty-two airmen, both men and women, en route to Nellis or some other Western air force base with a stopover in Nevada. They sat in sidewall seats, all dressed in ABUs—airman battle uniforms—made from service-distinctive camouflage fabric that deviated from army combat uniform design by including slate blue in its digital tiger-stripe pattern. As per regulation, each ABU bore name tag tape, rank insignia and occupational badges, with trouser cuffs bloused into sage-green suede boots.

The others talked among themselves, while carefully avoiding Bolan. He supposed they had received a hands-off briefing in advance, without details, since no one at McGuire had any knowledge of his mission or his destination, once he drove away from Nellis in the rental car that should be waiting for him on arrival.

He was extra cargo on this flight and nothing more. No reason they should think about the stranger in civilian clothes, or why he rated transport on their aircraft. Bolan knew they had to have questions, but they also had the discipline to keep from asking them aloud.

He kept an empty seat between himself and the young airman first class to his right, turning a little in his seat so that the youngster couldn't peer at Bolan's smartphone if he felt a sudden surge of curiosity. He had a four-and-one-half-hour flight ahead of him, enough time to review Brognola's files once more in transit and make sure he had it all down cold.

Yakuza in the United States had once been confined to Hawaii, by virtue of its Japanese population, but various families had spanned the Pacific to infest California in the early 1980s, branching out from there to Chicago and New York City. In California, they allied themselves with Chinese Triads and other Asian mobsters, including South Koreans and Vietnamese. Where feasible, they brokered deals with leaders of the Cosa Nostra, taxing Mafia gambling clubs and other rackets in Asian communities.

Another lure in the States was firearms, greatly restricted at home in Japan. Through the eighties, a simple $300 revolver could sell in Japan for $4,000 or more, and ammo averaged a dollar per cartridge to start. That blue-steel gold rush had faltered in the 1990s, as Japan suffered a gun glut of its own, but the Yakuza had expanded by then, importing methamphetamine, trying its hand at human trafficking, and infiltrating legitimate firms. The latter offered threefold benefits: as cover for taxation, covert money laundries and a foot in the door of industries such as gaming and pharmaceuticals, where the predators felt right at home.

The FBI had enjoyed mixed success in cracking the Yakuza stateside. In 2001, the Bureau had arranged for Tadamasa Goto, *oyabun* of the Fujinomiya-based Goto-gumi family, to receive a lifesaving liver transplant in Los Angeles. Goto had returned the favor with a $100,000 donation to the UCLA Medical Center and some titillating gossip on the rival Yamaguchi-gumi clan, before the story broke and raised a stink from Washington to Tokyo, with reports that scores of Los Angelenos had died waiting for livers while Goto got his, courtesy of the Justice Department.

Meanwhile, Goto had retired to enjoy his new liver and published a memoir, titled *Habakarinagara*—"While Hesitating"—that topped bestseller lists in Japan, in 2011.

Nowadays the FBI had a joint "working group" against the Yakuza, collaborating with Japan's National Police Agency, paralleled by Project Bridge with Interpol, and a Cross-Border Crime Forum coordinating operations with the Royal Canadian Mounted Police. None had made any significant busts, but they consoled themselves with gathering intelligence, interdicting meth shipments and waiting for the one big chance they needed to get on the scoreboard.

Mack Bolan, fortunately, wasn't bound by rules of evidence or any fat books filled with authorized procedures. He was free to strike an adversary when and where he liked, as long as certain basic guidelines were observed.

Avoid civilian casualties.

Spare cops, even the dirty ones, from use of deadly force.

Minimize collateral damage to property owned by innocents.

The third rule could be dicey, but he did his best.

Vegas would be different from Atlantic City, both in climate and the risks involved. The Yakuza out there couldn't be certain they were next in line for trouble, but they had to be smart enough to brace themselves for ripples from the detonation in New Jersey. Bolan would have to hit the ground running, stay in motion and shake his enemies until their house came tumbling down. Along the way, if he could pick up more intel, so much the better.

Satisfied for now, he stowed the smartphone, settled back into his seat and closed his eyes. The other passengers were free to watch him if they liked. He wasn't going anywhere until they landed.

And from there, only the Universe could say what happened next.

East St. Louis Avenue, Las Vegas

JIRO SHINODA FUMED over his *oyabun*'s terse words and lack of courtesy, but there was nothing he could do about it at the moment. He was a subordinate within the family, condemned to follow orders until such time as the *oyabun* retired or made some critical mistake, leaving himself open to challenge from the ranks.

And that might happen sooner than his rude master imagined. If the rumors out of Tokyo were true, Kazuo Takumi's son and heir was weak, distracted from the business and perhaps even unwilling to succeed his father when the old man died or stepped aside. How that had to gall Takumi, knowing that he'd raised a wastrel who was glad to spend his money but would not exert an ounce of effort to maintain the empire.

Call it poetic justice for Kazuo Takumi's arrogance.

Meanwhile, however, there was wisdom in the old man's orders. If Machii's murder in New Jersey was a part of some larger conspiracy against the Sumiyoshi-kai, Shinoda should be prepared for trouble on his own turf. Only fools trusted that storms would never threaten them.

He believed he was secure on almost every legal front, with well-placed spies on Nevada's Gaming Control Board and the Las Vegas Metropolitan Police Department. A secretary in the local FBI office was close to turning, presently enraptured by a young *shatei* who wined and dined and bedded her on Shinoda's dime, but she had not delivered anything of value yet. When that panned out, he would be covered on all law enforcement fronts.

But now, he might be forced to deal with something else.

Noboru Machii's death and all the rest of it, back East, could not be blamed on the police or Feds. Shinoda was well aware that lawmen often violated laws, and some of them were murderers, but mayhem on that scale surpassed all plausible deniability. He thought some rival syndicate was to blame, and he could not defend himself against that kind of threat with high-priced lawyers.

It required brute force.

That was a problem in Las Vegas. From its earliest beginnings, with construction of the Fabulous Flamingo under Bugsy Siegel after World War II, the city fathers of Las Vegas had been willing to accommodate known felons if they played by certain basic rules. The first of those was sharing what they skimmed with those in charge. The second was to do their bloody business elsewhere, so that Vegas could preserve a shiny "clean" facade.

The second rule had filled southern Nevada's desert with a host of shallow graves over the decades, while dictating that high-profile executions had to be carried out elsewhere. Siegel, when it was time for him to go, had been gunned down in Beverly Hills. A decade later, Gus Greenbaum—also a wheel at the Flamingo—had been butchered with his wife in Phoenix. Tony Spilotro, in the 1980s, had been carried off to Indiana, bludgeoned and buried alive in a cornfield.

That explained Merv Mendelbaum. The obstacle in Jiro's path had vanished from Los Angeles, not Vegas, Reno or Biloxi, where his gambling resorts appeared to be secure, above reproach. Investigators were examining the outposts of his far-flung empire, but they would be disappointed.

Shinoda's difficulty now was that he did not know his enemy. He could not reach out from Las Vegas to Atlantic City, or wherever else Noboru Machii's killers might be at the moment, to eliminate them. He could only sit and wait until they came for him, and that meant blood spilled in Las Vegas, if he was not very, very careful. That could blow up in his face and ruin everything that he had worked for since arriving in the States. The agents he had bribed would turn against him if he violated their most basic rules.

He sipped a glass of Chivas Regal whisky, pondering the problem set before him. There was still a chance the storm in Jersey might not reach him, that some local grudge was settled with Machii's death. Or, on the other hand, it might blow past him, leaving his preserve untouched and moving on toward Tokyo. But neither outcome was predictable.

Shinoda had told his *oyabun* the truth. He was prepared for anything, and if a spark flared on his turf, it would be smothered instantly. The threat to him—and to the image of Las Vegas—would be neutralized. That was the only way to save his life.

CHAPTER SEVEN

It was late morning when the Globemaster touched down on concrete shimmering with heat haze underneath the desert sun. The landing wasn't smooth by airline standards, but the military passengers weren't likely to complain. They rose and lined up, lugging their deployment bags, and Bolan waited for the line to move before he joined it, stopping to reclaim his bags before he followed the others down the cargo ramp and out into the sunshine.

It was hot out there, and nowhere near the day's predicted high.

The night, if Bolan had his way, would wind up being hotter still.

Two uniforms had seen him off in Jersey, and another pair waited to greet him now. Apparently, he only rated a first lieutenant, backed by a grizzled staff sergeant. They both saluted him without enthusiasm, waiting for him to return the gesture.

"I'd begun to wonder if you'd made the flight, sir," the lieutenant said. "We thought you might be first up to deplane."

"I'm not the pushy type," Bolan replied.

"Sergeant Jacoby, help the colonel with his bags."

"Yes, sir."

Bolan did not object as the staff sergeant took his mobile arsenal, seeing the man wince a little in surprise. Bolan carried the duffel with his clothes inside it.

"This way, sir," the lieutenant said, already moving out. "If you'd like to refresh yourself, we have all the amenities."

"No need, Lieutenant."

"As you wish, sir. In that case, your vehicle is over here."

"Here" was a short walk from the runway to a prefab building painted beige, like all the others Bolan saw, as a concession to the desert heat. It cast no shade to speak of on the silver Chevrolet TrailBlazer parked out front, the only ride in sight that didn't bear a military license plate.

"It's a civilian rental," the lieutenant said. "We got it from McCarran International. You can return it there, or bring it back here when you're finished. At your pleasure, sir."

Bolan received the keys and popped the Chevy's door locks. Whoever had brought it from the airport on the far side of Las Vegas had seen fit to leave the windows rolled up tight, and it felt like an oven in the SUV. Bolan turned on the Duramax 2.8-liter diesel engine, powered down the windows all around and turned the air-conditioning on full blast to break the killer heat.

"Where would you like your bag, sir?" the sergeant asked.

"In the backseat, thanks."

As soon as that was stowed, Bolan deposited his smaller duffel with it, and he was good to go.

The officer was squinting at him, fighting sun glare, saying, "Sir, if you require any directions—"

"I can find my way around, Lieutenant. Thanks for everything."

"A pleasure, sir," the lieutenant replied, clearly not meaning it.

The Chevy's air-conditioning was powerful. When Bolan slid into the driver's seat, he could already touch the steering wheel without a risk of contact burns. He shut the door behind him, sealed the windows against hot air intruding and got out of there.

The TrailBlazer was larger than the rented cars he normally preferred, and it would cost him extra for the diesel fuel, but Bolan wasn't paying out of pocket, and he might appreciate the Chevy's off-road capabilities and ramming weight before he finished up his mission in Las Vegas. As for being too conspicuous, that wasn't an issue. Flashy cars were all the rage in Vegas, whether you were lucky at the tables or just wanted lesser mortals to believe you were.

A good start, overall.

He would've liked a shower and a meal, but Bolan didn't want to hang around the base a minute longer than he had to, drawing more attention to himself and generating the inevitable gossip, causing anybody to remember him. Besides, sweating would help him fit in with the tourists, not to mention local working stiffs who kept the desert city running like the vast money machine it was. And he could always find someplace to eat in Vegas, search online for restaurants of any style, cuisine and price range, from buffets in the casinos to a mom-and-pop café that had been overshadowed by the glitter palaces.

His stomach started growling on North Main Street, heading downtown from the base. Bolan checked the Chevy's dashboard clock and saw that it was early yet for rousting Yakuza thugs who would have spent a long night working angles on their turf or partying to welcome in the weekend. Vegas never slept, and while most of its denizens were forced to crash eventually, many of them led a vampire's life, shunning contact with daylight.

Early afternoon was soon enough to launch the second phase of Bolan's war.

He'd feed himself, and then go looking for his prey.

Azabu, Tokyo

Kazuo Takumi kept his face expressionless as Toi entered the study, shoulders slumped as usual, and sauntered over to the nearest easy chair. He dropped into it, slouching until it seemed that he might slide on to the floor, but stopped short of collapsing, lolling like an astronaut prepared for liftoff from the launching pad.

"You're late," Takumi said, his face still deadpan. It was an expression he'd perfected over decades, grown impervious to any aggravation, any threat. When he relaxed his features, let them mirror what he actually felt, those in his presence knew that he was either very pleased, or that they were about to die.

"Busy," Toi said, too lackadaisical to even form a sentence.

"Doing what?"

"Dono yō na." The contemptible American expression, always uttered with disdain. *Whatever.*

"When I summon you in future," Takumi said, tight-lipped, "you will stop *whatever* you are doing on the instant and immediately come where you are needed. Is that understood?"

"Needed?" Toi feigned confusion, putting on a half smile. "What do you need me for? You have Ando and your army. I can't measure up to that."

"And yet, I keep hoping that you will try."

That seemed to sting Toi for a second, but he brushed it off. "The great inheritance, you mean? The so-called family?"

"You've always taken full advantage of its privileges," Kazuo said.

"Why not? The money's there, and we can't take it with us."

"Are you going somewhere, Toi?"

"We all are. Sensei Kodama says—"

"Enough!" Takumi nearly shouted the command. "I have told you that we will not speak of this supposed holy man."

"Supposed?" When Toi echoed him, his voice dripped with contempt. "If you had seen what I have—"

"I've investigated this guru you idolize. I know more than you think, Toi."

"Sensei Kodama is an open book."

"Indeed. But there are chapters you have yet to read."

"Enlighten me," his son replied defiantly.

"Another time. Today, I must inform you of your cousin's sudden death."

Toi blinked at that. "Which cousin?" he inquired.

"Noboru Machii."

That got through to him, piercing the insolent facade. Noboru had been bound to Toi by blood, as well as through the Sumiyoshi-kai's familial network. Machii's mother was Kazuo's younger sister, Mariko. As children, Toi and Noboru had played together, attended the same private school, and it had obviously pained Toi when his cousin got the plum assignment in New Jersey.

Had that move started Toi's slide into farcical religion and disdain for all the other members of his family? It was a question that had to be postponed until another day.

"What happened to him?" Toi asked, his voice subdued.

"He died serving the family in the United States."

"Murdered, you mean."

"It was a hostile act, yes."

"Just another price of doing business, I suppose."

Takumi fought an urge to slap his son. "In fact," he answered, "it was most unusual. Unprecedented for our dealings in America."

"All right. I'm listening."

"I hope so. While we have no final answers yet, there is a possibility the trouble will continue, spread beyond New Jersey, even to our own home shores."

"As if you didn't have enough already," Toi replied.

He was correct in that. Japan's Diet had passed its first law banning corporate payoffs to the Yakuza in 2011, while police in Fukuoka made special efforts to break up public meetings of five or more family members. In June 2013, Yakuza were banned entirely from some of that prefecture's business districts, on pain of arrest if discovered. The National Police Agency had instituted a ratings system, ranking "combative" families in terms of danger to the public.

Trouble enough, indeed, and now Takumi faced a worse storm.

"I may require your help," he said.

"What can I do?" Toi asked him, seeming honestly confused.

"Stand with me. Learn from me and take your rightful place within the family. Help me command and save our people."

Toi considered it. He seemed to waver, sitting up a little straighter, then told his father, "They're not my people."

Takumi absorbed the insult and asked his only son, "Are we not flesh and blood?"

"That doesn't make us both the same. You feed on crime and suffering."

"And you eat from the same bowl, every day."

"Not for much longer."

"Oh? Are you to be emancipated now?"

"A change is coming, Father." Toi surprised Takumi, who could not remember the last time his son had called him that.

"What change?"

"There's no point in trying to explain it," Toi replied dismissively. "You wouldn't understand."

"Try me."

"There's no time. You have set a course that can't be changed."

"And what is your course?"

"You'll see that soon enough." He rose, brushing the wrinkles from his Saku three-piece suit that would have looked at home on any soldier of the Sumiyoshi-kai. So much for throwing off the chains of family. "I have to go now."

"You refuse to stand beside me, then?" Takumi asked.

"I will be standing on my own, to make a difference," Toi said, and left the room.

At least, Takumi thought, he stood a little straighter as he exited than when he had arrived.

Kato Ando responded to the intercom at once, emerging through a side door to the study.

"Hai, Sensei."

"Go after Toi," Kazuo ordered. "Find out where he goes and who he sees. Do not let him see you."

Ando nodded and hurried off to do as he was bid.

East Charleston Avenue, Las Vegas

BOLAN WOUND UP going for the mom-and-pop, a Mexican café two blocks off the main drag that didn't look like much but had a homey atmosphere inside and an extensive menu of dishes from south of the border. Once seated, with a longneck bottle of Corona beer in front of him, Bolan realized how long it had been since he'd last eaten, and he went for broke: a taco, tamale, enchilada, chile relleno, rice and beans. Why not, when he had no idea when he would have another chance to stop and feed himself?

The food was fast, delicious, and it set his mouth on fire, demanding backup on the beer. While Bolan ate, he looked over two maps of Vegas he'd collected from a gas station, en route to lunch. Both showed the city's streets and highlighted the various "resorts"—meaning hotel-casinos with their built-in shopping malls—but one also provided photos of the various attractions, which included Mendelbaum's Goldstone casino, midway down the Strip.

Vegas was always changing, at least superficially. It never hurt to brush up on geography before launching a new campaign, ensuring that he knew the various approaches and escape routes from his targets in advance.

Neither map highlighted Night Moves, the strip club that Jiro Shinoda called home, but Bolan had the address and had no trouble plotting it as he was scoping the battleground. East St. Louis Avenue was still six blocks ahead of him, driving away from downtown, toward the Strip, and by the time he'd finished his meal, he thought the joint should probably be up and running. Jiro might not show his face that early in the day, but Bolan had a home address for him, as well, in case they missed each other at the skin show.

He couldn't help Merv Mendelbaum, that much was obvious, and Bolan didn't waste time mourning for a mega-millionaire who'd gotten in over his head with players whom he didn't understand. Whether the hotelier's remains were ever found or not, Bolan assumed that he was dead. The odds against the other option—that he'd pulled a Howard Hughes and vanished voluntarily—were astronomical.

Case closed.

Nor was it Bolan's job to seek justice for Mendelbaum, whatever that might mean. A rich man's disappearance probably alarmed his friends in government, if for no other reason than cessation of his contributions to their various campaigns, but Bolan's mission was to stop the Yakuza from planting any deeper roots in the United States.

A futile task? Most likely, human nature being what it was. It would require a dedicated army to destroy the Sumiyoshi-kai, and they were only one of seventy-plus rival clans in Japan, all itching to expand their territory. Keeping them out of the States was an exercise in futility. But the Executioner could certainly discourage Kazuo Takumi's family and frustrate their invasion plans.

Beginning now.

He'd cleaned his plate, finished his second beer and left his money on the table with a handsome tip. Outside, the old familiar heat was waiting for him, taking over where the restaurant's air-conditioning let go of Bolan, with the closing of a door.

Donning a pair of mirrored sunglasses, Bolan headed for his rented ride and off into his war.

Asakusa, Tokyo

KATO ANDO HAD no difficulty catching up with Toi Takumi, trailing him to the subway stop nearest to Kazuo Takumi's apartment building and below ground, crowding aboard the next train heading northeastward. Toi never checked to see if he was being followed in the crush of foot traffic. The thought, apparently, did not occur to him.

He was a foolish boy.

Ando had been a member of the Sumiyoshi-kai since he was seventeen. He served the family, but loved his *oyabun* and would do anything within his power to preserve Kazuo's hold over the clan. Since no man lived forever, Kazuo Takumi was bound to pass someday, but he would not be taken out before his time if Ando could prevent it. That meant guarding Kazuo against all threats of any kind.

Even from an ungrateful, disrespectful son.

Rail transport in Japan could be a nightmare for the uninitiated. The trains were punctual, of course, their schedule so precise that "delay certificates" were often issued to passengers if a particular train ran five minutes late, thereby excusing any tardiness at work. Trains were also packed to the walls at rush hour, so crowded that uniformed "pushers" manned the subway platforms, jamming passengers into their cars like canned sardines, speeding each train on its way.

That kind of crowding naturally led to certain problems. Pickpockets had a field day on Tokyo's trains, but the most common offense was the groping of female passengers by men.

Ando had no fear of a groping as he squeezed into the subway car Toi had selected, keeping his target constantly in sight. His scowl and burly frame discouraged any crude advances, and if they were not enough, he would be pleased to break a groper's fingers like so many rotten chopsticks. He was also armed with a *tanto* blade and a *burakku jakku*—what foreigners would call a sap or blackjack—but deploying them in a sardine can would be difficult and would draw undesired attention to himself.

Ando had no idea where Toi was going, but his orders were to follow and report back to his *oyabun*, no matter where the trail might lead. He kept a sharp eye on the youth—in fact, no longer very young—and was prepared to leave the train as soon as Toi got off. Whichever stop Toi chose, the crowds would cover Ando's exit and permit him to continue surveillance of his mark.

He saw Toi edging toward the car's far doorway as they pulled into the Asakusa station. Ando started doing likewise at his end, meeting a measure of resistance from three businessmen who'd claimed the space before the door, until he jabbed one in a kidney with the stiffened fingers of his left hand, snarling at others in a tone that made them blanch.

The moment that the doors hissed open, Toi was out and moving toward the nearby escalator. Ando gave him room, then followed with the flow of foot traffic, maintaining visual contact without drawing too close for comfort. Moments later, they were on the street and moving east, then turning north.

Before Ando's time, Asakusa had been Tokyo's chief entertainment center, famous for its theaters, until American bombers had rained hellfire on the Japanese capital. These days, it was best known for the Sensōji Temple, hung with *manji* banners—backward swastikas—that paradoxically served as emblems of a peaceful faith.

Tourists flocked to photograph it, and to purchase souvenirs from countless tiny shops. Locals gravitated, in turn, to Kappabashi Dougu, lined with stores selling kitchen and restaurant supplies.

Toi Takumi had no restaurant to furnish, and he had not come to spin a prayer wheel in the Buddhist house of worship. Ando trailed him northward, past the looming Sensōji kodomo Library. A block beyond it, Toi turned east again, along a side street, and immediately ducked into a stairwell on his right.

Ando slowed and crossed the street. He would not permit the stripling to outwit him with a simple dodge, but if the building was Toi's destination, Ando needed to find out what drew him there.

He found a point directly opposite the stairwell, dawdled with his back turned to it, window-shopping, while the polished plate glass served him as a mirror. He saw no one lurking in the stairwell, watching for a tail, and turned at last to double-check directly. Satisfied, he plunged through traffic, trusting the city's noise-conscious drivers to lay off their horns.

Reaching the entryway he sought, he paused again and checked the stairs from top to bottom. Reaching underneath his jacket, he stroked the handle of his sheathed *tanto* blade, and then began his cautious climb.

Toi Takumi knocked twice on the plain door, simply labeled "9," and waited with a heady feeling of anticipation that came over him each time he visited his master. He had already put his father's lecture out of mind, dismissing all the crap that the old man shoveled in defense of his corrupt, pathetic Sumiyoshi-kai. No matter what his father thought, Toi had found another path.

The door opened, no sound of anyone approaching,

and the master stood before him. "Welcome," Susumu Kodama said. "Please, enter freely, and without constraint."

Toi bowed, then stepped across the threshold, relaxing as the door closed behind him. The smell of incense—sandalwood and benzoin—instantly enveloped him, accompanied by subtle music playing in the background at low volume. Toi could not have named the melody, but it took only seconds to accommodate the rhythm of his pulse.

In the foyer, Toi slipped off his Gucci loafers and replaced them with a pair of soft felt slippers that awaited him. Kodama knew his size and always was prepared. The master moved directly to a low divan and sat, while Toi settled into a bentwood chair directly opposite.

"You were detained," the master said, not asking. Not accusing, like Kazuo.

"I was summoned by my father. I am sorry, Master."

"There is no need for apology. We give priority to family."

"Saikosai Raito is my family," Toi said. "I owe nothing to him."

"Except your life."

"An accident of birth, Master."

"That accident determines who you are, and what you may become."

Toi was beginning to feel flustered. "You guide my becoming, Master."

"But the raw materials were all within you at the start, were they not?"

Toi could not argue with the master's logic, so he simply bowed again.

"Was it an urgent matter?"

"He supposed so. Deaths related to his rotten business in America." Toi felt a pang of guilt as he dismissed Noboru Machii out of hand, but it was fleeting, there and gone like a mosquito's stab.

"Does he expect the trouble to continue?"

"All he cares about is losing money."

"Might this trouble cross the water?"

"I don't know, Master. What if it does?"

"It might become our golden opportunity."

"As a diversion?"

"Possibly. How goes preparation of the cleanser?"

Toi admired his master's flare for euphemisms.

"All on schedule. We shall meet the quota."

"And the apparatus for delivery?"

"Tested with satisfactory results."

"No more than satisfactory?" Kodama almost seemed to chide him.

"My apologies. I should have said 'successful.'"

"Without suffering?"

"None was observed." Toi saw no need to inform the master that his chosen subjects had been prostitutes, self-medicated to the point where feelings were irrelevant.

"Good news," Kodama said. "You never disappoint me, Toi."

"I hope not, Master."

"Nor will you, on the great day of our revelation to the world."

Toi wasn't quite so sure, on that score. It was one thing to accept the master's message, recognize the need for sweeping change, and to prepare for doling out divine judgment. Taking the final step, however, from the preparation to the execution, called for greater strength, greater resolve, than Toi had ever found within himself.

He was, in fact, the very spoiled man his father thought he was. From childhood, Toi Takumi had assumed the best of everything was his by right, because his father was a man of influence. Master Susumu and the Saiko-sai Raito had redeemed him from that wasted life, but was he strong enough in fact to justify his master's faith?

And if he failed Susumu Kodama at the Great Reckoning, then what? Would he be excluded from the joys of Paradise on Earth?

"All shall be in readiness," he promised.

"Is it feasible," Kodama asked him, "to accelerate the schedule?"

"Accelerate?"

"Move up," Susumu said.

"I don't know, Master. Shall I ask?"

"Please, do. Preparedness, as you well know, encompasses all possibilities."

"Hai, Masutā."

"Excellent. Will you stay and share my lunch?"

Lunch with the master was an honor, but Toi understood that more was now expected of him. "I should speak with the technicians, Master."

"Your devotion is appreciated, Toi."

Flushed with pride, Toi rose and bowed again. Kodama saw him to the foyer, where he traded slippers for his shoes and bowed one final time before taking his leave.

Accelerate the schedule.

Tokyo was in for a surprise, and no one in the city would be more astounded than his father.

CHAPTER EIGHT

East St. Louis Avenue, Las Vegas

Vegas was a self-styled town that never slept, but there were lulls in the frenetic action. Strip clubs, like casinos, operated around the clock, but daylight had a tendency to thin the crowds seeking a lap dance or a cuddle in some tacky "VIP" room. On the seamy side of Vegas, which was most of it, the two requirements for a VIP were money and a willingness to part with it, but even those guys had to work or sleep sometime.

Night Moves did what it could to lure the lonely when they were between shifts from serving others, offering a chance for them to be served while their cash lasted, before they headed home or off to work. In case they tried to leave with pocket change, a bank of slot machines located in the strip club's lobby beckoned with the hope of instant riches if they just spend one more quarter, one more dime, before they hit the street.

All smoke and mirrors, in a town that lived by sleight of hand.

Bolan walked into Night Moves at 11:35 a.m., its painted-over door closing behind him with a sigh that could have been interpreted as ecstasy or terminal fatigue. A bouncer manned the register inside, the club's logo silk-screened across his T-shirt, strained by pumped-up pecs, with lightning bolts tattooed on each side of his shaved scalp.

"Morning, sport," he growled. "Five dollars cover."

"Is the boss around?" Bolan inquired.

"Ain't seen him."

"So, is that a yes or no?"

That made the bouncer blink, slow wheels revolving underneath his shiny dome, deciding how rude he should be to a potential paying customer. Like most Vegas inhabitants, he came down on the side of money. "If you're lookin' for him, best to come back in a couple hours."

"No, that's fine. I came in for the show."

"Okay. Five dollars cover, like I said."

Bolan brushed his jacket back, as if to reach for a wallet in his right hip pocket, then revealed the MP-5 K on its shoulder sling, muzzle extended by the black suppressor. "No cover today," he said.

"Hey, easy, man, awright? You want the till, it's yours. There ain't much in it, though, and I don't got the combination to the safe."

"Don't have," Bolan corrected him.

"Say what?"

"Just lead the way." A waggle of the SMG directed him.

"Whatever, man. Just take it easy, huh?"

A padded door muffled the music pulsing from the club's main showroom, volume rising as the bouncer pushed through, Bolan giving him sufficient distance so that he couldn't spin and slam the door in Bolan's face, but staying close enough that neither could he bolt and run.

The showroom wasn't dark, exactly, but the lights were muted, keeping customers' attention on the long stage where a single dancer went lethargically through moves she'd made a thousand times before. Four customers were widely spaced along the catwalk, nursing drinks and watching with as much enthusiasm as the stripper showed for them.

Apparently, they saved the star material for prime time at Night Moves.

"Office," Bolan said, raising his voice to make it heard over the strains of Jackyl wailing "Down on Me."

The bouncer tipped his head in the direction of a curtained doorway, barely noticeable at the far end of the showroom's bar. The bartender was cleaning up and didn't seem to notice them, eyes on the dancer while he ran a towel along the bar. They reached the curtain, slipped through and proceeded past the restrooms— "Hounds" and "Foxes"—to a staircase, climbing to a door marked PRIVATE.

"You should think about this, man," the bouncer warned. "You don't know who you're messin' with."

"Inside," Bolan replied.

"Your funeral."

His escort turned the doorknob without knocking, stepped across the threshold and to one side, saying, "Mr. K, you got a visitor."

Hal Brognola's file had not contained a photo of the Yakuza thug behind the office desk, but if it had, he probably would not have looked as startled in it as he did right now, first interrupted at his work, then staring down the muzzle of a gun.

"What's this?" he asked, remaining seated, both hands dropping out of sight below the desktop.

"I'll take whatever's in the safe," Bolan replied, "and leave a message for your boss."

"Who says I'm not the boss?"

"You're up too early. Safe. Now."

Mr. K turned toward the bouncer, swiveling his chair.

"You disappoint me, Rico. When I'm done here, we'll discuss your future."

Something in the man's tone tripped a switch in Rico's head. His face and scalp flushed crimson, as he spun toward Bolan, growling through clenched teeth. Bolan triggered a short burst, point-blank range, that made a bloody ruin of the bouncer's left shoulder, flinging him back against a bank of filing cabinets before he hit the floor.

Mr. K was covered well before his hidden pistol cleared the desktop. "Make it count," Bolan said, finger on the subgun's trigger. "If you're up to it."

"You will regret this, you son of a bitch."

"Flattery will get you nowhere. Last chance for the safe."

Mr. K set down his piece and rose, an unimpressive five foot six if that, and crossed to where a wall safe stood exposed above the filing cabinet closest to his desk. "Take my advice and spend this money quickly. It's the last you'll ever see, *gaijin*."

The safe door opened, showing stacks of banded currency. Mr. K stepped back and faced Bolan with a mocking smile.

"This isn't Tokyo," Bolan said. "You're the *gaijin* here."

The narrowing of the man's gaze signaled a coming move.

Cutting it short, the Executioner shot him in the face.

Button Willow Drive, Las Vegas

JIRO SHINODA MISSED his soldier's first knock on the bedroom door. It took another, more insistent rapping to cut through his dream of lounging on his party boat, cruising Lake Mead, and drag him back to bleary-eyed reality.

"What the hell do you want?" he croaked, as he sat up in bed.

"Boss?"

The bedroom door was open six or seven inches. Yoshinoro Shiroo had his face wedged in the crack with one eye showing.

"What, for God's sake?"

"We've got trouble, boss," his number two told him, as he stepped inside and shut the door.

Shinoda waited for a moment, then said, "Well?"

"Somebody hit the club. They took out Koichi and cleared the safe. The morning bouncer's messed up, too."

Koichi Choshu ran the club in Shinoda's absence. He had been in Vegas longer, but the *oyabun* had passed him over as *kyodai* in favor of Jiro. A loyal family underling, he hid his disappointment well and followed his boss's orders to a T.

"When you say took him out—"

"He's dead, boss. That's confirmed. The cops are there."

"Have they called here?" Shinoda asked.

"Not yet."

"Well, when they do, tell them I'm coming down."

It wasn't far to drive. Shinoda lived in Summerlin, northwest of downtown Vegas, seven miles from Night Moves, give or take. His house was midsized for the ritzy neighborhood, running about eight hundred grand and offering a scenic view of Red Rock Canyon to the west. He kept a plane at North Las Vegas Airport, three miles east, but didn't feel a need to flee the state that morning.

Not yet, anyway.

Dressing in haste, but still with style, he hoped this was a simple robbery, the perp too stupid or high to realize who he had chosen to rip off. If that turned out to be the case, Shinoda would flip a coin, decide whether he left it to the local police or put his soldiers on it. Either way, the punk responsible was dead as soon as he learned his name.

But if it *wasn't* simple, if this was the trouble he'd been warned about, then he was in deep trouble. All eyes would be watching him from Tokyo, to see how Shinoda handled it, and there was only one acceptable outcome. He had to identify the enemy, eradicate him and preserve his standing in the family.

Shinoda had completed the required eight-hour firearms training course to earn a nonresident carry permit, and he had no intention of leaving his pistol at home, even though he traveled with armed guards, all similarly licensed. In his own mind, it enhanced his status to be packing, and it certainly enhanced his confidence.

Choosing a Beretta 8000 from his small but diverse collection of pistols, the Yakuza crime boss clipped its nylon holster to his belt, secured the weapon and smoothed the lines of his tailored jacket to hide it as best he could. The license in his wallet meant he didn't have to hide it, necessarily, but Shinoda was a businessman in Vegas, not some gangbanger fresh off the boat, trying to wow the lowlifes.

"Ready, boss?" Yoshinoro Shiroo asked from the bedroom doorway.

"Ready. Bring three of our men and leave the others here to watch the house."

"I've got it covered."

Shinoda had to think about who would replace Koichi Choshu at Night Moves, but his priority right now was finding out who'd staged the raid and robbed him of his treasurer.

His treasurer, and some $300,000 from the strip club's safe.

Shinoda should probably have banked that money—some of it, at least—but he liked having cash accessible immediately, if he needed it, and IRS reports of cash deposits larger than $10,000 were a royal pain. If he couldn't get the money back, he'd have to compensate his *oyabun* somehow, and bringing back the bandit's scalp would only be a small down payment on that debt.

But it would please Jiro Shinoda greatly, all the same.

Akasaka, Tokyo

KATO ANDO HAD not been able to identify whomever Toi was visiting in Asakusa, much less to determine what they talked about, but he had marked the address and would make up that deficiency before reporting to his *oyabun*. The block, the building's number and the floor should be enough. He would locate the building's manager and use his powers of persuasion to find out who occupied the floor in question. Once he had a list of names in hand, the rest should not be difficult.

No one refused him, once they got a look into his eyes and understood that they were dealing with the Sumiyoshi-kai.

Once Ando realized that he could not trace Toi to a specific flat, he decided to wait on the street until his master's son emerged, then trail him back to Akasaka's metro station. It was good practice to follow him, avoiding being seen, although he wondered whether Toi would even recognize him if they had collided on the street. The young Takumi seemed to have so little interest in his father's business that he might not know members of the family he'd seen each week, for years on end. It was a shame, and Ando wished that he could spare his master any further pain on Toi's account.

With any luck, perhaps he could.

It was the same scene on the metro, always crowded, though the lunchtime rush hour was not on them yet. Tokyo's crowding made inhabitants susceptible to various diseases, ranging from the flu and colds to cedar pollen allergies, and many wore surgical masks while walking on the street or riding bicycles. Pollution also fouled the air, less visible at night with all the neon blazing, but by day it fogged the streets, producing fog reminiscent of nineteenth-century London. It was paradoxical, for such a tidy people as the Japanese, but that was the reality. The pollution did not bother Ando, born and raised inside the pressure cooker, but he wondered sometimes if it might cut into tourist dollars for the family.

At Asakusa Station, Toi chose the Sobu Main Line heading southwest. Ando was last to board the same car, nearest to the door for exiting when they had reached their destination, elbowing his way inside before the pushers had a chance to help him. One of them had seemed inclined to shove him all the same, but Ando's glare had stopped him short, the man wise enough to see the folly of putting his hands on this particular stranger.

The train sped toward its destination, still unknown to Ando. He had counted seven stops before Toi made his move, at Akasaka Station, stepping from the car and moving with the crush toward escalators on his left. Ando remained roughly forty feet behind him, keeping Toi in sight.

Akasaka was a residential and commercial district in the larger ward known as Minato. It was not a tourist draw but featured decent restaurants, including an abundance of Korean eateries that prompted locals to call the neighborhood Little Korea. Akasaka catered chiefly to businessmen and bureaucrats from the neighboring Nagatacho government center, while catching some nocturnal overflow from the Roppongi nightlife district. Also close at hand was one of Tokyo's most popular entertainment and shopping areas for young people, renowned for its shopping, restaurants and fashion houses. Overall, it might be called the hub of Tokyo.

And what drew Toi Takumi there, on this day, after quarreling with his father? Ando wondered.

He trailed his target to a relatively seedy side street, hanging farther back as the foot traffic thinned and he became more visible to any backward glance. Halfway down the second block, Toi slowed his pace and did look back, the first time he had shown any concern about security since bolting from his father's home. Ando feigned interest in a window filled with power tools, imagining what they could do to flesh, and watched Toi from the corner of his eye until the young man relaxed and ducked into a doorway numbered 35.

The building was commercial, renting space to lawyers and accountants, two temp agencies, several doctors' offices, one dentist and a driving school's headquarters, among other tenants. Ando reached the single elevator just in time to see its lighted indicator stop on the third floor, housing three offices and something called Saikosai Biometrics. Trusting logic, he decided that the floor had to be Toi's stop, and called the elevator back to follow.

South Las Vegas Boulevard

BOLAN PARKED OUTSIDE the huge Fashion Show mall to count his cash, leaving on the SUV's air-conditioning and watching passersby in case they tried to peer through the tinted glass. His take was larger than he'd hoped, $260,000 and some change, a total guaranteed to put Jiro Shinoda on the warpath. Anger muddled thinking, and if Bolan's luck held out, the Yakuza *kyodai* would begin to make mistakes.

Especially if Bolan pushed some more, to keep him off balance.

He could go directly to Shinoda's home, but that kind of work was better left for darkness, still some seven hours off by Vegas time. Another option was to find a room and sleep, but Bolan had already rested on the flight out from New Jersey and had energy to burn.

Brognola's file on Jiro Shinoda listed seven other local businesses he owned or had investments in, providing Bolan with a list of targets that could fill his afternoon if he was so inclined. Metro police would soon be on the case, if they weren't already, but they were spread thin in Clark County, with some 3,200 officers covering eight thousand square miles of territory, with two million year-round residents and an average 3.5 million tourists per month. Like any other force, its members split their time between guarding the rich and cleaning up after the rowdy poor, both of which Las Vegas had in abundance.

And now, it also had the Executioner.

Bolan had listened to the news since hitting Night Moves, and there'd been no bulletins about the shooting. Shinoda would have liked to keep a lid on it, no doubt, avoiding scrutiny and any nagging questions from the IRS about his looted safe, but that would have depended on who found the bodies in the upstairs office. Would the first call have gone out to EMTs, or to the boss?

Bolan considered it, deciding that the bouncer he'd left wounded was unlikely to be seen again in Vegas. That didn't bother him, but Bolan knew he had to try harder at his next stop, to create a stir and put Jiro Shinoda on the hot seat with authorities, fighting a two-front war to keep his little fiefdom safe and sound.

He ran Brognola's list of targets through his mind, deciding whether he should take them geographically, by value of the property or alphabetically. Avoiding any kind of pattern was essential, to prevent the Yakuza mobsters or the police from guessing where he'd turn up next. Shinoda would have an edge in that regard, already knowing every property he held in Vegas, but he couldn't know if his invisible assailant knew precisely what and where they were.

That is, until they stated falling like dominoes.

And speaking of invisible, Bolan would have to take into account hidden cameras from that point on. Las Vegas was a town obsessed with *watching*: naked women, dinner shows and circus acts, the action at selected high-stakes tables in the big casinos. Vegas also watched its dealers, croupiers, bartenders, cocktail waitresses, store clerks and shoppers, drivers and pedestrians, with cameras up the old wazoo and all around the town.

Evasion of the omnipresent closed-circuit TV cameras was not a realistic option. Neither could he wear the balaclava that had served him in New Jersey. That left working in disguise, an option Bolan very rarely used, but which he'd mastered long ago, during his one-man war against the Mafia.

Vegas helped him there. It was a show town, serving every manner of performer from full-monty strippers to circus clowns and the Blue Man Group. Costume and makeup shops were a dime a dozen in Vegas. He went online and found one of the largest, set the SUV's GPS for his destination and rolled out toward the next phase of his desert war.

Akasaka, Tokyo

"A CHANGE?" THERE was a note of budding panic in Tago Jokichi's voice. "What change? He hasn't called it off?"

"The opposite," Toi Takumi replied, trying to project a sense of calm for Jokichi's benefit.

"*Advance* the schedule?" He blinked at Toi through wire-rimmed spectacles that made him look owlish. With his thin hair, pasty complexion and his white lab coat, Jokichi resembled a mad scientist.

Exactly what he was, in fact.

"The Great Reckoning may occur this week," Toi said. "Within the next few days."

Another blink. "So soon? I didn't realize—"

"Events have overtaken us," Toi told him, interrupting. "When the time is ripe, there must be no delays. Will you be ready?"

Jokichi did not hesitate. "We're ready now, for distribution on a local scale. Volume is adequate. To cover all of Tokyo, as hoped for, we will need more personnel and aerosol dispensers, or another system of dispersal."

"You know the limit on our personnel," Toi said. The Saikosai Raito barely had one thousand hard-core followers prepared to make the final sacrifice. It was impossible for them to save the thirteen million citizens of Tokyo, spread over more than five thousand square miles.

"I do," Jokichi replied. "It's not too late to reconsider Lake Miyagase."

He referred to the primary source of drinking water for both Tokyo and Yokohama, which could theoretically expand their scope of mass salvation.

"No, Tago. Master Susumu has rejected it."

"But—"

"His command is law."

Jokichi lowered his eyes. "Of course. I meant no disrespect."

"None taken. But dispersal must be on the wind. A final, cleansing gift from heaven to our people."

"As the master says. In which case, we require a mechanism with much wider range than any handheld aerosol device."

"An aircraft?"

"Preferably more than one. It seems impossible, of course, but—"

"For the master and Saikosai Raito, anything is possible," Toi said.

In fact, he had an idea already. It would require some hasty planning and some daring action, but with Susumu Kodama's power, channeling almighty Bishamon, the god of righteous warfare, nothing lay beyond Toi's reach.

"Could you achieve the master's goal with, say, three helicopters?" Toi inquired.

Jokichi was wide-eyed now. "Three helicopters would be *very* useful, certainly. We would need time to mount the necessary hardware—storage tanks, nozzles and triggers—but with three, most of the city could be covered. If they aren't shot down, of course."

"Don't worry about that."

By Toi's calculation, most of Tokyo could be saved before authorities knew what was happening, much less who was responsible or how to stop Saikosai Raito's acolytes. And if defenders of the city rallied soon enough to bring down one—or even all three—of the helicopters, then what?

Any manna from on high would be dispersed on impact with the ground. More souls would instantly be saved, and if Master Susumu's followers fell short of their intended reaping goal...well, Toi believed Lord

Bishamon would still be satisfied with what they'd managed to achieve on his behalf.

"Forgive me, brother, but I feel compelled to ask," Jokichi said. "Do you have three helicopters?"

"Personally, no," Toi granted. "But I know where they are kept, and how I may procure them."

KAZUO TAKUMI WAS not a believer in Saikosai Raito. He may even not have known his son had joined the sect a year earlier, rising by virtue of his zeal and wealth to serve as the anointed master's strong right hand. But now, with the Great Reckoning drawing nearer, Takumi might serve the cause involuntarily.

The Great Reckoning.

Master Kodama had decreed it, Toi thought, speaking for the great Lord Bishamon, and no mere human could prevent it now. His father's recent difficulties in America would serve as a distraction, granting Toi the freedom he required to the cause and guarantee his place beside Master Kodama in the kingdom yet to come.

It would require finesse, something Toi had not cultivated in his life to any great degree, but with the proper inspiration he believed that he could fake it adequately. Those who served his father in the Sumiyoshi-kai were programmed to accept orders without objection or inquiry. What more natural than that the orders they obeyed, this time, should come from Kazuo Takumi's son and rightful heir?

"How much time will you need to fix the helicopters?" he asked Tago.

"If by 'fix,' you mean—"

"How long?" Toi cut in, not quite snapping at the man.

"It depends upon the model. Say, two hours, minimum, for fitting all the hardware into one aircraft, then twenty minutes each to fill the tanks. We cannot test dispersion without trial runs."

"No." Toi shook his head emphatically. "You have one chance at this, no more."

"Then, brother, we shall do our best and pray for satisfactory results."

Prayer couldn't hurt, Toi thought.

"And while you're at it," he suggested, "pray for guidance so that you don't disappoint Master Susumu or our Lord."

CHAPTER NINE

East Desert Inn Road, Las Vegas

Boom Town was a gun store and pay-by-the-hour target range where shooters could bring their own weapons and ammunition, buy rounds from the house or enjoy "the full-auto experience" with rented submachine guns burning ammo at a rate that left more holes in their wallets than in their targets. Tourists and local survivalists flocked to the warehouse-sized setup, enriching its owners as they shot for macho brownie points and fumed over mythical threats to the Second Amendment.

On paper, the place belonged to a couple of locals who swaggered around in tattoos and shoulder holsters, sporting long hair in the style of Wild Bill Hickok and directing buyers to the home defense equipment that was perfect for their needs. Their silent partner—and the real owner, in fact—was none other than Jiro Shinoda.

Boom Town made a killing in its own right, but its secondary function was supplying arms and ammunition to the Sumiyoshi-kai in Tokyo. Jiro Shinoda's accountants cooked the books, reporting certain weapons as "defective" and returned for credit to their manufacturers, while they were shipped out to Japan with phony bills of lading, for delivery to paper companies owned by the Yakuza. Each month, the shop also recorded higher ammo traffic than it logged in fact, paid all due taxes on the nonexistent sales and sent the extra rounds to Tokyo.

For Boom Town, Bolan tried one of the new disguises he had purchased. It consisted of a light brown wig with sideburns and a matching Fu Manchu mustache, a pair of oversized dark glasses and a realistic stick-on scar along his jawline, on the right. Once he had donned the getup, his reflection in the gas station's bathroom mirror made him think of outlaw bikers or a drifter who was going nowhere fast. When paired with an expensive charcoal suit, however, he was Vegas all the way and good to go, maybe a pit boss from the Strip concerned about his personal security.

Appearances.

There were three customers booking range time when he entered, one guy on the register, so Bolan dawdled past a long display case filled with pistols, waiting until the patrons got their tickets, ammunition and their earmuffs, vanishing beyond a side door where the crack of gunfire echoed.

Bolan moved up to the register, smiling. The guy behind it had a droopy 'stache much like his own, though he had grown his the old-fashioned way. "What can I do you for?" he asked, all smiles.

"Can you get Jiro on the phone?" Bolan inquired.

"How's that?"

"Your boss. Jiro Shinoda."

"Sounds like you're confused, friend. I'm the owner here. Half owner, anyway."

"I guess he can't advise you on our situation, then."

"What situation would that be?"

Bolan showed him the MP-5 K on its shoulder sling, suppressor leveled at the front man's chest. "The one where you clean out the register and crack the safe. No hinky moves, unless you want your day to end the hard way."

"Shit. You're kidding, right?"

"Not even close."

"You know that you're on camera?"

"I hope they get my good side."

"Okay, man. Don't get excited. This Jimbo Shinola—"

"Money, now," Bolan said, cutting through the bs.

"Sure, man, sure."

The register gave up chump change, about a thousand dollars, then the scowling clerk told him, "The safe's down by my feet. I gotta stoop to reach it."

"Wait right there," Bolan instructed, vaulting the display case to a perfect landing, well beyond the other man's reach. He didn't care about the palm print left behind, since no police department in the world had any of his prints on file. "Okay, crack it. If you come out with anything but cash, you're done."

"I hear you."

It took less time than expected, stacks of greenbacks stuffed into a worn gym bag that rested on a bottom shelf, close by the safe. When it was full and fastened shut, he took it from the Boom Town rat and told him, "All right, turn around."

"Hey, man, please, don't—"

"Do it!"

The guy turned, shoulders slumped in resignation, maybe thinking he should try to reach the Ruger SR9 on his right hip, but Bolan didn't give him time to find the nerve. A long step brought him close enough to swing the SMG against his target's skull, a solid *thump* that dropped the guy facedown, out cold before he hit the floor.

Hefting the satchel with his money, Bolan walked around the counter this time, paused to switch a hanging sign on the front door from Open to Closed and let himself out into blazing sunshine. A moment later, he was on the street and rolling toward his next appointment with the Yakuza, keeping his schedule and waiting for this day to burn down in the west.

East St. Louis Avenue, Las Vegas

IT WAS RISKY, coming back to Night Moves after what had happened there, but Jiro Shinoda made a point of never running scared. His soldiers had cleaned up the mess, taking Koichi Choshu and the bouncer out the back way, off to plant them in the desert ten miles west of town. The bouncer had been alive when they got to him, but it was a risk to let him stay that way, maybe deciding he should tell his story to police. So, two graves in the desert, where they'd have a lot of company, and neither one of them could cause any more trouble for the *kyodai*.

Shinoda hated incompetents. They pissed him off and cost him money. Someday, he imagined, one of them might get him killed. But in the meantime, he would not be scared away from working at his office, picking up vibrations of the bass line from the music rumbling downstairs.

Besides, lightning had struck the club already. Why should it strike twice?

That didn't mean he was relaxed, by any means. Four of his men were stationed on the strip club's second floor, with two more in the main showroom downstairs. Each of them wore Kevlar under their dark suits, over their tattoos, and each carried at least one weapon locked and loaded, ready for emergencies.

If Shinoda's enemy returned, he would be in for a surprise. The last one of his life.

The desk phone purred for his attention, drawing his focus from the ledger that Koichi Choshu had been working on before his brains had spattered the filing cabinets. Thankfully, there were no stains on the book itself, so Shinoda did not have to soil his hands.

"Hello?"

The voice that answered was excited, speaking Japanese. The caller was an underling, a cutout who controlled the men supposedly in charge of Boom Town and two other Vegas enterprises Shinoda owned, thus insulating him from any contact with the law. The cutout had bad news, of course—what other kind was there, this day?—and he applied no sugarcoating to it as he gave his boss the details.

Robbery, one man rendered unconscious at the scene, but no one dead this time. The bandit had escaped with $20,000, give or take, a pittance in the grander scheme of things. His image was preserved on video, for what it might be worth. Police were not involved.

Shinoda thanked the caller, cradled the receiver with a hand that trembled from his mounting rage and rose to pace the office that, while spacious, suddenly felt claustrophobic. Fury spun his thoughts out of control, until he reined them in and forced himself to face the situation rationally.

He was under siege, and the example of Noboru Machii told him he was fighting for his life. A face on video might help his soldiers find the man responsible, but that meant getting lucky when his soldiers canvassed local hotels and motels, showing the pictures around to see if Jiro Shinoda's nemesis had rented one of the city's 50,000 available rooms. And after all that work, he might be operating from a house, condo, apartment, or he could be living in his car.

How was he supposed to get a handle on one man—assuming that it *was* one man—before the bastard struck again?

Perhaps by luring him out into the open, where his only option was to die.

South Industrial Road, Las Vegas

PROSTITUTION WAS ILLEGAL in Clark County and in Reno's Washoe County, though Nevada law permitted the residents of fifteen other counties to permit commercial sex work under what was called a "local option." Some Vegas hotels arranged transport for randy high rollers to desert "ranches" staffed with female livestock, but for visitors who wanted to try their luck in town, Lost Wages offered fifteen "escort agencies" pursuing business under forty different names, while two dozen massage parlors negotiated the going rate for "happy endings."

Hal Brognola's file told Bolan that the Sumiyoshi-kai owned Star Escorts, also advertised in local phone directories as Midnight Angels and as Tiger Girls, all with the same office address and phone number. It was like phoning three cab companies to book a ride, hearing the same dispatcher on the line each time.

Star Escorts and its clones were strictly out-call services, no hookers on the premises, but Bolan didn't have a room, and he was not looking for company. He planned to shut down the operation and leave a message for Jiro Shinoda that would push the Yakuza lieutenant toward one careless move too many.

This time, Bolan wore a beard attached with spirit gum, balanced against a bald skullcap, with the same shades to mask his graveyard eyes. He wasn't after money, having bagged enough to let him carry on his

War Everlasting for a while yet, also knowing that an escort office dealt primarily in credit cards, over the phone. The girls—or guys—got "tipped," of course, and gave their pimps the lion's share, but Bolan had another kind of irritant in mind.

Star Escorts was about to be shut down.

He rolled in off the street, surprising a receptionist who could have worked out-call herself, and maybe did. She peered up at him, through false lashes that resembled spider's legs, and tried to form a happy face while asking, "May I help you, sir?"

"Be smart and help yourself," Bolan advised. "Go home."

"Excuse me?" Worry and confusion clashed behind her eyes.

"You need another job," he said. "This place is going out of business."

Bolan saw her reaching for the panic button underneath her desk, and made no move to stop her. When the two Yakuza hardmen suddenly appeared, scowling as if they'd practiced the expression in a mirror, Bolan turned to meet them with a stone face of his own.

"What the hell is this?" one of them asked.

"*Hell* sums it up," Bolan replied, raising the MP-5 K on its sling.

He had them cold but let them try for holstered pistols anyway. Three bullets zipped into the first gunner, and the same for number two, dropping the pair at the threshold of the door behind them. The receptionist let out a squeal and kicked back in her rolling chair, sobbing out, "Please, please, please."

"I warned you," Bolan told her. "Go."

She went, snatching her purse and bolting for the exit, bursting into sunlight and away. Bolan forgot her on the spot and stepped around the two corpses, moving deeper into Star Escorts. Another moment brought him to a room where two more women, older than the girl out front, were working telephones, one rattling off the measurements of someone she called Desiree, the other promising some john a "guaranteed good time." They both ran out of words as Bolan barged in on them, freezing when they saw his SMG, then magically regained mobility when he stepped to one side and nodded toward the exit.

The manager had missed it all, somehow, and Bolan took him by surprise, dozing behind his desk. He grumbled, turning as his door opened, trying to get his tough-guy face in gear and not quite making it.

"I don't know you," he said, maybe the understatement of his life.

"You want to live?" Bolan inquired.

"What do you want?"

"Carry a message to your boss."

"I *am* the boss."

"Spare me. Take the message to him, or *become* the message. Your decision. Chop-chop."

"Okay, sure. What is it?"

"Tell him if he's smart, he'll catch the next flight out to Tokyo and not look back."

"I hear you."

"Give it back to me."

The Yakuza repeated it, and Bolan said, "So, go."

Alone, but obviously not for long, he primed a couple of incendiary sticks, tucked one inside the top drawer of the nearest filing cabinet and left the other hissing on the manager's desktop. The walls were cinder block and should contain the flames until firefighters reached the scene. Smoke triggered the alarm before he cleared the lobby, clamoring for notice in the sterile desert daylight.

West Tropicana Avenue, Las Vegas

THE TOWN WAS going crazy, Mori Saigo thought. No, scratch that. Crazy was the recognized default position in Las Vegas for the tourists, entertainers and a fair percentage of the locals, even though they tried to talk it up as just another normal city.

Try this, then: the town was going craz*ier*.

Saigo was stuck at Apex Pawn, out of the action, when he yearned to join the hunt for whoever was dumping on his family. If he could get his hands on one of them…

But, no. The order had come down for him to stay exactly where he was and keep the business safe. He understood responsibility, the strict chain of command, and never tried negotiating when Jiro Shinoda was in one of his explosive moods.

Apex made decent money for the Sumiyoshi-kai. Up front, it was a straight pawnshop, dealing with suckers who had gone all in and lost their last dime, desperate to pawn or sell a watch, a car, whatever, for the pittance Saigo offered, get back to the gaming tables for the big break that they knew was coming, if they just played one more hand, or one more after that.

Morons.

Behind the scenes, Saigo negotiated larger loans, at rates of interest the law did not allow. His customers included showgirls nursing habits, contractors who'd fallen on hard times of late, truckers who had to keep their rigs roadworthy, Gordon Ramsay wannabes who saw their culinary dreams slipping away—in short, the usual. Saigo was pleased to help them, at a going rate of 10 percent for ten days' time. As long as they could pay the interest, he'd gladly leave the principal hanging over their heads from now until doomsday—or, if Jiro needed new investment properties, Saigo could cut another deal, keeping the strapped proprietors as lackeys or removing them entirely from the scene.

A few complained, but not for long, and never yet to the authorities. One who had threatened prosecution had a new position, fertilizing Joshua trees in Red Rock Canyon, west of town.

Saigo was drifting aimlessly around the pawnshop when the *gaijin* entered, looking like a backup roadie from a Lady Gaga tour: long hair, platinum blond, and some kind of tattoo wrapping around his neck in front. A pair of mirrored shades with glitter rims concealed what Saigo guessed were crazy eyes.

Same old, same old.

Saigo stood watching as his floor man moved to greet the customer. Before Tommy could say two words, the walk-in pulled a fancy-looking piece and stuck it in his face. Saigo immediately ducked behind the nearest showcase, shouting for his backup muscle.

Three of them came running, two with guns in hand, one carrying a metal baseball bat. The glitzy gunman swung his piece, clubbed Tommy to the floor and faced the other three before they had a chance to open fire. His shots were muffled, sputtering, no less destructive for the lower volume.

First, he took Adachi Kagemori's face off, punching him back through the doorway he'd just exited. The second burst spun Fuma Mitsuhara like the arm on a lawn sprinkler, this one spraying crimson everywhere. Gamo Teru was caught flat-footed with his useless bat, reared back to throw it at the gunman, but he never made the pitch. Slugs opened him from belt buckle to breastbone, spilling things Saigo had never hoped to see.

"Are we done now?" the gunman asked, turning back toward Saigo's paltry hiding place. "Can we get down to business?"

"What business?" Saigo asked him, rising to his full five-six on shaky legs.

"Tell Jiro that Vegas isn't healthy for him anymore. He needs to leave, like now."

Saigo summoned the nerve to say, "He won't like that."

Nodding toward Saigo's dead men, the man replied, "Tell him there's only one alternative. He's leaving, one way or another. First class, or the cargo hold."

Still trembling, Saigo blinked, and the intruder was gone.

North Decatur Boulevard

IN FACT, BOLAN had no desire for Jiro Shinoda to leave town. He wanted the *kyodai* stuck in Vegas, but away from downtown, preferably at his home in Summerlin, where Bolan could minimize collateral damage for the last act of his desert drama. Keeping the mobster pinned down in Sin City was his top priority.

Which brought him out to North Las Vegas Airport three miles from the city's heart on Fremont Street. North Las Vegas was an independent city, with its own mayor, police and fire departments, wastewater services and recreational facilities. Clark County owned the airport, though, with three asphalt runways and 686 aircraft in more or less permanent residence. Two percent of those were private jets, including a Learjet 55 owned by Jiro Shinoda.

It was Bolan's next target, to keep his prey grounded.

Bolan went off-road from Simmons Street, east of the airport, rolling over open desert, trailing beige dust in his wake. He stopped a thousand yards out from the nearest fence, say fifteen hundred from the runway, and stepped out into the waning heat of late afternoon, shadows stretching to meet him from westward. From the SUV's rear compartment, he removed the tool he'd chosen for this job and prepped it.

He was pulling out the stops this time, hefting a Barrett XM500 sniper's rifle. Chambered for .50-caliber Browning machine gun rounds, the Barrett was semiautomatic, a bullpup design, fed by a 10-round magazine behind the pistol grip, hurling its 750-grain projectiles downrange at 2,820 feet per second, with a killing range of 1,900 yards. To aid a shooter at that distance, it was mounted with a Leupold Mark 6 scope.

The APIT rounds Bolan had picked were special, too. The acronym stood for "armor-piercing incendiary tracer," used in combat to destroy armored fighting vehicles and concrete structures. They combined penetration with a payload that would light up any fuel or other combustibles found in the bullet's flight path.

Like a Learjet 55, for instance.

Bolan had no trouble spotting Jiro Shinoda's plane. Hal Brognola's file included photos of it, with the tail number clearly visible. All Bolan had to do was scope one of the fuel tanks, and he had no end of them to choose from: three in the tail, one in each wing, auxiliaries forward, under the passenger compartment and extending toward the cockpit—259 pounds of fuel in the tail cone alone.

He wasted no time setting up the shot, rested the Barrett's bipod on the SUV's hood and found his mark, way off across the desert and tarmac. Called it a moderate to easy shot from where he stood, requiring only clear eyes and a pair of steady hands.

The rifle bucked against his shoulder, and he held the scope's view, saw the flash of impact from the Learjet's tail before a larger ball of fire erupted there, enveloping the jet's rear section, dropping its twin Pratt & Whitney power plants on to the runway. Shifting slightly, Bolan fired through smoke to drill the starboard wing and spark its larger fuel tank, feeling echoes of the shock wave where he stood.

Mission accomplished. Jiro Shinoda wasn't flying anywhere in that $800,000 heap of twisted, smoking steel. But he'd be running, though.

The Executioner would bet his life on that, even at Vegas odds.

East St. Louis Avenue, Las Vegas

SHINODA GRIMACED WHEN he heard the news but managed to control his voice. "I understand," he told the caller. "Thank you. There will be a bonus in your envelope this week."

Nothing was free in Vegas, or anywhere else. Loyalty, he'd found, could be the priciest commodity of all.

Instead of phoning out, he rang for Yoshinoro Shiroo on the office intercom, already on his feet and moving when his number two came in. "What's up, boss?" Shiroo asked him.

"Some bastard just hit the Lear at North Las Vegas. It's scrap iron now."

"What do you want me to do?"

"I'm going home," Shinoda informed him. "Call in everyone, and I mean *everyone*. They're no good to me wandering around the streets or watching over strip clubs."

The truth be told, Shinoda was not convinced his soldiers would be any use to him, no matter where he stationed them, but if they had to die, then let it be defending him, at home. He did not plan on roosting there, of course, not with a madman—or a group of madmen—running wild around the city. He would pack whatever he required, empty his safes and hit the road as soon as possible.

Los Angeles was four hours away by car, but he did not intend to run that far. Instead, there was the cabin he had rented on Mount Charleston, half an hour from downtown, costing three grand a month for the occasional long weekend getaway: three bedrooms, two baths and a modern kitchen. His men could camp out on the sofas or the floor, assuming they had any time to sleep at all.

The thought of fleeing from an enemy galled him, but he did not plan to share Noboru Machii's fate, if that could be avoided. Gaining distance from the battlefield would grant him breathing room. He could regroup, consider all his options, weigh the merits of survival versus honor under the code of *bushido*.

By rote, involuntarily, he ran the code's eight touchstones through his mind: justice, courage, honesty, benevolence, politeness, honor, loyalty and character. Interpretation was the key, particularly in relation to the Yakuza, where normal standards of benevolence, justice and honesty received short shrift. Shinoda honored the code as he had learned it from his *oyabun*, placing his family—the sacred Sumiyoshi-kai—above all else.

Easy to say, until his life was riding on the line.

But this could be a valuable test. The world was his
to win, or lose, depending on his mastery of crisis. And
defeat by unknown adversaries was unthinkable.

CHAPTER TEN

Button Willow Drive, Las Vegas

Bolan sat downrange, slumped in the SUV's driver's seat, watching as Jiro Shinoda and his men got ready to evacuate. They worked efficiently, a flurry of activity, no motion wasted under supervision of a stone-faced supervisor whom he recognized from Hal Brognola's dossier as Yoshinoro Shiroo, Jiro's second in command. No guns were visible, but Bolan took for granted that the crew was armed, and he saw rifle cases being loaded into two black Hummers and the Cadillac XTS sandwiched in between them.

Bolan watched and waited while the Yakuzas walked their boss to the limo, shielding him with their bodies, then piled in around him, the leftovers breaking right and left to fill one Hummer or the other. Two young ones stayed behind, guarding the house, while three engines fired up in unison and the black caravan rolled out.

Bolan gave them a lead and saw the stay-behinds turn back toward Shinoda's sprawling house before he followed, running without headlights the first two blocks, like someone who'd forgotten them with all the streetlights blazing overhead.

Heading east, they turned on Anasazi Drive to West Lake Mead, then followed that eastward again to Highway 95. Given a choice, the caravan turned north and

Bolan trailed them, merged with traffic leaving Vegas on its way to who knew where. He had a full tank, wasn't worried about running out of gas before the Hummers sucked their own tanks dry, and found a station on his radio that played the "golden oldies" with a minimum of chatter between songs.

Six miles on Highway 95 brought them to Kyle Canyon Road, running west through Red Rock Canyon in the general direction of Pahrump and California, somewhere on the other side. Traffic was sparse there, and he doused the SUV's lights again, keeping the taillights of his prey in sight from half a mile behind. The next green highway sign he passed told Bolan they were headed for Mount Charleston—which, as he remembered it from other visits to Las Vegas, meant a dead end at the scenic peak.

He smiled at that, relieved that Shinoda wasn't heading out the long back way from Vegas, through Death Valley, toward Los Angeles. It would have been a long, fuel-wasting way to flee Nevada, but a fair choice if he wanted dark, wide-open desert to reveal a tail. Mount Charleston meant a hideaway of some kind, close enough to keep a finger on the pulse of Vegas, while the *kyodai* felt more secure.

That meant some hiking, probably through forest, over rough terrain. Bolan was up for that, accustomed from experience to doing things the hard way, and he carried all the gear he needed for a trek to hell. The only question now would be how many backup shooters waited for their leader, wherever he was going on the mountain. Twenty were riding with him in the three-car caravan, but Bolan was accustomed to the long odds stacked against him.

Ten more minutes remained, give or take, until they reached the mountain and began ascending. Bolan checked his rearview, saw no headlights coming up behind him on the two-lane blacktop and relaxed.

His enemy had picked the game, thinking the rules were under his control. The Executioner had a surprise in store for him.

With any luck, the last one of Jiro Shinoda's life.

Mount Charleston

THE SOLDIERS SHINODA had dispatched from town ahead of him were waiting when he pulled into the cabin's parking area, a graveled space with room remaining for another car or two, despite the Hummers and the Cadillac. Light shone from every window of the cabin, holding shadows from the dark forest at bay, and smoke curled from its chimney made of rough-hewn stone, scenting the air.

The *kyodai* followed procedure, waiting for his men to pile out of the Hummers and surround his limo, weapons ready on the off chance that an enemy had reached the mountain lair ahead of them. It was far-fetched, of course, but there was no such thing as too much caution in a shooting war.

The night was cool as Shinoda finally stepped from the Caddy, brushing at imaginary wrinkles in his London slim-fit suit from Burberry, tailored from virgin wool that had only cost him $2,195 on the Strip. It wasn't warm enough to spare him from the chill, however, and he wasted no time heading for the cabin, brushing past the guards who lined the front porch, seeking light and warmth.

Something was cooking in the kitchen, its aroma vying with the fireplace as a treat for Shinoda's senses. He guessed that it was something grilled on skewers, possible the Kobe beef he favored, globally renowned for tender succulence. Maybe seafood tempura on the side, to make it turf and surf. For just a moment, as his mouth watered, he almost believed the meal could compensate for being driven from his home.

Almost.

Reality caught up with him as Shiroo came in from the dark, issuing orders to the troops who filled the cabin's spacious living room. They'd planned the details in advance: how many men would be on watch at any given time, where they would be positioned, how the roving teams would circulate around the property. The first shift would be changing into warmer clothing, gloves included, since Nevada desert nights were cold at best, and colder still on mountain peaks. Sun-baked by day and chilled from dusk till dawn, it was a paradox that the mobster recognized without trying to understand.

"We're good here," Shiroo reassured him, when the soldiers had their various assignments. "Leave it to the police for now."

"I don't trust the police," Jiro replied.

"Of course not, but they're good at this. The only reason they exist is to protect rich people and their property."

"You think I qualify?" Shinoda made no attempt to veil his sarcasm.

"Why not? You pay taxes and bribes, like every other leading citizen."

"They tolerate us, but they value orderly procedure. Chaos frightens tourists, so it frightens the authorities."

"More reason for them to eliminate the problem," Shiroo said.

"Or blame us for it. They elect the prosecutor here, if you remember. He can frighten voters with the 'yellow peril.'"

"That's old-fashioned thinking. Not politically correct."

"What is correct about Las Vegas?" Shinoda challenged. "It's a monument to greed, built up by criminals who now pretend their hands are squeaky clean. They ban whoring to pacify the churches, but continue to protect it."

"So, our kind of town," Shiroo said, smiling.

"But we'll never fit the profile. Don't deceive yourself into believing otherwise."

"You know the saying, money talks."

"Money talks, all right," the *kyodai* agreed. "But a white man's money always has the louder voice."

"You're in a mood," Shiroo suggested. "We should have something to eat."

Shinoda acknowledged his second in command's wisdom with a nod. "The Kobe beef?"

"And lobster tempura, naturally."

"For the soldiers?"

"Nikujaga," Shiroo answered, a stew of meat and potatoes, seasoned with soy sauce and sugar.

Shinoda allowed his second in command a compliment. "You think of everything."

"That's my job, sir."

BOLAN WAS DRESSED in black, no camo necessary in the forest on a nearly moonless night. Instead of blackening his face with war paint, he'd put on the balaclava, topped with the night-vision goggles that immediately turned the shadowed woodlands green. His combat boots were tan rough-outs, temperate weather style, and laced up tight.

For weaponry, he'd brought along the Colt M4A1 with the under-barrel M320 launcher stripped away, backed by the Glock, now fitted with a SilencerCo Osprey suppressor that tamed the gun's bark to a wheeze. For truly silent work, he had a Mark I trench knife, cast bronze knuckle-duster handle, with a satin-finish double-edged blade honed to a razor's edge. Whether stabbing, slashing or clubbing a target, it got the job done. As a replacement for the M320, Bolan carried half a dozen M67 fragmentation grenades and two AN-M8 smoke canisters, in case he needed cover in the house or during his retreat.

From where he'd parked, the hike was uphill all the way. Bolan took his time, letting the Yakuzas get settled in and find their comfort zone, start to believe that they were free and clear from all the havoc they had left behind in Vegas. Shinoda wouldn't get much sleep this night, unless he was a cooler customer than Bolan thought, but his security detachment might believe they were untouchable out here, the molten lava sprawl of neon on the Strip and Glitter Gulch invisible despite their altitude, screened by tall trees.

There was no danger of civilian casualties on the mountain. Bolan knew the nearest town—also Mount Charleston—was located in a nearby valley, where its 350-odd souls, mostly Vegas commuters, were well insulated from racket, pollution and crime. They might hear distant echoes once the party started, might or might not make a call to Metro, but as far as guiding officers directly to the scene, they wouldn't have much luck.

Response time out from headquarters was forty minutes, average. A rover in the area might cut that time by half but still would need to search the mountain, listening and watching, to pinpoint the source of shots. Metro's air support consisted of seven choppers, different makes, and one Cessna Skylane search plane. The pilots were on call around the clock but still took time to scramble and respond, longer to mount effective searches. Time enough for Bolan to complete his mission on the mountain, if he managed to avoid a major snag.

Like getting killed.

SHINODA COULD NOT remember when he'd eaten better food or packed as much away. He knew that it was partly nervous eating, trying to distract himself from his oppressive troubles, simultaneously fueling up for battle, if it came to that. He could relax here, in his mountain lair, surrounded by his men—but only to a point. Solving the mess in Vegas was his top priority.

And in the process, he might save himself.

The second lobster tail had vanished, and he nearly took the chef up on his offer of another, smaller steak, but exercised a bit of self-control. He pushed his chair back, despite the fact that Yoshinoro obviously wasn't finished eating, stood and began to pace the dining room.

The cabin was a good size, sixteen hundred square feet with a second floor, but it was feeling claustrophobic now. Shinoda began to second-guess himself, wondering if he should have stayed in Vegas, either at his home or at Night Moves, to meet the threat head-on.

And then, what? Die like his manager *heishi*, who had been cut down without a chance to fight?

Logic would be irrelevant, if Kazuo Takumi put a hostile twist on Shinoda's moves. Depending on the point of view, his tactics could be seen as wise or cowardly, a brilliant bit of strategy or hiding from a fight he might have won, if he'd remained to lead his troops.

"We're going back," he blurted, almost surprised to hear the thought spoken aloud.

"What, now?" asked Shiroo, with his mouth half-full of lobster.

"Now. This minute. Tell the men."

Shiroo knew better than to argue. Rising from the table, dabbing with a napkin at his lips, he left to spread the word.

Running had been a momentary lapse. There was no reason why Kazuo Takumi should be told of it at all. Shinoda would personally take control of a relentless search throughout Las Vegas, peering under every manhole cover, into every sewer drain, if that was what it took to find his enemy.

He had eyes on the street, though they were sometimes blurry ones: users and dealers, thieves who sold their swag to Shinoda's fences, call girls and their lowly sisters of the street, cab drivers who conveyed sheep to the fleecing of their choice and kept their ears open along the way.

Someone knew something. It was guaranteed.

The *kyodai* retrieved his jacket, slipped it on, then patted the pistol holstered on his belt for reassurance. He had never killed a man with this specific weapon, but had practiced with it at Boom Town until he'd mastered it and shot tight groups consistently at twenty yards. What more could be expected of a man in his position?

Nothing less than absolute success.

He shouted through the cabin, seeking his second in command, interrupting him as he was asking questions via walkie-talkie, to a guard outside.

"I'm ready," Shinoda told him. Those who stayed behind to watch the place could clean up after he was gone.

"I can't reach Chu," Shiroo replied.

It took a moment, sorting through his mental photo gallery of underlings, to come up with a face. "The young one, with the Elvis sideburns?"

"Yes. He should be answering."

"Leave him behind, if he breaks discipline. I'll deal with him another—"

The explosion took out both living room windows,

spraying glass and splintered wood inside, its shock wave
slamming Shinoda to the hardwood floor. A jolt of pain
lanced through his hip, but he shook it off. He had no
time for mere sensations now, as smoke swirled in the
air around him, blurring his vision.

Hell had found him on the mountain. It was bellowing his name outside.

BOLAN HAD CAUGHT the first Yakuza hardman smoking in
the woods and slit his throat, easing the body down without a fuss and stamping out the cigarette. As he moved
closer to the cabin, scanning with the goggles, he saw
two men on the front porch, one armed with an AK-47
knockoff, while the other held a riot shotgun.

He could likely snipe them from the tree line with
his Glock, say thirty yards or so, but either one of them
might fire as he was going down and give the game away.
If there was going to be noise, Bolan decided, then he
might as well be making it himself.

He primed one of the baseball-size grenades and
pitched it overhand, dropping it more or less between
the lookouts on the porch, and six or seven feet in front
of them. One noticed it, was trying to identify the object that had dropped from nowhere, maybe thinking it
could be a pinecone, when the fuse ran down and smoky
thunder swept the porch. Windows imploded, and a shrill
voice somewhere in the cabin squealed, in either surprise
or sudden pain.

Bolan charged through the smoke and dust, his finger on the M4A1's trigger, shouting out Jiro Shinoda's
name. Why not, when he had literally blasted stealth to
smithereens? The Yakuzas wouldn't mistake him for a
member of their team, and anything that he could do to
spook them, maybe spoil their hasty aim, worked out to

his advantage. Some might even flee, if they thought their boss was the only target, but he wasn't counting on it.

Twenty men, at least. A slaughter, if he pulled it off; oblivion for Bolan if he failed.

He reached the porch and stormed across it, found the door already hanging open, jarred loose by the blast of his grenade and scarred by shrapnel. Bolan crossed the threshold in a fighting crouch, the carbine's muzzle leading, and immediately saw a face he recognized, despite its veil of blood.

Sweeping the room for other enemies and finding none close by, he crossed to Yoshinoro Shiroo, kicked the armed but wounded Sumiyoshi-kai lieutenant over on his back and pressed the carbine's muzzle to his bloody cheek.

"One chance," he said. "Where's Jiro?"

"Jibun de seikō iku, gaijin!"

"Wrong answer," Bolan announced, and blew the bloody face apart before the man could bring his weapon to bear.

A babble of excited, angry voices was converging on him from the cabin's two wings and the floor upstairs. No way to count them, sight unseen, but there were plenty to surround him if he didn't stay in motion, doing anything he could to throw them off and put them down. Jiro Shinoda was somewhere in the cabin still, unless he'd made it to a back door seconds after the grenade went off, and that was damned unlikely.

More Yakuzas closed on the cabin from outside now, making it a perfect death trap.

But for whom?

SHINODA HAD LEFT his second in command behind, wounded. There was no shame in that, per se. For all he knew, Shiroo was dead, his scalp wound gushing blood as if a faucet had been opened.

Dead or merely stunned, he was no good to his boss now. Self-preservation was the *kyodai*'s imperative, and he was running out of time.

The din of battle raged beneath his feet, sending vibrations through the floorboards. He had run upstairs, impulsively, and now cursed his own foolishness. Roaming along the second-story hallway, pistol in his hand, he shouted at the soldiers passing him, en route to join the fight downstairs. He wanted guns and bodies in between himself and whoever had come to kill him, somehow trailing him from Vegas to his eagle's nest.

Shinoda wondered if he could safely bail out from an upstairs bedroom window, land without breaking his legs on impact and escape into the woods. The cars outside were useless to him, their ignition keys all hanging where he'd ordered, on a row of pegs downstairs beside the front door. Jumping was obviously better than the grim alternative, but what if there were other enemies outside, waiting to cut him down?

Another blast rattled the cabin, raising dust devils around his feet. He heard more screams, more gunfire, and now imagined he smelled wood smoke. Was the cabin burning, or had shrapnel damage clogged the fireplace flue?

To shoot it out was one thing, but to wait upstairs and burn alive…

"Son of a bitch!" he snarled, and started looking for the nearest window he could find.

THE FIGHT DOWNSTAIRS was fierce, but took less time than Bolan had expected. It was fluid, constantly in motion from one smoky room into another, leaving dead

Yakuza gunners in his wake. They came at him from all sides, shouting, often firing well before they had a target marked, and twice he saw their bullets cut down members of the home team, crying out what felt like bitter curses as they died from not-so-friendly fire. Bolan used up two 30-round magazines clearing the living room and what most people would have called a rec room, though it didn't feature any games that he could see, short bursts dropping his adversaries as they came, spraying the log walls and the furniture with blood-spray patterns that would keep the CSI team busy for a week.

Rushing the kitchen from the rec room, he had used his second frag grenade—more screams in there—then dropped a smoker in his wake before he moved on, leaving any hardmen behind him to come groping through the man-made fog. A fear of fire might set some of them running, but if they found Bolan in the haze, eyes blurred with tears, he didn't mind that, either.

Through the storm of slugs his enemies laid down, Bolan emerged unscathed except for one small cut below his left eye, caused by flying splinters from a wooden chair. Some of his luck was owed to hasty fire from gunmen in a hurry, shaken and confused by the abrupt invasion of their mountain sanctuary. Most of it was Bolan: his experience, agility and combat savvy—knowing when to drop and roll, upend a table as a momentary shield, or spring from cover to attack when his pursuers thought that he was finished.

Killing was his business, and the trade was booming on Mount Charleston.

And when the shooting stopped, he hadn't seen Jiro Shinoda. Standing in a smoky hallway, wondering if echoes from the firefight had alerted any staffers at the mountain's famous restaurant and lodge, he froze in place and listened to the house.

Some damaged object toppled from a counter in the kitchen, finally surrendering to gravity, and shattered when it hit the floor. A couple of the dying gunners still moaned and muttered, maybe pleading with their fallen comrades for relief that only death would bring.

And then, he heard a creaking floorboard overhead.

Bolan retreated toward the stairs, wasting no time on stealth. He fed his carbine a fresh magazine, keeping a sharp eye on the second-story landing as he climbed. The corridor up there was empty, bedroom doors on each side of the hallway closed, except for one.

Judging the cabin's floor plan, Bolan thought the open room would have been more or less directly overhead when he'd first heard the noise downstairs. That didn't mean his quarry would be in that room, of course. The open door could be a trap to lure Bolan, while an enemy emerged behind him for the kill shot.

Bolan mulled it over while he drew a long, slow breath, then rolled the dice. He passed by five closed doors, drawn by more scuffling sounds beyond the open one. If Jiro Shinoda planned an ambush there, he'd obviously missed the memo on surprise.

Edging around the doorjamb, Bolan saw the Yakuza boss of Las Vegas grappling with a window that refused to open. On a nightstand by the room's large bed, the mobster had set a pistol just within his reach.

"Looks like you're stuck," Bolan observed.

Shinoda stiffened, then turned to meet him, glancing sideways at the gun, deciding not to try it. When he spoke, his voice seemed well under control.

"Are you my death?"

"Your executioner. I'm not in charge of what comes after, if there's anything."

"Should I repent?" Shinoda inquired, mocking the word.

"It wouldn't help you."

"May I see your face?"

"No time for introductions. Do you want that gun?"

Shinoda considered it, then nodded, slowly reaching for the pistol, offering no threat to Bolan.

"You'd allow me absolution through *seppuku*?"

Bolan kept the carbine's muzzle pinned to the man's chest as he replied, "Your call."

"This is not proper form, of course, but I don't have a *tanto* or a *kaishakunin* to attend me."

"If you miss, I've got it covered," Bolan said.

"In that case, with sincere regret for having failed my *oyabun* and ancestors, I leave this life."

Bolan was ready for a trick, but Shinoda wedged the weapon's muzzle underneath his chin, and he was smiling when he pulled the trigger, spattering the stubborn bedroom window with his brains.

Downstairs, Bolan dropped an incendiary stock dead center in the living room—a dying room, this night— and exited into the darkness, trailing smoke. Before he'd cleared a hundred yards, the place was burning, most of the ground floor engulfed in flames, a noon-bright beacon in the forest night.

CHAPTER ELEVEN

Tsukiji, Tokyo

From his penthouse, sixty floors above the traffic throng-ing Shin-Ohashi Don, Kazuo Takumi had a clear view of the famous Tsukiji Market, world's largest wholesale fish and seafood market, but the smell could not assail his nostrils. It amused him sometimes, watching *gaijin* tourists flock and gawk at dead fish in the outer market, while the inner circles were reserved for buyers from the city's countless restaurants and grocery stores.

Takumi had chosen his flat in Tsukiji as the one least likely to be vulnerable in his time of tribulation. His own-ership of the six-thousand-square-foot penthouse was a closely guarded secret, though he still might be betrayed, as *oyabuns* so often were, by traitors in the bosom of his family. To guard against that threat, he had six of his best soldiers in residence, with three more on rotating duty in the building's lobby, covering approaches to the eleva-tors and the service stairs.

And after hearing from Las Vegas, hours earlier, he had recalled The Four.

Kazuo had not recognized the name of the survivor from Nevada who had telephoned him, waiting while the call was shunted through relays to stymie traces, finally connecting with his *oyabun*. No one could memorize the names of twenty thousand little brothers and recall them instantly, on cue.

Yuji Ota, calling from Nevada in the middle of his night, had told the story simply and succinctly, sparing him no details on the scrambled line. While not personally present at the massacre—he'd been part of the team assigned to hunt Jiro Shinoda's nemesis through every nook and cranny in Las Vegas—he had received details from a detective now in mourning for the loss of weekly payoffs from the Sumiyoshi-kai. Jiro was dead, along with twenty-seven of his men, at someplace called Mount Charleston, where he'd gone for reasons Ota could not properly explain. It pained Takumi to believe his *kyodai* had run away from battle, and he hoped that Jiro had not died a coward's death.

The long and short of it: his two main outposts in America now lay in ruins, with the twin spotlights of law enforcement and the rabid media focused on Yakuza activities in the United States. The family's small colonies in Canada were safe, as far as he could tell—Canadians were much more civilized than Yanks, and far less prone to mayhem—but that situation, too, might change at any moment. More security would be required for operations in Vancouver and Toronto, while Takumi tried to learn exactly who in hell had fixed their sights on him.

And to that end, he had recalled The Four.

It posed no major difficulty, just a phone call to the pilot of his Bombardier Global 8000 over the Pacific, hurtling toward Los Angeles at fifty thousand feet, cruising at 640 miles per hour. It was no hardship to turn the jet, and no refueling should be necessary, since its range exceeded the planned trip's distance by some thirty-six hundred miles. The Four would not be disappointed by their detour, could not be, since they were strangers to all normal human feelings except fealty to Kazuo Takumi himself.

They made a perfect killing team, remorseless, expert, trained extensively in every aspect of their trade from martial arts to demolition. Ninjas of the old school in their mutual devotion to *bushido* and its rituals, The Four were also high-tech warriors when they had to be, well versed in cutting-edge techniques that Takumi grasped only in the broadest terms.

He wondered whether they could save him from the danger that, he now felt certain, would be crossing the Pacific soon, to menace him at home. His trouble would not end losing Vegas and Atlantic City, or the prosecutions that might follow as his secrets were revealed there.

Death was on its way. But it would find Kazuo Takumi well prepared.

McCarran International Airport, Las Vegas

THE FIRST THING anybody noticed at McCarran was the slot machines, more than twelve hundred of them flashing, jangling, playing vapid little tunes. No other airport in the world met travelers straight off the plane with such enticements to discard their money in a bid to get rich quick. So far, no one in history had scored a jackpot large enough to make him turn and fly back home a winner. Feeding the McCarran slots was like a rite of passage to Las Vegas proper, suckers paying their admission fee before they caught a ride downtown.

Bolan had dropped his gear at Nellis, leaving most of Shinoda's cash padlocked in a valise addressed to the Robert F. Kennedy Department of Justice Building. Brognola's name wasn't mentioned, or any specific department, but Bolan emailed Stony Man from his smartphone to set a pickup by whomever the big Fed might have on tap in the immediate vicinity. The loot should reach its destination safe and sound, but if it went astray somehow…well, easy come and easy go.

Bolan kept twenty grand to cover his expenses in Japan and drove from Nellis to McCarran, left his hot SUV in the long-term parking lot, and caught a shuttle to the terminal from there. A ticket on the next flight headed for Los Angeles, in business class, ate up the better part of seven bills for forty minutes in the air. He'd budgeted five grand from LAX to Tokyo, nonstop, and if it ran a little over, Shinoda would be picking up the tab. The rest should see him well armed, through a dealer Stony Man would recommend, and he'd be living off the Sumiyoshi-kai from that point on.

The language didn't worry Bolan, as he waited for his takeoff in McCarran's transit lounge. Most Japanese public schools taught courses in English, and Tokyo claimed the country's highest percentage of English speakers, due to its role as a center of government, commerce and tourism. From prior visits, Bolan knew that he could find his way around the city and communicate sufficiently with locals.

As for members of the Yakuza, he spoke another language they would understand.

A disembodied female voice called "preboarding" for Bolan's flight—a diplomatic way of saying that the wealthy, those who needed assistance, and those with kids could board the plane ahead of those who'd make the journey in "economy," wedged in their seats like livestock in a cattle car. No snacks except stale pretzels on a flight this short, unless you brought your own, and no distraction from a movie that wouldn't have the time to run its course.

He let the first-class flyers board ahead of him, then made his way to business class and settled in. The seats were smaller here, and didn't crank back into beds, but he had ample legroom and the drinks were "free," in theory. The seat-back pouch in front of him was stuffed with magazines, but Bolan planned to spend the short flight resting, and to do the same for most of his air time en route to Tokyo, as well.

Barring a dirt nap, who knew when he'd have another chance to sleep?

He watched the passengers file past him as they boarded, some of them dressed more appropriately for the swimming pool or thrift store shopping than for travel in the public eye, all focused single-mindedly on finding seats that would leave many of them feeling cramped and claustrophobic by the time they landed in LA. Bolan turned from them to the window on his left, and took his last look at the pyroclastic flow of neon, headlights and emergency flashers along the Strip.

Farewell to Vegas, for a while, at least. It might not be his final visit to the city built on broken promises, but he had seen enough—and done enough—for now.

Tsukiji, Tokyo

KATO ANDO HAD followed Toi Takumi from his last appointment back to the luxurious apartment where he lived in Shiodome, bankrolled with his father's money. Ando was prepared to wait there overnight, in case Toi went out again, but he'd received an urgent summons from his *oyabun* to meet him at another of his penthouses.

The boss was in a mood when Ando entered. Strangers would not have imagined he was raging on the inside, from the normal bland expression on his face, but

Ando knew the signs from long experience: a thinning of Kazuo's lips, though barely visible; a tiny wrinkle in the space between his straight eyebrows; a subtle flaring of his nostrils when he breathed.

Something was obviously wrong.

Instead of spilling it immediately, Takumi inquired, "What have you to report?"

Ando described Toi's movements and apologized for failing to identify the persons he had visited. Takumi stared into the distance and replied, "I know the first one. He pretends to be a spiritual man but makes me think of Shoko Asahara."

Ando was surprised at the mention of the old cult leader, sentenced to death years earlier, after members of his Supreme Truth sect released nerve gas on Tokyo's subway. Asahara sat in prison still, his execution stayed time and again as more of his disciples were arrested, slowly tried and locked away for life.

"And the other, Master?" Ando asked.

Takumi frowned, ever so slightly. "I know nothing of Saikosai Biometrics," he replied. "Investigation may be helpful."

"I shall undertake it," Ando promised.

"First, though…"

He listened as his *oyabun* detailed late-breaking events in the United States. Jiro Shinoda was among the dead, which secretly pleased Ando. He had always thought that Jiro harbored more ambition than ability, posing a danger to their *oyabun*, but he had kept that feeling to himself, waiting for solid evidence of treason to emerge. Now, he could put the weasel out of mind for good.

The rest of it was all bad news, of course: great losses in Nevada and New Jersey, fresh investigations pending in the wake of bloody murder. Takumi had managed to recall The Four, before they disembarked into the midst of that impending maelstrom. And, from what the *oyabun* was saying, it appeared they might be needed close to home, in Tokyo.

"You think the Inagawa-kai or Yamaguchi-gumi plan to move against us, Master?"

"Not immediately. War is costly for all sides. But if another enemy should come in to distract us, one or both of them might feel our fruit is ripe for picking."

"They'll regret it," Ando vowed.

"I would prefer avoidance of the conflict altogether. But without unknown enemies from overseas, we may not have a choice. Meeting the threat immediately, forcefully, shall be imperative."

"Whatever I can do…"

Takumi raised a hand to silence him. "I will direct our home defenses personally, with Tadashi Jo," he said.

"Of course, Master." Ando smothered the tiny spark of disappointment. Certainly, it was Jo's place, as first lieutenant of the Sumiyoshi-kai, to stand beside his *oyabun* in fighting for the family.

"Your task is more important," Takumi went on.

"Master?"

"I want you to continue watching Toi. With troubled times upon us, he must not become a liability. You understand?"

Not positively sure he did, Ando still nodded. *"Hai."*

"We must protect him from himself, if possible," Takumi said. "But first and foremost, we must keep the family intact and strong."

That made more sense to Ando. If the *oyabun*'s spoiled brat turned traitor, Ando might be able to eliminate him, at his own discretion. Maybe make the bastard disappear without a trace and leave his father wondering. That would be cruel, but doubt was sometimes preferable to the hard truth of betrayal.

"First, however," Takumi instructed, "find out more about this biometrics company. Toi has no interest in science or in commerce. I wish to discover who these people are, and what they do that interests him."

"It shall be done, Master."

"Speed and efficiency, old friend," Takumi cautioned. "For all we know, our time is short."

Terminal 7, Los Angeles International Airport

BOLAN WOUND UP with an hour to kill before his flight's departure, and he spent it watching people. Some of them looked shady, one had obviously served some time within the past few months, emerging with the jailhouse pallor that was unmistakable. Most of the passengers seemed happy to be traveling, though some—say 10 percent—looked dour, as if they'd booked one-way flights to their own funerals.

Bolan had been mildly surprised to learn that was the airport's number two international destination, after London, moving 1.3 million passengers yearly on eight different airlines. He was flying on United, hence his terminal, which was the airline's hub at LAX. Like every other major airport terminal in the developed world, Terminal 7 resembled a shopping mall, complete with nine shops, several restaurants and one full-service bar packed with travelers drinking their downtime away.

He wasn't hungry now, but would receive two meals of some description during the eleven-hour flight. His estimate for flying business class had been precise: $4,958 nonstop, round-trip. Big corporations picked that up and wrote it off without batting an eye. Behind him, in economy, the hoi polloi were flying "cheap" at $1,380 per head, not counting fees added for baggage.

He spent part of his dead time looking up the contact Stony Man had recommended for his hardware needs in Tokyo. His name was Kota Yuko, and he was a pawnbroker in the Roppongi district, with a shop two blocks from the former Azabu Police Station, no longer functional. Yuko had not been warned of Bolan's coming, but a code phrase was provided as a form of introduction.

"Watashi wa machi ni atarashīdesu," translated to "I am new in town."

To which Yuko should answer, *"Anata ga enjo o hitsuyō to suru baai ga arimasu."*

You may need assistance.

That assistance would be furnished in the form of weapons, ammunition and related items, at a price to be negotiated. After their transaction was completed, Bolan did not plan to see Yuko again. The dealer, for his part, would know that future business—and, indeed, his life—depended on his personal discretion.

A robo-voice announced arrival of his plane from San Francisco. It would be refueling, undergoing all the normal preflight checks, cleanup and stocking of its larder prior to boarding. Say another twenty, thirty minutes, anyway. Bolan began a set of breathing exercises, helping him relax in preparation for the long nap in his window seat, awakened only twice with any luck, for "gourmet meals" he could have bagged at any supermarket chain in town.

And when he woke the third time, during their approach to Tokyo's Narita International Airport, the last phase of his mission would begin. He'd be on foreign, hostile soil, squared off against a twenty-thousand-member private army, and some forty thousand Metropolitan Police.

Long odds, indeed, but Bolan had his own advantages. Surprise was one. The Sumiyoshi-kai might know someone was coming to upset their rotten apple cart, but they had no idea who they were looking for, or how many opponents were involved. Each day, flights from thirteen major American cities touched down at Narita International, each airliner disgorging two or three hundred passengers. It was impossible for either Yakuza or the police to shadow every visitor arriving on a given day, and passing time increased their number exponentially.

Bolan's other great advantage was the nature of the man himself. He was a warrior, pure and simple, on the surface: savage when he had to be, but also capable of mercy; cold as glacial ice when choosing and eliminating targets, but with a crusader's zeal. No Yakuza still living had experienced what Hal Brognola once called the Bolan Effect, but some were about to.

Whether they'd be living afterward was open to debate.

Over the North Pacific

CLOUDS SCREENED THE vast ocean fifty thousand feet below, but Shoei Sato didn't mind. He'd flown this route before, more than a dozen times, and knew that there was nothing to be seen. No archipelagos, no lonely atolls, no great reefs—nothing but water, from Japan to the United States.

The only novelty about this trip, so far, was turning back. It was the first time he had been dispatched to do a job, then summoned home without completing his appointed task. That did not bother Sato either, since he would be paid in any case, but it suggested danger waiting for him back in Tokyo.

No problem. He lived for danger: the excitement of it and the compensation he received for making rich men's troubles go away.

He glanced around the plane's passenger cabin, marking each of his companions in their window seats. The good thing about flying on a private jet was that they all got windows, but that only helped if there was something to be seen.

Sato did not believe the difficulty in America had magically resolved itself. Barely a week had passed since his last visit to the States, killing the *gaijin* in New Jersey with his whores and pitiful security. Since then, from what he heard—and he heard *everything*—his master's operation in Atlantic City had been decimated, and Nevada had been lost, as well. Sato and his three brothers of the sword had been dispatched a second time, to find the enemies responsible and take them out.

But now, without a word of explanation, they were turning back.

Clearly, the *oyabun* had changed his mind, but why?

In normal circumstances, Shoei Sato would not care. He had been trained to follow orders without asking questions, and that regimen had never bothered him before. Even this day, it would be an exaggeration to say Sato was concerned. But he *was* curious, a trait that could be perilous.

Some explanation, doubtless, would be offered when they landed back in Tokyo. Whether Tadashi Jo told them the truth or not was something else entirely. Sato understood that masters withheld information from their servants as a matter of routine, but he was paid to risk his life and spill the blood of others. In that trade, disclosure—though, perhaps, not *full* disclosure—was essential.

He could kill a man, woman or child without compunction, without knowing why or even knowing names, but information was required in certain cases to complete the task efficiently. If Sato was assigned to stage an accidental death—one of his specialties—it helped to know whether the target drove a car or was a pilot, if he swam or skied, if he enjoyed skydiving or kept vipers in his home as pets.

Knowledge was power, in its way. And ignorance could kill.

Sato was not afraid of death. He had no more belief in any kind of afterlife than in the basic goodness of humanity. Still, he was in no hurry to explore the final mystery himself.

When he—when *they*, The Four—received their new assignment, he would ask specific questions, couched in terms that let Tadashi Jo know the information he requested was essential to completion of the task. Jo, as first lieutenant of the Sumiyoshi-kai, was wise enough to know that soldiers needed preparation in addition to their skill and weapons.

Preparation *was* a weapon, possibly the most important of them all.

The long flight to America might well have bored another man. Returning midway through the trip might add frustration to the boredom, making tempers flare. Sato felt none of that, and recognized his stoicism as another sign that he was not entirely "normal." Coupled with his total lack of conscience, whatever that was, and his tolerance for pain, it made Shoei Sato a special kind of warrior.

Not unique, the other three were proof of that, but very special all the same.

In Tokyo, The Four would prove themselves again, and make their master proud.

CHAPTER TWELVE

Terminal 1 South Wing,
Narita International Airport

The airport was chaotic, as expected. Bolan claimed his check-through bag and saw no evidence that it had been disturbed, besides the normal scuffs and scrapes that baggage handlers left on most luggage. He joined the sluggish human river bound for Immigration, with his passport and arrival card in hand.

The documents revealed nothing about himself. The name they bore was "Matthew Cooper," tagged to an address in New York City that did not exist. He had nothing to declare for Customs. Cooper's reason for the flight to Tokyo was business, otherwise unspecified.

Appearances were everything in brief encounters with authority.

From there, Bolan moved on to get his rental car. Matt Cooper had a Honda Stream on hold, a compact five-door minivan in silver, right-hand drive, and bought the full insurance package just in case. His bags went in the backseat, and Bolan found his way onto the Shinjuko Expressway, joining swarms of traffic for the fifty-minute drive to Tokyo.

Roppongi was southwest of downtown Tokyo, in the Minato district. Best known for its nightlife, Roppongi was the place to go for watching gangsters and celebrities. Pachinko parlors and illicit gaming rooms alike fleeced visitors, which guaranteed that pawnshops also did a thriving trade.

Kota Yuko's establishment was relatively modest, for the neighborhood. Its signage promised fair deals, spelling out the terms in half a dozen languages. Its windows, covered with protective grates, displayed musical instruments and jewelry, leather and wicked-looking knives.

Inside, there was a musty smell about the shop that spoke of age and hand-me-downs. Bolan spotted the white-haired owner from his photo in Brognola's file, making his way past cases filled with cameras and watches, toward the register. Kota Yuko glanced up at his approach and asked, in English, "May I help you?"

"I am new in town," Bolan replied, in fairly decent Japanese.

Without missing a beat, Yuko said, "You may need assistance."

"Hai," Bolan agreed.

Yuko beckoned to an assistant, issuing instructions in a tone that sounded rude but seemed to have no adverse impact on the younger man. That done, he turned to Bolan and said, "Please to follow me."

They left the main sales floor, passed through a storage area, then downstairs to a basement where Yuko unlocked a smaller room and stepped inside. Bolan followed into the dealer's armory. He was surprised by the diversity of weapons on display, from pistols to grenade launchers and a QJG-02 heavy machine gun manufactured by Norinco, out of China.

Bolan browsed, selecting what he needed, starting with a Steyr AUG assault rifle. For greater range, he chose a DSR-1 bolt-action chambered for .308 Winchester rounds, with a custom suppressor included. Pistol-wise, he took a Glock 22, the .40 S&W model, with a threaded muzzle and suppressor of its own. For heavy punches, Bolan picked a 40 mm Milkor multiple grenade launcher, together with a mix of HE, buckshot, smoke and incendiary rounds. A case of Russian RGD-5 frag grenades joined the arsenal, and a *tanto* dagger topped it off, leaving cash enough to fill the Honda's tank and dine out for a week or so, if Bolan stuck to fast-food restaurants.

He bagged his purchases and paid Yuko without dickering over price. No tip, since that would be an insult and a waste of time. Once action started in the city, Yuko might decide to make a call, but not to the police. He'd curry favor with the Yakuza, up to a point, though he could not identify his *gaijin* customer. Against that, he would weigh the possibility of retribution from the CIA and other foreign clients, if they ever learned he had betrayed one of their own.

It was a devil's choice, and either way, if Yuko tried to sell him out, Bolan would never know. He would be dead by then, if the betrayal worked. And if it didn't, well, what difference did it make?

Bolan left the pawnshop a hundred pounds heavier, stowing the gear in his Honda, and left Roppongi behind for the moment. His first destination lay elsewhere.

It was time to light the fuse.

Akasaka, Tokyo

KATO ANDO DID not resent his orders. It was true that he would have preferred to join the fight against his *oyabun*'s opponents, but he had a duty to perform, and he did not deceive himself by thinking that he could accomplish anything The Four could not. They were beyond the pale of normal soldiers, members of a breed apart.

It was near the end of business for most offices as Ando took his post to watch Saikosai Biometrics from across the street. Foot traffic flowed around him, as if he had been a boulder in the middle of a stream. He watched the third-floor windows, saw their lights go out at last, and memorized the faces of the four young people—two men and two women, no one smiling—who were next out of the building, turning as a group in the direction of the nearest metro station.

Would there be a watchman left behind in darkness? Ando doubted it.

He waited for the crossing signal, made it to the other side and tried the front door of the office building. Open. It was possible a janitor might come around and lock it while he was inside, but Ando was not worried about being trapped. No door had ever yet defeated him.

He shunned the elevator, used the service stairs and moments later stood before the door of Saikosai Biometrics. This one was locked, and he moved along the hallway, checking other offices to satisfy that none were occupied, before he doubled back and went to work with lock picks. Once inside, he looked for keypads, any sign of an alarm, but found nothing.

What was he looking for? Something that would explain the operation to his *oyabun*. Some explanation as to why it lured Toi Takumi. He started with what seemed to be a private office, one more locked door vanquished. More locks on the filing cabinets, but Ando knew the trick to beating them, tipping each cabinet and reaching underneath to press the master disconnect. Inside, he found files filled with formal business correspondence, none of which meant anything to him, and ledgers filled with formulae that might as well have been composed in ancient Greek.

For all he knew, they were.

He couldn't spend the whole night here, searching for some small clue he might not even recognize. Ando considered taking one of the ledgers—or maybe some pages selected at random from each—but what would his *oyabun* do with them? Did Kazuo Takumi have contacts who could translate scientific blather?

Almost certainly.

He drew his blade and was about to slit a page from the first ledger, when the lights hummed on above him. Ando turned to face two men approximately half his age, both holding guns with silencers attached.

"Silent alarm?" he asked.

"It's motion-sensing," one of them replied. "Keyed to the light switch by the door."

"Don't tell him that!" the other grated.

"Why not?" the first one asked. "He isn't going anywhere."

Kabukicho, Tokyo

BROTHELS FLOURISHED IN JAPAN, although the Anti-Prostitution Law of 1956 strictly prohibited payment for sexual intercourse. Enforcement of that law gave rise to alternate activities, including "fashion health parlors" that featured intimate massages, and the soaplands, where clients reclined on waterproof beds, smeared with lotion, while prostitutes writhed atop them without penetration. By recent estimates, the legal sex trade in Japan raked in some $24 billion per year, and Kabukicho was the hotbed of activity in Tokyo.

Most locals called it "Sleepless Town." A recent police inventory counted more than a thousand Yakuza members in Kabukicho, with at least 120 different enterprises under their collective thumb. The controversial installation of fifty closed-circuit street cameras had reduced theft and mugging in Sleepless Town, but sex workers still serviced johns around the clock.

One of the sleeplands owned by Kazuo Takumi in Kabukicho was Joirando, which Bolan understood to mean "Joyland." No subtlety required, when customers came looking for a quick fix or the next best thing to love. To emphasize the point, neon outside the club portrayed a blue lotion bottle gripped by a pink hand with red-lacquered nails. Every thirty seconds or so the hand squeezed, and the bottle ejected a creamy white geyser.

Pure class.

Bolan entered and was greeted by a lounge lizard he assumed to be the manager. The guy spoke English perfectly, none of the cliché problems with the *l*s and *r*s.

"Good evening, sir. Time to come clean!" He gave a little chuckle that Bolan didn't share. "The price for ninety minutes is twelve thousand yen."

Bolan converted that in his head, $126 give or take some change. "You take Amex?" he asked.

"Of course, sir."

Reaching underneath his jacket, Bolan said, "How about Glock?"

The lizard stiffened, lost his artificial smile. "You don't know what you're doing, *gaijin*," he advised.

"Seems pretty straightforward to me," Bolan replied. "Show me the office."

"*Hai*. It is, as you might say, your funeral."

"Not yet."

He trailed the manager, saw one hand rise to the lizard's lapel and let him key the panic trigger. Better to dispose of any muscle now than have them springing at him from the shadows as he left.

Two of them emerged from a door to Bolan's left before they'd reached the office. Both were armed with pistols, but they clearly didn't want to shoot their boss if they could help it. That gave Bolan all the edge he needed, firing two quick shots over the lizard's shoulder, dropping both hardmen where they stood, before they had a chance to use their guns.

His escort gaped, aghast at the display of blood and brains in his establishment, where other fluids were the stock in trade. The lizard doubled over, spewed his dinner on to his patent leather shoes and finished gasping, hands braced on his knees.

"Is that it?" Bolan asked him. "Are we done?"

The guy managed a shaky nod.

"Okay, then," Bolan said. "I'm on the clock. Let's get to work."

LIEUTENANT KENICHI KAYO studied the first pair of corpses, letting the CSI team wait for him. He had been summoned to the Joyland murder scene after firefighters had answered an alarm there, only to discover that there was no blaze beyond a metal trash can in the bloodstained hallway, spewing smoke from burned-out bedding.

It had been enough to clear the place, too many feet trampling the scene as clients fled, before emergency responders finished off the job. No one had actually touched the two dead gunmen lying in the corridor as far as he could tell, but cursory examination might not be enough.

Two head shots, relatively neat and clean as such things went. Whoever had dropped the gunmen had not bothered to collect their weapons, though a closer look revealed that both had lost their magazines. Kayo frowned at that, puzzled. Was it a bid to make the pistols safe, in case someone lifted them from the scene? Or did the killer want more ammunition for himself?

Impossible to say.

"You recognize them?" the lieutenant asked Hiromi Inoue, the first detective on the scene.

"They're Sumiyoshi-kai, sir. Small-time muscle."

"Outclassed, I would say, on this occasion."

"Yes, sir."

"Where's the manager?"

"This way."

Kayo trailed the man who'd called him out to Joyland, reached another door that stood open, and stepped into an office rank with death. A body's sudden relaxation at the final instant vented all manner of unpleasant smells and substances. The manager propped in a high-backed chair behind a cluttered desk had left his home this evening thinking he was dressed to kill.

As it turned out, he had been dressed to die.

It was another head shot, almost carbon copy. Whoever their shooter was, he didn't hesitate and didn't miss—at least, from ten feet out.

"Cartridges?" the lieutenant asked.

"Three .40-caliber," Inoue said. "We'll check for prints, of course, but…"

"Hai." But nothing. They'd be lucky to retrieve a greasy smudge, if that.

A small, stout safe stood open in a corner of the room, behind the desk and lolling corpse. Kenichi's frown deepened into a scowl. "Three dead, for robbery?"

"The two resisted, sir."

"And this one?"

"Leave no witnesses."

Kayo nodded. "Cameras?"

"In place and functional," Inoue said, "but someone took the disk."

"Of course they did. Print every surface from the office to the entryway."

"Yes, sir."

"Was there anyone remaining when you got here?"

"They were wise enough to flee."

"And damned unlikely to come forward now. They'll call Tadashi Jo before they'd speak to us."

"You'll question him, sir?"

"On what grounds? Does his name appear on any lease for this establishment?"

"I doubt it."

"And without that link…"

"He's bound to squeal harassment."

"Certainly harassment, at the very least. I think, Hiromi, we must treat this as a simple robbery gone wrong. Pursue such evidence as may remain after the buffalo stampede, and wait to see what happens next."

"Is this a war beginning?" the detective asked.

"I couldn't say," Kayo answered.

But I can always hope, he thought to himself.

Shiodome, Tokyo

TOI TAKUMI'S SMARTPHONE blared its ringtone from the coffee table in his living room.

He did not recognize the number showing on the phone's screen, so he answered cautiously. *"Sore wa daredesu ka?"*

His master's voice spoke softly, as it always did. "We have a difficulty, Toi."

"Difficulty?"

"We have caught a spy prowling the laboratory. It appears your father sent him."

"Mazāfakkā!" Toi was instantly embarrassed by his use of the obscenity. "Forgive me, Master."

Susumu Kodama's voice was soothing. "This is a surprise, I know, but one that I should have foreseen."

"Has he confessed?"

"He was reluctant, but the flesh is weak. He calls himself Kato Ando."

"He's my father's lackey."

"And a killer, eh?"

"No doubt. What shall be done with him?"

"He claims to have learned nothing, but he was surprised while stealing files. We cannot risk releasing him."

"Of course not, Master. But will eliminating him cause further difficulty?"

"You would be the better judge of that, I think."

"My father will expect to hear from him. When he does not, he will send others to investigate."

Kodama did not answer for a moment. When he did, his voice was calm as ever. "Thankfully, our work is nearly finished. We no longer need the office or laboratory. I shall purge the files tonight and leave nothing behind for other spies."

"A wise decision, Master. And Ando?"

"He will simply disappear. Such things are common in the city, as I understand it."

"Forgive me for the inconvenience of my father," Toi pleaded.

"On the contrary, Toi. He helps us by accelerating our plan. You should thank him."

"I give thanks that he and all his rotten family will soon be gone."

"A vengeful spirit does not suit you, Toi. Bear in mind that we visit this judgment on the city out of love."

Chastened, Toi answered, "Yes, Master!"

"And you'll be available, to play your part?"

"I will."

"God's love to you, Toi."

"God's love to you, Master."

Toi cut the link and stared through his apartment window toward the Shiodome city center, a collection of thirteen skyscrapers housing billion-dollar firms such as Fujitsu, Nippon Airways, Bandai Visual, and SoftBank. In his mind, he pictured the great towers crumbling, rotten from within, burying thousands of their zombie slaves as they collapsed.

His father had conspired to ruin everything, as usual, but this time he had met a force that guns and money could not overcome. Accustomed to eliminating any obstacle with bribery or brute force, how would Kazuo Takumi fare against the mighty wrath of Bishamon?

Toi smiled, imagining his father's face when the great *oyabun* discovered everything he'd done in the pursuit of wealth and power was a waste of time. The day was coming when no private army, no corrupted judge or politician, could protect him. If Kazuo Takumi were allowed to see the future, would he plead for mercy? Beg forgiveness for his crimes?

Toi doubted it. And secretly, that pleased him.

Let the old man die with all the other sinners.

Toi hoped that his father would die screaming.

Haneda Airport, Tokyo

TADASHI JO WAS waiting when the Bombardier Global 8000 landed, right on time. The pilots knew their master well enough to understand that no delays were tolerated in emergencies.

Haneda Airport—formally known as Tokyo International—had been the city's primary international airport until 1978, when Narita siphoned off much of the commercial airline traffic. Nowadays, Haneda was the hub for Japan Airlines, All Nippon Airways and various low-cost domestic carriers, with private charter flights. It remained the second-busiest airport in Asia and the world's fourth busiest, moving sixty-nine million passengers yearly.

No one would notice The Four.

Watching the 110-foot jet taxi closer, Tadashi Jo rehearsed his instructions to Kazuo Takumi's elite assassins. He wanted no confusion, nothing to retard a swift solution to his *oyabun*'s concerns. Above all else, he wanted to be firm and in control while giving orders to The Four.

The truth was, they intimidated him. He'd never seen them work, but knew some of the things they'd done in service to the Sumiyoshi-kai. As individuals, they would be feared exterminators. But together, as The Four, they were approaching legendary status.

Shoei Sato. Koyuki Masuda. Nakai Ryo. Tamura Min.

Each had his specialty—explosives, blades, poisons, the bow—but all four had been rigorously trained by masters in *ninjutsu* and kung fu, as in firearms, edged weapons, scuba, hang gliding and a host of other skills. For "graduation," Kazuo Takumi had made arrangements for a twenty-member strike team of the Japanese Special Forces Group to hunt The Four through five hundred square miles of virgin forest in Honshu's Shirakami-Sanchi preserve, with orders to pull no punches, take no prisoners.

The result had been catastrophe—for the soldiers. Three had died, chalked off to "training accidents," while the remaining seventeen were hospitalized, four with injuries necessitating their retirement from military service. Takumi contributed to their disability pension and arranged a promotion for the colonel who had authorized the exercise.

Such men as these were dangerous in the extreme. But if their loyalty held fast…

Tadashi Jo watched them disembark, leaving their bags for someone else to carry. He had brought a Toyota Century Royal to accommodate The Four and their luggage, chauffeured, with a shotgun rider along for security's sake—an almost humorous inclusion, now that he considered it.

No casual observer would have thought The Four were special. Certainly, they moved with an athletic grace most humans did not share, and were possessed of quiet confidence, but if a passing stranger on the street were asked to guess at their profession, he would probably have called them young accountants, brokers, maybe up-and-coming lawyers. Perfect form, enhancing their invisibility.

Jo knew better than to shake hands with any of The Four, or waste their time with pointless pleasantries. He bowed in greeting, ushered them inside the limousine and was the last to enter. Perched on a jump seat facing his passengers, he said, "You may be curious about the cancellation of your mission."

No reply from any of The Four.

Jo forged ahead. "Your boss considers that the trouble in America may be beyond redemption for the moment, while the family is threatened here, in Tokyo."

"By whom?" Tamura Min inquired.

"That is unclear. Part of your task is to identify the enemy."

"We're not detectives," Shoei Sato said.

"That's understood," Jo granted. "Others are at work to name the targets. If they strike in Tokyo, however, it is hoped you may be able to pursue them and…eliminate the problem."

Koyuki Masuda smiled and answered for The Four, "It's what we do."

CHAPTER THIRTEEN

Nihonbashi, Tokyo

Someone was working late at Kazoku Investments when the Executioner arrived. *Kazoku* translated as "family," and in this case, that meant the Sumiyoshi-kai. The firm consisted of accountants and advisers moving money for the Yakuza, "cleaning" it in the process, while a board consisting of six oath-bound, tattooed members of the Yakuza issued the orders from their *oyabun*.

Nihonbashi was Japan's "Kilometer Zero," official heart of the country from which all mile markers were measured. It earned that honor in 1603, with construction of Tokyo's first bridge across the Nihonbashi River, and remained a major business district, though the heart of commerce in the capital had moved on to Hibiya. Billions still passed through the offices and vaults of Nihonbashi, and while Bolan didn't plan to tap that golden flow this night, he did intend to put a major crimp in Kazuo Takumi's piece of it.

Across the street from Kazoku Investments, one block south of Eitai Dori, Bolan sat on top of another high-rise, peering through the scope of his DSR-1 sniper's rifle. Conceived as a specialized piece for police sharpshooters, later adopted by Germany's GSG 9 counterterrorist unit, the weapon was a bullpup design, fed from a 5-round detachable box magazine behind the pistol grip.

Its stock was fully adjustable, as was the cheek piece. A spare magazine was mounted within easy reach, between the trigger guard and the adjustable fore grip. The rifle's fluted, free-floating barrel was shielded by a ventilated aluminum hand guard and fitted with a muzzle brake. This night, it also wore a tactical suppressor, attached to the muzzle brake with a quick-release lever.

Across the street, six Yakuza directors sat around a long gleaming conference table, manila folders stacked in front of them as they discussed whatever passed for business at Kazoku Investments. Moving money here and there, skimming the cream, deciding which firms they should infiltrate, which ones were ripe for looting to the point of bankruptcy. There'd be no passing thought for innocents caught in the grinder, only profits for the Yakuza machine.

Six targets for a 5-round magazine. That suited Bolan well enough, since he intended to leave one witness alive.

Hal Brognola's file had shown him photos of the six men seated at the table, listed their rap sheets, addresses and unlisted phone numbers. Watching them through his scope, he dialed one of those numbers now and listened to the phone ring, saw one of them reach for a cell phone and respond.

"Hai?"

Bolan had rehearsed the phrase, knowing his accent wouldn't pass a close inspection, but it didn't matter. Speaking to his wireless headset, he said, *"Inagawa-kai kara no go aisatsu."*

Greetings from the Inagawa-kai.

His first shot drilled the glass downrange and struck a target seated across from the man with the phone at his ear. Blood sprayed across the polished table from the head shot, spattering the second mobster's face and crisp white shirt. The corpse toppled forward and struck the table with a face-plant that splashed more blood to his left and right.

Before the others could recoil or come to grips with what was happening, Bolan cycled the DSR-1's precision bolt and fired again, turning another face to crimson gruel, painting the wall behind the dead man's chair with gleaming shades of red and gray.

The *crack* of Bolan's shots echoed around him, as his 165-grain bullets broke Mach 1, hurtling along at 800 meters per second despite the suppressor. No problem, since diffusion in the concrete canyon would prevent ear-witnesses from pinning down the source.

Five shots, five shattered skulls draining their contents on the tabletop, with blood streams dribbling to the floor. The sole survivor had already disappeared beneath the table, hiding out, and Bolan left him to it as he packed his rifle and moved out.

The message was delivered. Whether it accomplished anything was up to Kazuo Takumi.

At the very least, it would instill confusion, maybe turn the Sumiyoshi-kai against their arch competitors, instead of hunting a *gaijin*. If not, at least he had disrupted operations of the family's top money mill and laundry. For the moment, that would do.

Until he hit the next target in line.

Tsukiji, Tokyo

KAZUO TAKUMI'S SEVENTH call to Kato Ando's cell phone went directly to voice mail, as the others had. He muttered an obscenity and was about to set his phone aside, when it began vibrating in his hand. The unexpected feeling nearly made him drop it, but he managed not to, recognized Tadashi Jo's cell number on the screen and answered, "Yes?"

It was rare for his first lieutenant to sound rattled, but Tadashi Jo almost sounded out of breath. "You haven't heart the news yet?"

"What news?"

"Of the shooting?"

"Organize your thoughts and speak coherently," Takumi ordered.

"Yes, I'm sorry," Jo said. "A sniper has attacked the Nihonbashi office and killed five of the directors. Only Adachi is alive."

Adachi Nagaharu, that would be. One of the six directors Takumi had selected to ride herd on Kazoku Investments and ensure the constant flow of profits to his family, no matter what travails beset stock markets, East or West.

"How fortunate for him," Takumi said.

"He's being questioned by police," Jo said. "He has a lawyer with him, Tsuda Adinori."

Adinori was one of several top attorneys on retainer to the Sumiyoshi-kai, skilled both in criminal and civil law.

"He's keeping quiet, then."

"Of course. But Adinori passed a message to me. Just before the shooting started, Adachi received a phone call."

"And?"

"A voice he did not recognize said, 'Greetings from the Inagawa-kai.'"

"And you believe they are responsible for this?"

"They are our enemies."

"You state the obvious. But would they strike us now, in such a public way, just when we've had our difficulties in America?"

"Why not?"

"I'm not a great believer in coincidence."

"Who is to say they aren't responsible for all of it? They envy us, being the second-largest family."

"That envy is traditional. What makes it so acute, just now, to prompt so much bloodletting in Japan and the United States?"

Jo sighed and answered, "I don't know."

"Consider it, while you investigate. Do not ignore the Inagawa-kai, but bear in mind the possibility of a diversion."

"Hai!"

"Have you heard from Kato in the past few hours?"

"No, sir. Shall I try to reach him?"

"Never mind," Takumi said. "I'll deal with it."

He cut the link, more curious than ever as to why he could not reach his strong right hand. Was Kato's sudden and unprecedented unavailability connected to the Nihonbashi murders in some way and to the rest of it? Rephrased, was there a possibility it *could not* be related?

Takumi craved *sake* but denied himself the sweet relief it offered. He would stay alert, on edge, ready to strike the moment that a target was presented to him.

And he would not grant himself the liberty of fear.

Kazoku Investments, Nihonbashi

"SORRY FOR THE second call-out," Hiromi Inoue said.

Lieutenant Kenichi Kayo waved off the apology, scanning the massacre scene from his place near the conference room's doorway. It did not take a supersleuth to spot the bullet holes in laminated plate glass.

"Armor-piercing rounds?" he speculated. "At the very least, full metal jackets for such tidy holes."

"The rest isn't so tidy, Lieutenant."

"No," Kayo granted. "Head shots normally aren't neat and clean, unless they use small calibers up close."

"We'll have ballistics after the autopsies. If the rounds were AP, even FMJ, we may get something."

"Useless, still, without the weapon."

"Hai."

"When you disturbed me, I was browsing on the internet," Kayo said.

"For what?" Hiromi asked.

"News bulletins," Kayo said, "from the United States."

"Work, then, not pleasure."

"Were you aware of the attacks on Sumiyoshi-kai members in both New Jersey and Nevada?"

"No."

"You should educate yourself," Kayo chided him. "We've lost Noboru Machii and Jiro Shinoda, with a number of their men."

"Too bad." Inoue did not sound disturbed.

"Kazuo must be grieving for his protégés," Kayo said. "Have you spoken to Tadashi Jo yet, Lieutenant?"

"I'm looking for him," Kayo replied.

"Well, it seems you've found him."

Kayo turned in the direction of Inoue's gaze and saw Tadashi Jo standing, restrained by officers in uniform, beside the elevators. With him were two younger, blank-faced men whom the lieutenant did not recognize.

"With bodyguards, no less," he said.

"I'm not surprised, considering."

"Get photos of them with your phone, will you? I'd like to find out who they are, specifically."

Kayo left his underling to it, staying well to one side as he went to greet the first lieutenant of the Sumiyoshi-kai.

"Tadashi Jo."

"Do I know you?"

"How quickly they forget. I have arrested you three times," Kayo said.

"But never once convicted me. I don't dwell over trivia."

"Not like this mess, eh? Five of your top men lost face tonight, in the worst way."

"I don't appreciate your humor," Jo told him.

"It is an acquired taste. How did you learn of the shooting?"

"As you must know, there is a survivor. I've provided him with an attorney, to prevent him being further traumatized."

"I doubt we'll shoot him," Kayo stated.

"He's a victim in this case."

"A material witness, in fact. We may detain him for a reasonable time, in furtherance of our inquiry."

"And the chief of police will decide what's reasonable, I suppose?"

"Barring a complaint from the attorney you've provided. Meanwhile, it occurs to me that you are listed as an officer of Kazoku Investments. What is your title, again?"

"CFO," Jo replied.

"Chief financial officer. It's lucky that you missed the board meeting tonight. Lucky for you, at least."

"I normally get briefings on the morning after."

"Not a hands-on leader, then."

"I have multiple interests," Jo stated.

"Indeed. Can you imagine anyone who might desire to murder your directors?"

"Communists, perhaps," Jo said. "They hate all corporations."

"Something more specific? Possibly more personal?"

"Sorry. My mind's a blank."

"That can't be helpful, for a CFO. We'll speak again."

"I live for nothing else," the Yakuza first lieutenant said, then turned back toward the elevator with his flankers close behind.

Akihabara, Tokyo

AKIHABARA'S NAME TRANSLATED as "autumn leaf field," but a person wouldn't know it, moving through the crowded streets. Nicknamed "Electric Town" after the last world war, when it served as a major shopping center for household appliances and black market contraband, nowadays Akihabara was the heart of Tokyo's *otaku* culture—obsessive pursuit of video games, anime and cosplay. Condos in the district were expensive and attracted a younger crowd than certain other parts of Tokyo.

Or, in Tadashi Jo's case, mobsters trying to feel younger than their thirty-something years.

Bolan was moving up the ladder of command, ready to make a move on Kazuo Takumi's number two. Finding the *oyabun* himself would be a knotty problem, with his multiple addresses and no office where he regularly made appearances. Bolan possessed Takumi's two unlisted phone numbers, but wasn't ready yet to force the top Yakuza's hand. Before he got to that stage, Bolan wanted the man off balance, panicked and with a sense of desperation snapping at his heels.

What better way to spike the *oyabun*'s blood pressure than to take one of his bishops off the chessboard?

It was too early for Tadashi Jo to be tucked up in his condo, and it seemed unlikely he'd be getting much sleep anyway, after the hits his family had taken since that afternoon. Instead, Bolan made for his home away from home, an office on the second floor of an expensive "maid café," one of the trendy restaurants where waitresses were dressed as maids to serve their "masters," commonly costumed as their favorite anime heroes or villains.

The place was like a mini-Comic-Con year-round.

Jo's place—the Blushing Maid—was situated one block off Kuramae-hashi Dori. A person didn't need a costume to go in and grab a bite, but Bolan figured what the hell, why not? As long as masks were commonplace, he might as well fit in.

He parked behind the Blushing Maid and walked back to the street entrance. His balaclava didn't mesh with manga, strictly speaking, but the outfits Bolan saw around him on the sidewalk were diverse and colorful enough to draw most eyes away from him, unless somebody focused on his height. Black garb, black raincoat overall to hide the Steyr AUG beneath his right arm, and he passed unnoticed through the younger folk in search of some excitement.

And the Executioner was happy to oblige.

The café's inner layout was a mystery to Bolan until he cleared the threshold. Then, amid the crush of tables with a bar in back, he saw stairs to his left, two Yakuza guards who could have been in costumes of their own, grim-faced, with skinny pinstriped suits hiding their full-body tattoos.

A hostess greeted Bolan, but he dodged her, heading for the staircase, paying no mind when she squeaked a protest at his back. The lookouts saw him coming, muttered something back and forth, bracing themselves for trouble.

Bolan mumbled something that was vaguely close to Japanese, causing the watchdog on his left to lean a little closer, frowning, asking, "What was that?" He choked on

Bolan's rigid fingers, left hand knifing up into his larynx, and went down, gasping in vain for air. The other man was a little quicker, reaching for his pistol, but the Steyr's muzzle stopped him, prodding at his navel.

"Upstairs," Bolan commanded, adding *"Ni-kai"* from his phrase book, just in case the Yakuza gunner was short on English. Something worked, because the shooter turned, scowling, and started climbing toward the second floor.

Minato, Tokyo

THE CHINESE EMBASSY in Tokyo was a seven-story blockhouse guarded day and night by uniformed police outside and by crack soldiers of the People's Liberation Army once you cleared the gates. It was a drab building, nothing to recommend it from an architectural standpoint, but art did not concern Susumu Kodama as he approached the embassy on foot, past demonstrators chanting for some cause he did not recognize.

Kodama showed his pass three times in all: first to a clutch of Tokyo Metro Police officers outside the embassy gates, next to a pair of Chinese soldiers wearing QBZ-03 assault rifles slung across their chests, and finally to a plainclothes security guard whose jacket barely concealed his QSZ-92 service pistol. Kodama was passed through each checkpoint in turn, escorted from the last one to the office of Colonel Fulian Sun, representing China's Ministry of State Security.

Colonel Sun was a short man, heavyset, stopping just short of what a Westerner might call roly-poly. He wore no uniform, preferring finely tailored suits from Punjab House in Hong Kong. His thinning hair was slicked back from a round face with a double chin, tufted with a goatee that seemed more accidental than precisely planned. A pair of wire-rimmed spectacles framed eyes like slivers of obsidian.

Kodama and the colonel bowed across Sun's desk, in lieu of shaking hands. Sun waved his guest toward a chair facing the desk, and sank into his larger chair positioned on a hidden riser to provide a sense of dominance.

"Thank you for seeing me on such short notice, Colonel," Kodama stated.

"I was surprised to hear from you so soon."

"That is the reason for my visit. We are going to advance the schedule."

Sun's moon face tilted slightly to the left. "Advance it?"

"Move it up."

"I understand the word. Why change it now?" he asked.

"We have an opportunity," Kodama replied, "that I'm reluctant to ignore."

"Explain."

He ran it down: the Sumiyoshi-kai's surprise dilemma, war in the United States, now spreading to the streets of Tokyo, facilitating Toi Takumi's grand betrayal of his father and the Yakuza.

"And this inspires a change of plan, because…?" Sun queried.

"The public will be focused on corruption and the mayhem it produces when we strike. It sets the stage. Salvation follows rampant sin."

"I wonder how much of this dogma you believe."

Kodama wondered that himself, sometimes. "Motives should not concern you, Colonel," he replied. "You desire disruption and deniability."

Sun nodded, a procedure that compressed his second

chin. "That's true, of course. But if, through no fault of your own, you should be captured…"

"You will not be implicated," Kodama assured him. "If my goal was martyrdom, I would select a better path than being killed in prison by some triad soldier working for your ministry."

"We understand each other, then."

"From the beginning to the end, Colonel."

"And is there anything you need, in aid of your accelerated schedule?" Sun asked.

"Nothing. The material you furnished has produced—what do the Americans say? A bumper crop? The final preparations for dispersal are in progress, using vehicles linked to the Yakuza."

"An interesting twist," Sun granted, not quite smiling.

"You shall not be disappointed."

"I sincerely hope not. If we're finished now…"

Kodama's escort led him back the way he'd come, out to the street. He passed unnoticed by the demonstrators, wondering how many of them would still be alive the next day.

The Blushing Maid, Akihabara

THE CLOCK WAS RUNNING. Bolan knew the café's hostess had to have seen him take down the lookout, even if diners were preoccupied or thought it was part of the joint's floor show. She could be on the phone by now, either calling upstairs to warn her boss, or bringing reinforcements to the scene. The least likely scenario: a call to the police.

She would have known better than that.

The second guard was talking as they climbed. "You making big mistake, believe me. This not going well for you."

"I'm touched by your concern," Bolan replied, and jabbed him with the Steyr's flash suppressor, instantly rewarded with a curse.

They reached the second floor, turned right and ran into another guard. He saw what was happening and tried to reach his shoulder-holstered weapon, but he never made it. Bolan fired a 5.56 mm NATO round into the first hood's back, piercing his torso and erupting from his chest to slam the second shooter backward, blowing scarlet bubbles from a throat wound.

Leaving them to thrash and die without him, Bolan stepped across their bodies, tried the knob and felt it turn. He shouldered through the doorway, following the echo of his shot muffled by flesh, and caught three men around a desk, just turning from a city map of Tokyo.

None of them was Tadashi Jo.

"Your boss around?" Bolan asked.

The tallest of them, to his left, said, "Who the fu—?" before a round from Bolan's AUG cut off the question. Now the other two stood frozen, gaping at him, hands frozen en route toward hidden weapons.

"Is your *boss* around?" he asked again.

They blinked at him like fish for a second, then scrambled for their hardware.

"Never mind," he said, and killed them where they stood. A plan was only useful if you had the choice of scrubbing it when it went south. He'd have to seek Tadashi Jo somewhere else, instead of wasting time with Yakuza muscle determined not to answer, even if it killed them.

He started back downstairs, thinking the hostess hadn't phoned a warning to the office gang. And that meant—

Halfway down the stairs, he heard the startled cries of

café diners, nothing like amusement in their voices now. Reaching the bottom of the staircase, Bolan spotted half a dozen Yakuza gunners with pistols out, wearing their shades despite the hour, ready to receive him. There were more outside, preventing any new arrivals from entering until their work was done inside.

"Hey, boys, you're late," he told the firing squad.

And the Executioner ripped them with a 5.56 mm buzz saw, firing from the hip.

CHAPTER FOURTEEN

Two of the gunners went down immediately, likely dead before their bodies hit the floor. The others scattered, flipping tables in a quest for cover, while the costumed diners screamed and shouted. Most of them were dropping, too, some clutching cell phones, texting furiously. One of them, dressed up in a karate *gi* with bandages disguising half his face, went for the nearest gunner with what appeared to be a pair of plastic nunchucks. For his trouble, he received a bullet in the face at point-blank range.

Bolan returned the favor, taking out the killer with a clean shot through his temple from a range of twenty feet. A short hop landed Bolan at the bottom of the staircase, crouching, shouldering the AUG and tracking targets as they scrambled. At the same time, from the sidewalk, the remaining goons were barging in, more pistols drawn, one of them hauling out a Micro-Uzi from an armpit holster.

Bolan took the Uzi man down first, two NATO rounds drilling his chest, punching him backward, out the way he'd come into the Blushing Maid. His two companions broke in opposite directions, one ducking behind a cigarette machine, the other diving for the cover of a table someone else had overturned.

The diver almost made it, but he wasn't fast enough. A foot or so before he would have been concealed, Bolan reached out to tag him with a 3-round burst that flipped him through a clumsy somersault, landing face-up and blowing wet red bubbles from his lips.

That still left four, and some of them were firing at him now, though not effectively. Their shots went high and wide, thrown out in hopes of getting lucky when they should have aimed. He spotted one, hunkered behind a small square table, and the NATO rounds cut through its plastic top as if it had been made of cardboard, instantly raising a dying scream.

Three left, and every second Bolan spent disposing of them brought police or more Yakuza that much closer. He was fifteen feet from freedom, but to cross that open ground he'd have to lay down cover fire, and that meant jeopardizing innocents whose cries and sobbing made the Blushing Maid sound like the viewing chamber at a mortuary.

Plan B had been to exit through the café's kitchen, out the back door and along an alley lined with garbage bins. To reach the kitchen, Bolan had to travel forty feet, already littered and obstructed with the dead and wounded, toppled furniture, discarded costumes. Could he make it, while the three surviving hardmen were still disoriented?

There was only one way to find out.

He bolted, dropped and slid on the linoleum floor as pistols started tracking him, firing too late instead of leading him as they should have. The Sumiyoshi-kai were fighters, obviously, but they'd cut their teeth on drive-bys and back-alley executions, learning little about marksmanship while they were at it. If they couldn't take a victim by surprise or while he was restrained, their aim went straight to hell.

A lucky break, but nothing Bolan could rely on in relatively cramped space. Stray rounds were as deadly as a sniper's finest bull's-eye, if they found their mark by accident. He had to keep the shooters hopping, take them out if possible, or at the very least confuse them until he'd reached the kitchen and slipped out.

Sliding, he squeezed off half a dozen shots at no one in particular, keeping the Steyr's muzzle elevated to avoid the café's cringing diners. Every shot elicited more screams from innocents, more rasping curses from the gunners as Bolan kept them under cover, likely also worrying about the cops by now.

He reached the kitchen door, rolled through it and ignored the cooks who cowered in the shadow of their grill and fry vats. Bolan hit the back door, ready for a Yakuza reception party, but the alleyway was clear. He turned right, sprinting toward the nearest cross street and toward the spot where he had left his Honda Stream. He had no doubt the Yakuza gunners would follow him, but it would be a game of catch-up now, and Bolan had a narrow lead.

LIEUTENANT KENICHI KAYO was psyched. Halfway back to headquarters, he'd turned, deciding that he needed more time with Tadashi Jo. The mobster would not tell him anything of value, naturally, but Kayo wanted to annoy the smug, arrogant bastard anyway, to let him know that some of Tokyo's police regarded him as scum and were devoted to the task of putting him away.

What would the lieutenant gain from that? A sense of satisfaction—and, perhaps, a reprimand if he pushed hard enough to make Jo file a citizen's complaint.

So be it. He'd decided it was worth the risk, and he was tired of watching the Yakuza run rampant in his city, flaunting its contempt for law and order.

Tadashi Jo would not be at home, so the lieutenant steered his unmarked Mazda RX-8 patrol car toward the

Blushing Maid café. The Mazda had originally been a sports car, when it premiered in 2001, but Tokyo's Metro Police liked its speed, its handling and its lines. The RX-8 had ceased production in 2011, but the cars remained in service while city hall dragged its feet on negotiations for new rolling stock. Kayo's unmarked version fooled no one with any street sense whatsoever, but he still enjoyed driving the little sportster and would miss it when the Powers That Be replaced it with some other model.

There were risks involved in cornering Tadashi Jo on his home turf. Surrounded by his men, the weasel would be cockier than ever, and on edge about the loss of his compatriots. Still, even hard-core Yakuza thought twice about molesting the police, aware that any breach of etiquette might see them stripped of favors they had purchased.

Going in, Kayo knew that he would be outgunned. Most Yakuza were wise enough to leave their guns at home on normal nights, but this was not a normal situation. For self-defense, the lieutenant had his .38-caliber Smith & Wesson Model 64 revolver, a small telescoping baton and his training in mixed martial arts.

Kayo was a decent shot, of course. Japanese police trained thoroughly with firearms at the National Police Academy, spending sixty hours of practice compared to an average thirty hours for American cops. Unlike their Yankee counterparts, however, they never carried high-capacity semiauto pistols, had no shotguns in their cars and were required to leave their sidearms at headquarters while off duty. The flip side of those restrictions was intensive martial arts training—ninety hours each in judo and kendo stick-fighting—with many officers holding black belts.

A burst of clicks and static from the Mazda's two-way

radio demanded Kayo's attention. The dispatcher came on air, directing units in Akihabara to the Blushing Maid café, where a shooting was in progress.

"Goddamn it!"

Even as he cursed, Kayo was accelerating, wondering if he had missed his chance to prod Tadashi Jo and make the mobster's life a bit more difficult. For all he knew, that life had ended, and Kayo would be faced with yet another cleanup operation, asking questions which the Sumiyoshi-kai would never answer in a million years.

The lieutenant was a block from the café when he saw gawkers milling on the sidewalk, peering through the windows at whatever lay within. They were not fleeing for their lives, which indicated that the shooting had subsided, but he planned to take no chances.

Slowly braking, he was startled when a car roared past in front of him, jumping the light at the next intersection. Seconds later, it was followed by another speeding vehicle, jammed full of young men whom Kayo recognized as standard-issue Yakuza muscle.

He reached out for his dashboard microphone, then hesitated. Backup was the way to go, of course, but sudden curiosity compelled him to ignore the rule book. Why? If questioned on it—which he likely would be, later—he could not have said. Something compelled him to give chase, see what was happening, try to identify the men involved.

And he could always call for backup later.

If he lived that long.

BOLAN SAW THE chase car's headlights closing as he reached Kuramae-hashi Dori, charging into traffic without waiting for the light to change. Two eastbound drivers hit their brakes in time to keep from T-boning his

Honda, one of them forgetting courtesy to give Bolan a
sharp blast from his horn. Whether the snarl would slow
his pursuers, Bolan couldn't say, but he was leading for
the moment, and he meant to take advantage of it.

Even now, in flight, he thought about the next stop
on his hit parade, wondering where he'd find Tadashi Jo
in Tokyo. Taking Kazuo Takumi's second in command
wasn't obligatory, but he'd set the goal and hated to abandon it without another try, if he could pin the target down.

Meanwhile, he had to stay alive and ditch the hunters, or dispose of them. They'd made it through the intersection to Kuramae-hashi Dori, somehow, and were
burning rubber to catch up with him. Headlights behind
them showed him four or five heads in the black sedan—
enough to do the job, if Bolan gave them any opening
at all.

He didn't plan on doing that, but every firefight was
a gamble. Like in Vegas. Like Atlantic City. Some gamblers bet their paycheck, house or car. Mack Bolan played
for higher stakes.

The were rolling east toward the Sumida River and another waterfront of sorts, not the dilapidated kind where
Bolan tried to stage a fight if one was handy, but at least
the hour should ensure that workmen had gone home.
About a dozen bridges spanned the Sumida, but he didn't
want to take the chase on any one of them, where he
would be confined and forced to fight amid congested
traffic.

Better to find open ground, if there was any left in
Tokyo, and do his killing there.

The spot he had in mind was a large parking lot behind a factory, screened off by trees from view of drivers
on the five-lane highway leading to the nearest bridge.
It wasn't perfect, but it offered some degree of privacy

and ought to be deserted now, unless there was an after-hours cleaning crew at work.

His exit lay four hundred yards ahead of Bolan, on his left, after he'd crossed the six-lane flow of Edo Dori with its traffic running north and south. The intersection there gave him trouble, red lights glaring at him overhead, but he blew past them, leaning on the Honda's horn and trusting speed to get him through.

A pileup now, especially if he was trapped inside the car, meant death.

A green-and-yellow taxi grazed his rear bumper when he was almost clear. The scrape shuddered through Bolan, but he kept a firm grip on the Honda's steering wheel and brought it back on course before he jumped the sidewalk on Kuramae-hashi Dori. Using that momentum, he veered across two lanes of traffic to his left—more squealing brakes—and set himself up for the left-hand exit drawing closer by the heartbeat.

Luck was with the hunters, too. The caught a green light at the intersection where he'd nearly met disaster, gaining ground and closing on his taillights. So far, they had not been close enough to take him out, but they were quickly narrowing his lead.

The exit, when he saw it, meant another dash across oncoming traffic, headlights lancing Bolan's retinas. He couldn't see the startled drivers, couldn't hear their curses, but he hoped they had enough control of their respective vehicles to let a madman pass.

And if they stopped the shooters who were tailing him, Bolan could live with that.

He made the exit, dipped below the level flow of traffic, braking slightly as he rolled into the parking lot behind its screen of trees. Two semitrailers occupied the far end of the lot, and Bolan made for them, pulling around behind the second one and immediately switching off the Honda's engine, scrambling for his weapons as he bailed out of the car.

Kenichi Kayo knew he was in trouble as he chased the two cars toward the river. Cursing his foolishness, Kayo almost grabbed the dashboard-mounted microphone, but stopped himself a second time. He'd traveled more than half a mile by then. His violation of procedure was already serious enough for a demotion. If he struck another vehicle, it meant the end of his career. If he struck a pedestrian, he could be sent to prison.

He should stop now, let them go, Kayo thought. No one knew he was in the area or would expect him to be near the Blushing Maid, much less in hot pursuit of fleeing fugitives. He could abort the chase, go back to headquarters and clock out for the night.

But if he did, Kayo would not sleep. He'd lie awake, fuming over the gunmen who'd escaped from him. And if they went on to kill someone else this night, those deaths would be on his account. His soul was bruised and stained enough already, without adding insult to the injury.

Crossing Edo Dori, the lieutenant thought he was about to watch a massacre on wheels. The lead car made it, barely, with a kiss in parting from a taxi, then the lights changed and the second car in line breezed through as if the thugs inside it had been blessed by Fate. Kayo took his chances, hands white-knuckled on the Mazda's wheel, no flashing lights or whooping siren to assist him in pursuit.

"I am such an idiot!" he muttered, and knew that every word was true. Even if he survived the chase and managed to arrest two carloads of Yakuza, well armed and belligerent, how was he going to explain the one-man exercise in foolishness?

He'd worry about it if he lived, he thought, just as he saw the two cars veering across lanes of traffic, seeming to be angling for an exit on the left. Kenichi followed, one more risky move in the fast lane toward professional suicide. He reached down with his right hand, verified the Smith & Wesson's presence on his belt unnecessarily.

Six shots, against how many guns?

Kayo carried two speed loaders, eighteen rounds in all, and wondered if he would have time to use them when the shooting started. That it *would* start, he had no doubt whatsoever. Ambulances had been summoned to the Blushing Maid. So had the medical examiner, which meant at least one death. Why would the gunmen willingly surrender, when conviction on a murder charge might send them to the gallows in the Tokyo Detention House?

What did another trifling murder mean, when they were fitted for the noose?

Kayo was rehearsing lessons from his early firearms training as he swerved to make the left-hand exit. Line up front and rear sights on the target's center mass. Don't jerk the trigger; squeeze it. Beat the recoil with a firm two-handed grip.

All fine in theory, but he'd never fired the .38 except in practice, never tried to wound or kill a man. Tonight would be his first time, if it occurred.

And Kayo was not sure that he was up to it.

BOLAN KNELT IN the shadow of a semitrailer with the Steyr at his shoulder, peering through the telescopic sight with its simple black ring reticle and range finder designed so that a target completely filled the eyepiece at three hundred meters. Call it half that distance to the entrance of the spacious parking lot, where he was focused on the Yakuza chase car.

His first shot drilled the black sedan's windshield, where Bolan hoped the driver's face would be. The glare of headlights ruled out a precision shot, but it was close enough. One round, and Bolan saw the car swerve sharply to his right, the driver's left, and speed on toward collision with the nearest elevated curb. One of its front tires climbed the pavement and the car hung there, its engine growling as if anxious to resume the chase.

He fired a round into its right-front fender, angling for the engine block, rewarded with a screech of grinding metal as his NATO slug smashed something critical. The engine stuttered, spluttered, died. No more pursuit for this machine.

The Yakuza hardmen were bailing out now, on the far side of the black sedan. A dome light showed him three men in the backseat, staying low and scrambling one behind the other to get clear. There was some kind of scuffle in the front, the shotgun rider grappling with the driver, maybe shifting his deadweight to clear a path, maybe exacerbated by the driver's safety belt.

Bolan resolved it with a double tap through safety glass, the right-front window raining pebbles while the shotgun rider lurched and slumped against his dance partner. Two dead, maybe two wounded. Bolan couldn't tell from where he was, and had three more to think about before he checked the two stuck in the car.

The Sumiyoshi-kai were firing back now, not precisely sure where Bolan was, but trusting random semiauto fire to pin him down. Their odds would have been better if he wasn't screened by semitrailers that absorbed the probing rounds. Bolan ducked around and ran the full length of the trailer, to its east end, circling back to bring the chase car under fire from that direction.

The hardmen weren't stupid. Pinned down as they were and maybe close to panicking, they still had sense enough to know their enemy would flank them if he could. One of them had the west end of the semitrailers covered, with another covering the east end. The third was busy wrestling bodies from the black sedan's front seat to clear it, maybe trying to discern if either of the soldiers wounded there was still alive.

Bolan could rush them, but that meant crossing a no-man's land of open pavement, thirty yards or so, with automatic weapons tracking him. That smelled like suicide, but it was only marginally worse than waiting where he was, time flitting by until police showed up and ended it.

So, move.

To take them down and walk away from it, he had to flush the Yakuza killers from cover, and he wouldn't get that done by sniping at the car they hid behind. There was a way, however...

Bolan palmed one of the RGD-5 frag grenades, eleven ounces in his hand, one-third of which was TNT. The rest consisted of a pyrotechnic fuse and an internal fragmentation liner scored to cast 350 bits of shrapnel with a killing range of eighty feet. Once Bolan made his pitch, detonation would follow in three to four seconds.

And he would be doing it left-handed.

Not a problem, under normal circumstances, but the Yakuza gunner assigned to watch the chase car's rear spied Bolan as he stepped from cover, winding up his throw. A burst of submachine-gun fire came rippling toward him, diving back to cover as he pitched the dimpled green egg overhand. He'd barely started counting when the blast came, drawing Bolan back to join the fight.

He was surprised to find three hardmen charging the semitrailers, two with automatic weapons blazing, while the third one—obviously wounded—hobbled toward their target with a pistol raised. Bolan went prone beneath the storm of fire, spotting the nearest shooter first and plugging him above his belt buckle, center of mass. The hardman dropped to his knees, then toppled over to his left, the SMG he held still spitting death. His aim was shot, though, bullets wasted as they cut a zigzag pattern in the semitrailer's corrugated side.

Two left, and Bolan shifted past the wounded gunman toward his more agile, more lethal pal. That one had spotted him, but had already spent his last rounds on the charge around the black sedan. Now he was trying to reload, cursing nonstop in Japanese, until a 5.56 mm mangler drilled his throat and silenced him for good.

Bolan was swinging back to drop the pistol shooter when the flat *crack* .38 rang out and the last Yakuza soldier went down. Turning to face the sound, he saw a stranger watching him from twenty yards, revolver lowered at his side, a wallet raised in his left hand to let illumination from the parking lot's tall lamps glint from a badge.

Police, damn it.

"I am Lieutenant Kenichi Kayo. We need to talk."

CHAPTER FIFTEEN

Roppongi, Tokyo

Captain Takahira Amago once had felt at home among Roppongi's all-night revelers—the young and wasted, *gaijin* tourists looking for an after-hours thrill—but that had been so long ago, as a patrolman for the Metropolitan Police, that it seemed foreign to him now. He knew his way around the neon zoo, of course, old ways were not forgotten, but he had moved on to better things.

This night, Roppongi felt particularly alien for his appointed rendezvous.

The message had arrived by telephone, and it was not for him to question, but it still felt…wrong. Why would Susumu Kodama insist on meeting there, and in one of the district's trendiest nightclubs featuring foreign performers at that?

No matter. He'd been summoned, and it was his duty to obey.

The place was called Genesis for reasons that he never grasped. Perhaps Kodama had selected it for some symbolic reason or, more likely, for the crush of drunken bodies that would render him anonymous, unrecognizable.

Captain Amago paid his cover charge and squeezed his way into the club, blinded by strobe lights for a moment, then navigated his way to the corner booth where Kodama had promised to meet him. At first, he barely recognized the man he'd come to see, his shaved scalp hidden underneath a frizzy perm wig, horn-rimmed glasses distorting his mesmeric eyes.

Amago sat before he bowed. "Master."

"Thank you for meeting me, Takahira."

"To hear is to obey."

"I would expect no less."

"How may I serve, Master?"

"The schedule for the Great Reckoning has advanced."

Despite the humid atmosphere inside the club, Amago felt a chill. Three years had passed since his salvation by Saikosai Raito from a course of drunken sloth that would have ruined him, perhaps led him to suicide. A fire had claimed his wife and children while Amago was at work, wasting his time on one more fruitless effort to disrupt the Yakuza drug trade. He had come home to ashes and despair, a grim resolve that nothing mattered in this life beyond the moment. On his path to dissolution, he'd been rescued by Master Susumu Kodama, who had recognized a soul worth saving.

Even then, it had been difficult at first, grasping the concept of the Great Reckoning would be apocalyptic, but he'd come to recognize its absolute necessity, drawing upon his own frontline experience with human decadence and the corruption of society at large. Nowadays, for saving souls, nothing but shock and awe would do.

"Advanced, Master?"

"The materials are ready. We shall have the means of adequate dispersal in a day or two, at the outside."

"So soon."

Kodama eyed him through the horn-rims. "Are you not prepared?"

"Of course, Master."

Truth be told, Amago had a relatively minor role in

the Great Reckoning. His part was to direct the manhunt, steering it away from Saikosai Raito toward the Sumiyoshi-kai. Master Kodama had an acolyte inside the clan—old man Kazuo Takumi's son, no less—who would, without his knowledge, naturally—make the perfect scapegoat. At one stroke, the nation would be stunned, grief-stricken, then would rise in righteous fury against those who had transformed Japan into a sewer of corruption.

Cleaning house was sometimes drastic. As the purge began, those who survived would naturally question their allegiance to the ineffectual religions of their youth. Shinto, Buddhism and imported Christianity would all be seen as failures. None had cleansed the country or prevented the apocalypse. Only a new prophet could lead the way to new awakening and ultimate release from sin.

Master Kodama was prepared to take the lead. And when that moment came, Amago would be standing at his right hand, ready to do anything within his power for the cause.

"What should I know about the actual event, Master?" he inquired.

"We shall be using helicopters owned by Toi Takumi's father. Is it not perfect?"

"Perfect, Master."

"On the day—you'll be informed of time and place—your aircraft must not intervene too soon."

He was referring to the Metropolitan Police Department's fourteen Falcon helicopters, employed for everything from monitoring traffic and pursuing fugitives to search-and-rescue work. In extreme emergencies, the helicopters could be armed and used as gunships, but the changeover took time and an order from the department's Public Security Bureau, issued by someone with a captain's rank or higher.

Someone like Takahira Amago.

"The response can be delayed," he told Kodama.

"Excellent. And when the helicopters are shot down, when they have been identified, it drives the final nail into Kazuo Takumi's coffin."

"Brilliant, Master."

"I must give the credit where it's due. Toi suggested the refinement. I almost regret the need to sacrifice him."

"But—"

Kodama smiled. "I said, 'Almost.'"

Ueno, Tokyo

BOLAN HAD FOLLOWED the policeman's car to a small coffee shop near the Ameya-Yokochō street market, adjacent to Ueno Station. The cop went in, returned with steaming cups of coffee, black, and sat in Bolan's car. It could have been a trap, an ambush hastily arranged by radio while they were traveling en route, but Bolan saw no SWAT teams lurking in the shadows anywhere nearby.

"Okay," he said. "So, talk."

They had already introduced themselves, after a fashion, at the river shooting scene, but there'd been no time for discussing anything beyond a basic plan to chat when they had gained some distance from the dead. Bolan had glimpsed Kenichi Kayo's ID, and had introduced himself as Matt Cooper, a name he could discard at need.

"I serve with the department's Organized Crime Control Bureau," Kayo said.

"Must keep you busy."

"Not as busy as I'd like. Mostly, I clean up after *bōryokudan* Yakuza fights and arrest what you call small fry. Some go to prison, most escape with fines. They kill each other and I do not mourn."

"Frustrating," Bolan said.

"It seems that you have found a way to circumvent frustration," Kayo pointed out.

"Have I?"

The lieutenant smiled at Bolan. "I have known assassins, and you do not fit the mold. Who are you, Mr. Cooper?"

"Just a soldier."

"From America."

"I'm not part of the alphabet," Bolan assured him.

"Arufabetto?"

"CIA, FBI, DEA, ATF, NSA, DIA. The alphabet."

"Am I to think you are a solitary vigilante?"

"Just a soldier, like I said."

"A soldier follows orders from superiors," Kayo stated.

Bolan considered his reply, judging the officer beside him. Finally, he answered, "Can we say I'm off the books and let it go at that?"

"Deniability. Of course, the concept is familiar. Our Public Security Intelligence Agency is much the same."

"I told you, I'm not—"

"With the alphabet. I understand. Your target is the Sumiyoshi-kai." Not asking.

Bolan nodded, cautiously. "There have been incidents at home."

"Atlantic City and Las Vegas. Yes, we do get CNN. Noboru Machii and Jiro Shinoda will not be missed in Tokyo. I wonder, Mr. Cooper—may I call you Matthew?"

"Suit yourself."

"I wonder, Matthew, if you might need any help."

"What did you have in mind?"

"Advice, perhaps. Or aid in navigation, though I must

admit you've chosen targets well enough, so far." Kayo dropped the smile. "Direct participation, if you think it feasible."

"You've seen the way I work," Bolan replied.

"Indeed. It is impressive."

"You're a cop," Bolan reminded him.

"Yes. And getting nowhere with the job I'm paid to do."

"Frustration's no excuse to throw your life away."

"Have you lost yours?"

"I have," said Bolan. "More than once."

"Perhaps I'm ready for the sacrifice," Kayo said.

"You need to be damned sure about that. And I need to know you mean it."

"You are not under arrest. I have not called for reinforcements. How else can I demonstrate my earnestness?"

"There's only one way," Bolan said. "And once you take that step, you can't turn back."

"The blooding. *Hai*. I understand."

Bolan had always been a fairly decent judge of human character. He used that judgment now and said, "Okay. Here's what I have in mind."

Akihabara, Tokyo

IT HAD BEEN a near miss at the Blushing Maid café. Tadashi Jo had been fifteen minutes out, when he'd received the warning of a raid on the café, an unknown number of his soldiers dead or wounded, others in pursuit of the *gaijin* attacker. If he had been there when the maniac arrived, most likely he would lie among the corpses now.

Jo settled for a drive-by at the scene, peering at the

police cars and the gawkers through the tinted window of his Cadillac CTS-V. There was no risk that anyone would recognize him passing by, distracted as they were by death and destruction inside the café. Like ghouls, they flocked around the scene, most of them drunk or high on something peddled by his dealers, leering at catastrophe.

Jo should have been there, would have been a dead man, if he had not stopped to see Shiori on his way to deal with business. She had several techniques that always managed to relax him, even at the worst of times, and while he'd only lingered with her briefly, he'd felt better on the drive from her apartment to the Blushing Maid café—until he saw what he had missed.

"Get out of here!" he told his driver, slumping down into the Cadillac's backseat.

"Where to, sir?" the wheelman asked.

Jo had to think about it for a moment, while they covered half a block and slowed to idle at the intersection, red light glaring at him like a baleful eye. His first order of business was to tell Kazuo Takumi what had happened, hoping one of the police on-site had not beaten him to it. That would look like negligence, the very last thing that Jo needed at the moment.

"Hinode," he said, naming an all-night club he visited approximately once a month, not frequently enough to make a pattern, as he saw it. It was popular, but not controlled by any family, although Jo had considered muscling in to claim a portion of the business. Now, with every operation of the Sumiyoshi-kai at risk, procrastination was its own reward.

His driver waited for the green light, turned when it was clear, and set the course. Jo found his cell phone, grimacing as he speed-dialed Takumi's number at the penthouse in Tsukiji, hoping that his boss had not moved yet again. He did not recognize the voice that answered, certainly not Kato Ando's rasp, but he was put through when he gave his name.

"What's the news?" Kazuo Takumi said. "What word?"

Jo opened, as had recently become his habit, with apologies for bearing more bad news. That done, he told Takumi what he knew about the Blushing Maid attack and waited for his *oyabun*'s response.

"How many dead?" Takumi asked, no outward sign that he was seething like the lava in Mount Meakan.

"I'm not sure yet. I have a call in to police," Jo lied. Something for him to rectify as soon as he got off the line with his *oyabun*.

"And have you gathered any information on our enemy?"

"Not yet, godfather." A little fawning never hurt in situations such as this. "All of our eyes and ears—"

"Seem useless. Can you explain that?"

"It tells me the man or men we seek are strangers, probably foreigners."

"Not Inagawa-kai?"

"There's nothing to suggest it but the phone call."

"Which you disregard?"

"No, sir. But—"

"Never mind," Takumi said dismissively. "I'll handle that myself. What are your plans?"

"To speak with the police," Jo said. "Increase security around our other properties, and—"

"Fine. Do that." The *click* of Takumi ending their conversation struck Tadashi Jo like a slap across the face. He blushed with anger and embarrassment, thankful his soldiers could not see it in the Caddy's dark interior.

Jo knew that he was running out of time in which to prove himself. And he was running out of tricks.

His only hope, it seemed, lay with The Four.
And where were they?

Tokyo Heliport, Koto

TOI TAKUMI DID not personally know the four Saikosai
Raito members who were trailing him through cavern-
ous Shin-Kiba Station, but he trusted them because they
came with Master Susumu Kodama's endorsement. Three
of them were helicopter pilots, he'd been told. The fourth
had come along to supervise, in case something went
wrong.

Toi saw no reason why there should be any problem
with the helicopters, but his arrogance was not so great
that he believed himself to be infallible. He did not know
the men who were assigned to watch the aircraft on the
night shift, and would be bracing them with nothing but
his name to make them grovel and obey his orders. If they
doubted him, if one of them decided it was best to verify Toi's orders with his father, it could ruin everything.

He had a pistol tucked beneath his belt, rubbing
against his spine, a Walther PPQ. Toi did not plan on
shooting anyone, but carrying the weapon made him feel
more serious, substantial, like a person to be reckoned
with. The others might be armed as well, for all he knew.
It had not been his place to ask.

Access to the heliport was through Shin-Kiba Station, Toi showing his corporate ID to an attendant at the
entryway. The clerks there were accustomed to his father's pilots showing up at any hour of the day or night,
requiring access to the Bell 206L LongRanger helicopters owned and registered to Oatari Enterprises. Sign-
ing in was a formality. Toi did not care that he had left
a paper trail. Tomorrow or the next day at this time, his

father and the lackeys he controlled would have much more important things to think about.

The helicopters were identical, as far as Toi could see, aside from the distinctive registration numbers stenciled on their waspish tails. All three were navy blue with white piping, their twin rotor blades drooping slightly while at rest. Toi knew the three aircraft had cost his father something like a million dollars each—another loss for the old man to tabulate when he was adding up the final score.

There should have been one pilot and one mechanic at the heliport, on standby if the *oyabun* required their services. They might be sleeping now, though it was early by Toi's standards, and he would be pleased to wake them, might even expect them to be more compliant in a groggy state. He would transmit his father's orders, fabricated from thin air, and if the loyal retainers balked… well, they could be the first of many sinners sacrificed for the Great Reckoning.

Toi told himself that he was equal to the task, and wondered whether that were true.

The pilot and mechanic were not sleeping in the office leased by Oatari Enterprises. They were playing Gomuku, an abstract game of strategy employing black and white stones on a board with 361 squares, each trying to outwit the other and present an unbroken row of five stones horizontally, vertically or diagonally. Both looked up from the board as Toi entered, trailing his small retinue.

He spoke before they had a chance to question him. "Do either of you recognize me?"

Both were on their feet now, bowing. *"Hai, Toi-san,"* one of them said. "How may we serve you?"

"There is an emergency," Toi answered, following the

script he had rehearsed. "My father needs the helicopters. Are they ready?"

"Which helicopter, sir?" The man was still deferential, but confused.

"All three," Toi said. "As I explained, it's an emergency."

"Yes, sir. But we need more pilots."

"My companions will be handling the machines. Begin your preflight preparations."

"But—"

"But *what*?"

"It's nothing, sir," the mechanic replied, his eyes downcast. "I thought I knew all of your father's pilots."

"You were wrong."

"I apologize, sir."

"There is nothing to forgive," Toi said, magnanimously. "You were simply being conscientious. I will tell my father how you guard his property. Now, get to work."

Ikebukuro, Tokyo

"Most of my fellow officers don't realize this place belongs to Kazuo Takumi," Kenichi Kayo said. "They think the Kyokuto-kai own all of Ikebukuro, as in times past."

"What changed it?" Bolan asked.

"Some years ago, Kyokuto-kai were feuding with the Matsuba-kai from Asakusa, outnumbered with two thousand soldiers against their twelve hundred. The Sumiyoshi-kai offered assistance, in return for certain concessions, and the alliance was victorious."

"That sounds familiar," Bolan said.

They were parked in Bolan's Honda Stream, a half block south of what appeared to be a stylish sushi restaurant. According to Kayo, the establishment was fishy in another way, fronting for Sumiyoshi-kai loan sharks who preyed on working men and women of the district, holding them in thrall while interest on their initial debts piled up beyond hope of repayment.

That cut close to home with Bolan, who had lost his family to Massachusetts loan sharks at the start of his long war against the Mafia. He wasn't grieving, wasn't angry anymore about that bitter loss, but he would never pass a chance to kill leeches feasting on the innocent.

"All right," he said. "Let's do it—if you're serious."

Kayo checked his .38, returned it to his holster, frowning at the Milkor MGL in Bolan's lap. "I'm serious. And so are you, apparently."

"I'm loading smoke and buckshot, no HE," Bolan replied. "We won't be bringing down the house on anyone who came for dinner."

"No, what you call it, collateral damage?"

"Not if I can help it."

With a nod, the lieutenant stepped out of the car. Bolan, on his side, tucked the MGL under a lightweight raincoat, pressing it against his side. The 40 mm weapon weighed twelve pounds and measured less than two feet with its stock folded. A steady hand could empty its 6-round swing-out cylinder in two seconds flat if the need should arise, wreaking havoc on targets with any munitions the shooter elected to load.

"I feel like your John Dillinger," Kayo said.

"That was before my time," Bolan reminded him.

"A stickup, yes? Reach for the sky!"

Now he was sounding like the James gang. "Just relax and take it easy," Bolan said. "The less confusion going in, before we meet the manager, the less chance you'll be seeing any of your colleagues when we leave."

"That would be terribly embarrassing," Kayo said,

but he was smiling as he spoke. "I fear my reputation would be tarnished."

"Or you could be dead. It's time to focus and remember this isn't a game."

Kayo lost his smile as they drew closer to the restaurant. Its name was Sea Breeze. "You may trust me when I say that I am absolutely serious. What have I got to lose?"

Bolan considered mentioning his life, but let it go. Kayo might be frustrated, pissed off or even desperate. He wasn't stupid.

At the door, a hostess greeted them. The lieutenant spoke to her in Japanese and showed his badge, discreetly, shielding it from nearby diners at their tiny tables. No one seemed to notice, all of them engrossed in sucking down raw fish.

The hostess nodded and escorted them beyond the kitchen to a closed door where she knocked, announced the visitors and waited for an answer from within. When it came, Kayo sent her on her way and led Bolan into the office, where a gray-haired man with sunken cheeks sat watching them across a desk.

Bolan raised the Milkor, held it steady in both hands, its muzzle gaping at the startled manager. Addressing him, Kayo switched to English. "We are here for the collection."

"And who are you?"

Kayo nodded toward the 40 mm launcher. "Does it matter?"

"Not to me," Gray Hair replied. "But the owner will not be amused."

"Tell him his turn is coming," Bolan interjected. "Now, the money."

"As you wish."

The safe was buried in concrete, behind the desk.

Bolan covered the manager with buckshot in the Milkor's chamber, twenty pellets, each tipping the scale at close to half an ounce. Call it three-quarters of a pound of lead, with little chance to spread before it ripped through Gray Hair's slender body.

But he played it straight, came out with cash and nothing else, removed a satchel from beneath his desk and quickly filled it. "That is all I have," he said.

"Remember what I said, the message for your boss," Bolan said.

"I assure you, *gaijin*, he will get the message." Gray Hair smiled as he spoke.

Kayo moved like lighting, whipping out a flexible baton and slashing it across the man's face, dropping him without a sound.

"A little lead time, yes?" he said, and started for the door.

CHAPTER SIXTEEN

Tsukiji, Tokyo

Tell him his turn is coming.

Kazuo Takumi played the *gaijin*'s crude threat over in his mind, imagining the voice as heard by his subordinate from Sea Breeze. It had been difficult to understand the man at first, when he had phoned. A shattered nose could do that, making conversation almost comical at times, laggard and frustrating at others.

But the message had been clear enough. So had the theft of some four million yen, the rough equivalent of forty thousand US dollars. That was an affront to Kazuo Takumi, a mere mosquito bite in terms of cash, but a deliberate assault upon his dignity, demanding retribution.

There had been no mention of the Inagawa-kai this time, a puzzle that Takumi had to solve before he could proceed to find and crush his enemy. The other puzzle was a *gaijin* working with a man his Sea Breeze manager had described as native Japanese, with the demeanor of a cop.

That was strange—not that a cop would steal, since some were no better than thugs themselves—but the cooperation across racial lines, a homegrown Japanese collaborating with a foreigner to strike against the Sumiyoshi-kai. What could he hope to gain from that? Could he be crazed enough to think four million yen would make him safe against Kazuo Takumi's vengeance?

No. Something else was happening, and once he grasped the measure of it, Takumi would know precisely where to strike, whom to eliminate. But first, he had to scratch the nagging itch that had been plaguing him since the assault by sniper fire on Kazoku Investments. He must satisfy himself, in fact, that this was not a hostile overture by rivals in the Yakuza.

After he drank a second cup of *sake* to compose himself, Takumi dialed a number one of the policemen he employed had given him. He rarely had occasion to communicate with Onoue Horie, godfather of the Inagawa-kai. They saw each other now and then, no more than once or twice a year at formal gatherings, but otherwise maintained no contact.

This was different.

The phone rang twice before a soft voice said, "Kazuo, you honor me."

"The honor is entirely mine, Onoue," he answered, finishing the dance.

"I hope you will accept my most sincere condolences for all your recent difficulties," Horie said.

Of course, he would be keeping track. Whenever one godfather suffered injury, the others celebrated, seeking ways to profit from the misfortune of their rivals. The polite facade meant nothing, and to penetrate it, Takumi knew he had to be direct.

"Thank you," he replied. "You are aware, I take it, of the shooting at Kazoku Investments?"

"Shocking," Horie said. "Deplorable. At least one of your men survived."

"And brought a message to me, from the sniper."

"Oh?" Horie was feigning ignorance, Takumi thought. The Inagawa-kai had law enforcement agents on its payroll, just as he did, feeding Horie any news they thought might interest him and earn a bonus for their efforts.

"The caller offered greetings from your family," Kazuo said, and listened as the silent seconds passed.

"Did he, indeed?" Horie inquired at last. Kazuo thought his evident surprise was genuine, but every *oyabun* held faces in reserve. "That is…peculiar."

"And distressing, as you may imagine."

"If you thought my family might be involved somehow."

"It was the implication."

"You recall our treaty, do you not, *Takumi-san*?"

He was referring to the peace agreement that had settled the last feud between Kazuo Takumi's family and Horie's. Nineteen men had died, three others vanishing without a trace, before the godfathers had sat down and drew lines on a map of Tokyo, delineating territories for their rival gambling operations. That had been six years ago, the start of an uneasy peace.

"My memory has not deserted me," Takumi said.

"I am relieved to hear it. Why would I betray our confidence?"

The thief was asking why he might decide to steal. It almost made Takumi smile.

"I felt obliged to mention it. No doubt, you understand."

"As I would, if the circumstances were reversed. You have my solemn word that none of this unpleasantness began with me."

His solemn word, whatever that was worth. Takumi frowned, considered it. Before he could respond, Horie added, "I hesitate to ask, but have you given thought to treachery at home, within your family?"

Takumi did not take offense. Most murdered godfathers were slain by their lieutenants. "If that were true," he said, "they would have come for me directly."

"Perhaps. But I was thinking of your blood, not the extended family."

That shocked Takumi into silence. What was Horie saying?

"You are probably aware of Toi's involvement with the Saikosai Raito. I personally do not trust the new, unorthodox religions. They demand too much, in my opinion, and subvert the order of our lives."

"If you know something…"

"Only rumors," Horie said, "which are available from any gossip on the street. This so-called prophet treasures his connections to the high and mighty, once removed. But is he simply living well at their expense? Or does he have something more sinister in mind?"

"I shall consider what you've said, Onoue, and take your words to heart. Your promise, above all."

"Sincerely made," Horie replied. "Good night, my friend."

Cutting off the call, Takumi tried Kato Ando again and got his voice mail.

Where was he? Where was Toi?

Exactly what in hell was happening?

Ebisu, Tokyo

"How shall we spend the four million yen?" Kayo asked.

"You keep it," Bolan answered. "Put it in your retirement fund."

"Am I retiring?"

Bolan shrugged. "I don't tell fortunes, but you sounded like you're giving up on the police department."

"I have not decided yet. Perhaps they shall make the decision for me."

"Maybe so."

Ebisu, one stop from Shibuya on the JR Yamanote Line, had only come into its own over the past two decades, with construction of Yebisu Garden Place, a stylish and expensive planned community, including concert halls and two museums, and a five-star Westin Hotel. Dozens of bars, boutiques and restaurants lined the Yebisu Skywalk's covered moving walkway, and the neighborhood catered to other clientele, as well.

"Where is this place?" Bolan asked, prowling in the Honda Stream.

"Two blocks, then turn right on Meiji Dori. It's next door to the Hotel Siesta."

"Seriously?"

"We are very international in Tokyo," Kenichi said.

Bolan drove on and made the turn, spotting his target on the right. It was another nightclub, this one said to house a large casino, banned by law, beneath its main showroom. He found a place to park and reached back for the Milkor MGL, slipping it underneath his raincoat as he exited the car.

They spent Takumi's money on the cover charge and went inside. Kayo whispered something to the young hostess who greeted them, chuckled at her response, then followed her with Bolan on his heels, skirting the showroom where an all-girl group was singing on a blue-lit stage.

The hostess led them to an elevator guarded by two gunmen whose suits were straining at the seams, stretched to the limit by their girth and hidden weapons. More discussion Bolan didn't understand, before one of the watchdogs made a gesture indicating both of them should raise their arms for frisking.

In a flash, Kayo had the muzzle of his .38 jammed under one gunner's chin, while Bolan pressed the Milkor into number two's expansive stomach. If he had to fire at that range, they'd be cleaning Yakuza out of their hair for days.

The guards delayed just long enough to show how tough they were, then called the elevator car and got in first, both of them wedged together under Bolan's 40 mm eye, letting Kayo punch the buttons.

When the door opened again, the sounds and smell of a casino greeted them. The place had slots, roulette, card tables, craps, a fair variety of games. Small for Vegas or Atlantic City, but for Tokyo, it was a good-sized carpet joint. Business was booming, young and old alike packed in together, all hoping to beat house odds.

"Where are the stairs?" he asked Kayo.

The lieutenant passed his question to the Yakuzas. One of them answered grudgingly. "The southwest corner," Kayo stated.

Better. Bolan didn't plan on being trapped below ground if the elevator was denied to them.

"Okay. Get out," he told the hardmen.

They understood him well enough to leave the elevator car, but one of them misjudged him, going for a gun as soon as they were clear. The Milkor belched its buckshot storm and both of them went down, leaving wet red tendrils on the nearest wall.

That spectacle set players screaming, scrambling for their lives. The next three 40 mm rounds were smoke, and Bolan triggered them in rapid fire, his launcher angled toward the far wall, laying down a fog bank as the canisters exploded. Chaos turned to pandemonium, gamblers colliding with one another, stumbling, reeling, some lunging for chips in a frenetic bid to profit from the moment.

Bolan scanned the room and saw two shooters moving toward them, both already holding pistols. "Here we go," he warned Kayo.

"Ready," the lieutenant said, his .38 steady in a two-handed grip.

And he was smiling as he squeezed the trigger.

Asahi Sutorito, Minato

COLONEL FULIAN SUN listened to the police scanner, mentally translating its broadcasts from Japanese to Cantonese. He spoke nine languages and had no difficulty understanding from the urgent messages he heard that hell had broken loose in Tokyo.

Unfortunately, it was not the hell he'd planned.

Not yet.

China and Japan had been at odds—and often at war—since the nineteenth century. Old wounds were not forgotten or forgiven in Beijing, nor were the modern insults suffered when Japan chose to support America in criticizing China's moves against Taiwan in 2005. Much talk of "ice-breaking" and "ice-melting" had produced a Treaty of Peace and Friendship between the two nations in 2008, threatened two years later by a naval incident near the disputed Senkaku Islands and severe cutbacks in Chinese exports of rare earth metals to Japan.

China's Ministry of State Security engaged in spying on Japan, of course, through traditional channels and with the aid of hackers such as the "Luckycat" group, inserting Trojan viruses into emails reporting details of the Fukushima Daiichi Nuclear Power Plant meltdown, but Colonel Sun's plan was the most ambitious of all.

He had seen through the heart of corruption in Japan, recognized the government's collusion with corporate and criminal elements that were often indistinguishable, and had devised a scheme to shame the nation that had victimized his own so often throughout history. His plan was relatively simple: take a homegrown cult—or, in this case, *create* one—and equip it for a major terrorist attack in Tokyo. Aside from loss of life, the panic and resulting loss of confidence in government, dissection of the plot would lead directly to Japan's second most powerful Yakuza family, exposing its long-term relationship with politicians, business moguls, judges and police. The scandal might drag on for years, while China sat behind a Great Wall of deniability.

The plan seemed perfect, until unknown players chose the moment of fruition to ignite a war against the Sumiyoshi-kai in the United States and Tokyo. Colonel Sun did not regret the deaths or tabloid headlines screaming for investigation of the Yakuza. All that might ultimately work to his advantage. What he hated was the sense that he had lost control, that all his hard work might be slipping through his fingers now, when supervision of his chessmen on the board was paramount.

Susumu Kodama, that old fraud who would have sung the devil's praises if it put yen in his pocket, seemed to have no sense of what was happening. The gangster's son, their patsy in the game, cared nothing for his father's outlaw trade beyond destroying it—sweet irony—and had no explanation for the fresh, untimely interference from abroad. Sun's headquarters in Beijing could offer no advice, claiming their sources at the CIA and NSA were ignorant of any ripples on the vast Pacific pond.

So be it. Sun would have to carry on alone, protect himself now that the wheels were set in motion and a deadline was approaching.

Put the emphasis on *dead* for thousands scurrying around the streets of Tokyo.

Old debts would soon be settled, scales rebalanced, and a new day would begin.

Toshima, Tokyo

"LET US BEGIN AGAIN," Tamura Min said.

"I have told you everything I know," the old man muttered, not quite weeping. "This is all a terrible mistake."

"You saw the men responsible for this attack," said Shoei Sato, "and they let you live. Can you explain that?"

"I already answered that. Sending a message to our Father."

The gray-haired manager of *Shiokaze* was a scrawny specimen without his clothes, duct taped into a metal folding chair. His nose had already been broken when they took him, but the other injuries were new. So far, he had not lost much blood. None of the damage was irreparable.

"What did they look like?" Nakai Ryo asked. No matter what the circumstances, members of The Four worked as a team.

"I've told you—"

Koyuki Masuda drove a fist into their captive's side, below the ribs, wrenching a squeal from bloodied lips. Nakai gave the old man a chance to catch his breath, then asked again, "What did they look like?"

"One was a foreigner, around six feet, dark hair. He had the weapon."

"Describe it for us once again," Tamura demanded.

"I don't know guns so well. It reminded me of those machine guns on the old American TV program *The Untouchables*."

"*The Untouchables?* You mean a tommy gun?" Masuda asked him.

"Only bigger. Like a shotgun of some kind, but bigger still."

Sato glanced at Tamura, saw him shake his head. The

man was useless when it came to weapons. He had started as a pimp, knew how to beat his girls with a sap, then had been promoted to loan-sharking when he demonstrated a facility with numbers. Sato knew all this from questioning Tadashi Jo before they snatched the old man and began interrogating him.

This inquisition was his gift for twenty years of faithful service to the family.

"Describe the other one," Masuda said. "The Japanese."

"He smelled like a cop," the old man replied. "Cheap suit, the way he acted, and the club he hit me with."

"Tattoos?"

The captive thought about it for a moment. Shook his head. "None that I saw. He didn't strip for me, of course."

"He made no mention of the Inagawa-kai or any other family."

"Nothing. I've told you that."

"We find the truth through repetition," Sato said. "Reviewing first impressions. Rooting out the memories a trauma may suppress."

"But I have told you everything!"

"And then," Tamura added, "there is still the matter of repayment."

"What repayment?"

"To your Father. Four million yen," Masuda explained.

"Four million? I don't have that kind of money!"

"Not since you gave it away," Sato said.

"I was robbed," replied the old man, very close to weeping now.

"You've told us you were struck *after* the robbery. Was that a lie?" Sato asked.

"I've only told the truth!"

"That means you offered no resistance," said Tamura.

"You gave up your master's money in a bid to spare yourself from injury."

The old man saw that he had walked into a trap, but he recovered. "Would you rather I had fought them and they killed me? Who would give you their description, then?"

"Your hostess. Diners from the restaurant," Nakai replied. "These robbers, as you call them, were not wearing masks."

"Are you blind?" the old man asked, getting angry now. "You all see what they did to me."

"But for what reason?" Sato asked him. "You did not resist. Was striking you, perhaps, a way to make it seem that you are innocent?"

"Did you arrange the robbery?" Masuda asked, before the hostage could respond to Sato's question.

"No! I swear to you!"

"And if we take your word for that…there's still the debt," Tamura said.

They stood around the old man in a basement room, beneath a vacant pencil factory. His folding chair sat on a plastic tarp, spread out to catch his blood. From the expression on his battered face, he knew that it was hopeless now.

"Go on and kill me, then," he said, his voice already lifeless. "All the talk about your bravery, and still—"

The muffled shot from Sato's pistol cut off whatever the old man planned to say. The bullet drilled his forehead, blood and other fluids instantly released at death, raining on to the tarp. As he removed the pistol's sound suppressor, Sato considered that the old man had, in fact, shared everything he knew about the robbery. Of course, that made no difference.

Their *oyabun* demanded vengeance. This was minor, and misguided, but at least it was a start.

Harajuku, Tokyo

BOLAN WAS PARKED outside another nightclub, this one in the district internationally known as a center for Japanese youth, their culture and fashion. The place was called Earthquake, and from the volume of the music audible outside, the tag was no exaggeration.

"Takumi thought this place would rope his son into the business?" Bolan asked.

"At first," Kayo said. "But he proved irresponsible. He became the bar's best customer, although he never thought to pay for anything. His father, as I understand it, was about to take the club away from him, when suddenly Toi changed."

"Changed how?"

"Began to pay attention and apply himself. Stopped chasing every woman in the place and making profits."

"So, the prodigal returns."

"Not quite. The rumor is that much of what he earns here is donated to a New Age sect, Saikosai Raito."

"Never heard of it," Bolan replied.

"There is no reason why you should have. Membership is presently confined to Tokyo and Yokohama. It appears to be innocuous enough, the standard game where acolytes donate their worldly goods to let a guru live in luxury."

"That must be irritating to Takumi."

"He still dotes on Toi, despite a string of disappointments."

The *oyabun*'s weak spot. His son and heir might know where Bolan and Kayo could locate the old man, and if not, grabbing the kid might bring his father out of hiding. Either way, it was their best shot for a wrap-up when their target had already gone to ground, hiding in one of six or seven high-rise homes in Tokyo, or someplace that Kenichi's street informants couldn't name.

It was a simple mission, on its face: pick up a callow youth and squeeze him just enough to make him talk. If he was still at odds with Daddy, Toi might play along with no need of draconian persuasion. Otherwise, he'd serve them as a hostage, root the old man out that way.

Bolan had no intention of assassinating Toi Takumi, come what may, but scaring him was something else. He was a mobster's son, spoiled all his life on money earned from drugs and human misery. A little shake-up wouldn't hurt him. It might even help, if his newfound religion didn't do the trick.

Armed only with his silenced Glock, Bolan followed Kayo from his parked car to the throbbing entrance of the club, forked over some of Kazuo Takumi's ill-gotten gains to pay the cover charge, and passed into the warehouse-sized interior, roaring with so-called music from a trio of competing heavy metal bands. The din was deafening, making him picture herds of deaf kids roaming through the streets of Tokyo, slack-jawed and glassy-eyed.

"You'll know him when you see him?" Bolan asked Kayo, shouting to be heard.

"We'll try the office first," Kayo hollered back.

There were no guards to deal with in the club, just sweating bodies jammed together on a dance floor, gyrating and shrieking as the music battered them from three sides. Bolan trailed Kayo down a narrow echo chamber of a hallway to a private office, where the lieutenant barged in without knocking first.

Three young men stood around a desk, one of them pointing to a map of Tokyo. Their conversation died at sight of the intruders, who had shut the office door and blessedly reduced the blare of music from outside.

"Who are you?" one of the young men demanded.

Showing them his badge, Kayo answered, "Toi Takumi, you will come with us."

The one who'd spoken first backed up a step, the others moving forward to protect him. "Why should he go anywhere?"

"Official business," Kayo said.

"Sounds more like official bullshit."

"I'm afraid he has us there," Kayo said to Bolan.

"We won't allow this," the third young man said.

"And how do you propose to stop us?" Kayo asked.

They were quick, drawing knives and moving forward, but the Executioner had time to pull his Glock and drop them both with head shots, leaving Toi Takumi with a stunned look on his face.

"You...you..." he stammered.

"You will come with us," Kayo told him. "One way or another."

Handcuffs snapped around the young man's trembling wrists, and Bolan locked the office door behind them as they passed back into screaming chaos in the showroom.

CHAPTER SEVENTEEN

Aoyama, Tokyo

"So, you learned nothing from him?"

"There was nothing to be learned," Nakai Ryo replied. "The man was innocent."

"No one is innocent," Tadashi Jo corrected him.

"Of the offense that you suspected," Shoei Sato interjected, "this man was."

The Four had always made Tadashi Jo nervous, even though—in theory, at least—he was their master and could order them to sacrifice themselves if necessary for the Sumiyoshi-kai. He never felt at ease while in their presence, knowing what they'd done and might do if unleashed. Even a simple conversation with them could be daunting, as they finished one another's sentences, their faces bland, emotionless. It was one reason he had called this meeting on a busy street corner, instead of someplace with more privacy.

"I see," Jo said. "He knew nothing of value, but you killed him anyway?"

"Examples must be set," Tamura Min explained. "He failed our godfather."

"And we're no closer to the enemy than when you started," Jo said.

Koyuki Masuda chimed in. "We believe the cop is the key."

"The policeman?" Jo stopped short of mocking the notion. "How do we know he *was* from the police? Give me an hour, and I can have a dozen badges for you."

"This one had authority," Nakai replied. "Your man was certain of it. We assume he had experience with the police?"

"He did." In fact, the former manager of *Shiokaze*, now a corpse, had been arrested ten or fifteen times, though never once convicted on a major charge. "So, what?"

"He knew a cop when he saw one," Sato answered. "Or, as he said, smelled one."

"So?" Jo asked again.

"If we find the policeman, we find the foreigner," Sato said, as if it should be obvious.

"And how do you propose to do that?" Asking all of them at once.

"You know which higher-ups serve the family," Tamura said. "Find a commander and inquire if there is someone he suspects."

"Or give us names," Nakai suggested. "We can make our own inquiries."

"No!" It came out louder and more forceful than Jo had intended. "Now, of all times, you must not interfere with the police."

Stone faces stared at him, none answering. Jo had no clue what thoughts were simmering behind those masks, but he trusted The Four to follow orders. And he had new orders for them now.

"Our godfather is troubled by another matter. It seems minor by comparison to these attacks, but it preys on his mind."

"Speak, and the matter is resolved," Sato said.

"You all know Kato Ando?" No reply. He took their

silence for assent and forged ahead. "He was assigned to carry out a small investigation and has disappeared. Our godfather wants one of you to find him. I suggest beginning at his last known destination."

"Which was…?" Sato prompted him.

"Saikosai Biometrics. I have the address in Akasaka." As he spoke, Jo took a folded piece of paper from his pocket, held it out to no one in particular.

"I'll do it," Masuda said, pocketing the paper without opening it.

"The rest of you, consider where this foreigner gets his weapons," Jo ordered.

"If he's working with a police commander, weapons are no problem," Sato said.

"Check dealers anyway. If you require a list—"

"We know them," Tamura replied.

"I won't detain you any longer, then." Jo turned back toward his Cadillac CTS-V, which was still idling at the curb outside a trendy restaurant. His guards stood waiting, one already opening his door.

Joi fought an urge to glance back at The Four, to see if they were watching his retreat. Each time he met with them, he felt as if he was handling snakes without protective gear. If one of them turned on him, he suspected, all four would join in.

For now, though, he was in command, at least in theory. They were following his orders, out of loyalty to Kazuo Takumi or to the Sumiyoshi-kai, if not Tadashi Jo personally. All that mattered was results. They took the risks, while he reaped the reward.

He did not pretend to understand the business with Saikosai Biometrics. His leader had commanded an investigation, while refusing to explain. Jo viewed the exercise as a distraction, but he only followed orders, like The Four.

And hoped his loyalty would not turn out to be the death of him.

Nakano, Tokyo

"Who else knows about this safe house?" Bolan asked Kayo, as he turned onto a residential street from Waseda Dori, passing homes he ranked as working class.

"My captain."

"Do you trust him?"

"It's irrelevant," Kayo said. "He won't know that we're using it."

Behind them, lying covered with a blanket on the backseat's floorboard, Toi Takumi had been silent since they put him in the car. A strip of duct tape helped with that. Kayo had already checked to see if Toi was breathing, and pronounced him fit.

For what?

They needed information from the mobster's son, and Bolan was determined to obtain it. He had never cared for torture, knew from personal experience that it was both repugnant and counterproductive, but in a pinch he'd use a variation of the tools available to see his mission through.

The safe house had a small attached garage. Kayo keyed the opener and Bolan drove the Honda in, sat waiting while the door came down again and his companion found the light switch. Pulling Toi out of the car was easy, but he started wriggling as they walked him toward an exit to the house, kicking and squirming, grunting like an animal behind his duct tape gag.

Kayo settled him before Bolan could deal with it, produced the flexible baton once more and whipped it down across Toi's kneecap. Grunts turned into squeals, and he collapsed, Bolan supporting his left side, Kayo on his right. They got him in the house, survived some awkward moments on a staircase leading to the basement and deposited him on a concrete floor.

Bolan yanked off the silver tape, their captive gasping as it stripped some peach fuzz from his lips and chin.

"Who are you?" Toi demanded, all indignant. "Why have you abducted me?"

"We are in need of information," Kayo told him.

Toi sat up, wincing at fresh pain from his knee, glaring at each of them in turn. "You won't learn anything from me. I took an oath."

Kayo bent down, ripping at the captive's shirt, revealing pale skin underneath. "You haven't been initiated," he observed. "No ink."

"Is that it? You think I am Sumiyoshi-kai." Toi yelped a laugh. "You're fools."

Kayo frowned at Bolan and turned back to their prisoner. "What oath, then?" he demanded.

"Never mind. You're too late, anyway," Toi answered.

"Then it won't hurt if you tell us, will it?"

"Do your worst," Toi said, sneering. "My master and Lord Bishamon protect me."

"Your master," Bolan said. "Not Daddy?"

"Idiot *gaijin*! I've told you I'm not Yakuza."

"What are you, then?"

"A savior to my people. Hail Saikosai Raito!"

It was Bolan's turn to glance at his companion. Toi's remarks meant nothing to him, but they'd clearly had an impact on Kayo.

"It's true, then. You are a member of the cult," Kayo said.

"Cult? Ignorant cop! It is the only true religion."

"And we've come too late to interfere with what?" Kayo prodded.

"With the Great Reckoning," Toi replied, grinning triumphantly.

"A reckoning with whom?" he asked of Toi.

"With everyone, of course. Lord Bishamon demands homage. No one escapes his wrath but the elect."

"And you are...?"

"Chosen," Toi said proudly. "I have done my part. Whatever happens to my flesh is meaningless."

"Where shall this reckoning occur?" Kayo asked. "In Tokyo?"

"The seat of all corruption. Can't you smell it? But a cleansing wind is coming, a divine wind. *Kamikaze!*"

It was turning into gibberish, from Bolan's point of view, but now Kayo couldn't let it go. "I want to know what you have planned," he said. "You'll tell me, or—"

"Never!" Toi growled, and twisted where he sat, dropping to slam his chin against the concrete floor. At first, Bolan considered it a clumsy try at suicide, but then Toi spit a severed portion of his tongue on to the floor and rolled to face them, smiling, drooling blood.

Bolan reached out to grip Kayo's arm, holding him back from swinging the baton at Toi Takumi. "That's enough!" he said. "We've lost him. What's this all about?"

"I'm not sure yet," Kayo said. "But I know someone who can tell us."

Akasaka, Tokyo

KOYUKI MASUDA FOUND Saikosai Biometrics easily enough. Entering the building after hours was a bit more difficult, but he was skilled in penetration, among other things. There was no overnight security in place, and he was masked, no need to fret about surveillance cameras recording him.

His destination lay on the third floor. With the building's elevator shut down for the night, he used the service stairs. The climb relaxed him, burned off energy and gave him time to think about the next step of what seemed to him a tedious and time-wasting inquiry. What did he care about Kato Ando or his small investigation gone awry? Nothing. But the assignment came down from his godfather, and he had volunteered. That obligation meant Masuda would apply his best effort and see it through.

The office locks were adequate, but nothing that he could not crack. Inside, he found the security keypad, green light flashing, counting down the seconds until it sounded an alarm and summoned the police. Masuda pulled a six-inch crowbar from his stash of tricks and pried the keypad from its moorings, disconnecting crucial wires before the clock ran down.

So much for the high-tech alarm.

He swapped the crowbar for a penlight and began to search the office, bypassing the small reception area in favor of an office with a bank of filing cabinets. He opened each in turn, riffled through papers that meant nothing to him: bills of lading, correspondence with more companies he'd never heard of, notebooks filled with calculations that were gibberish. Next door, there was a lab of sorts, with shelving on the walls and two long tables in the middle of the room. Masuda recognized an incubator and refrigerator, scores of petri dishes and a heap of plastic food containers, all stained red inside. He stopped with one foot on the threshold when he saw a pair of yellow hazmat suits hanging from wall hooks to his left.

This was beyond him, and Masuda knew it, but he needed answers. The lab suggested that whoever ran Saikosai Biometrics might not want police prowling their premises. What was the purpose, then, of the alarm? What else, but to alert the tenants to a breach?

Masuda turned back to the entryway, holding the penlight in his teeth while he deftly replaced the wires he'd disconnected without damaging them. On again, the green light started flashing, the interrupted countdown starting over. When the light turned red, and no alarm went off inside the office, he retreated to a nearby chair and settled in to wait.

It was a gamble. If he'd misinterpreted the lab equipment, squad cars might be rolling toward him while he sat there, killing time. Masuda doubted it, but if his guess proved wrong, he had no doubt that he could deal with two, three, even four policemen easily enough. Their judo and batons were child's play next to his skills, and they were harangued throughout their training to avoid the use of deadly force whenever possible.

Masuda, for his part, observed no such restrictions.

Fifteen minutes after he had reset the alarm, he heard footsteps rushing along the corridor outside. One person, trying to be stealthy, failing miserably in his haste. Masuda rose and stood to one side of the door, where it would shield him as it opened. He had drawn no weapon yet, trusting surprise to do the job.

There came a fumbling at the lock, the door eased open, and a small man eased it shut behind him. Eyeing the alarm pad, dangling from its mount, the green light turned to red now, he reached out and switched on the fluorescent ceiling lights.

Behind him, killing close, Masuda said, "We need to talk."

Taito, Tokyo

EASTBOUND ON KOTOTOI DORI, toward Asakusa, Bolan said, "Let's hear the rest about this Saikosai Raito."

"The name translates to 'Supreme Light' in English. All the New Age cults have names like that, you know— One Way, The Truth, The Golden Path. Such arrogance."

"Sounds typical of all religions," Bolan said. "What makes this any different?"

"Its leader," Kayo replied. "Susumu Kodama. He presents a bland, innocuous facade, but I've researched his background. He's served time in prison for assault and fraud, is suspected of more serious offenses that were never proved against him."

"Such as?"

"Thirteen years ago, he led another cult. *Kisei*, he called that one. Homeward Bound. Most of his followers were elderly. Some changed their wills in favor of Kodama and the cult. Three of them died within a few weeks afterward. All accidents, of course, in the official version."

"So, a con man and a killer, maybe," Bolan said. "What's this about a reckoning?"

"Saikosai Raito is what we call an apocalyptic cult. You've heard of them, no doubt."

"Like Heaven's Gate and Jonestown," Bolan said.

Kayo nodded. "Or, in our case, *Aum Shinrikyo*. 'Supreme Truth,' in translation. You're familiar with it?"

"Sarin in the subway," Bolan answered. "What, twenty years ago?"

Another nod. "Thirteen dead, more than fifty seriously injured, with a thousand others suffering minor effects. In related attacks, a policeman was shot, and a Yakuza assassin killed *Aum*'s so-called minister of science on the street, outside cult headquarters. *Aum*'s guru, Shoko Asahara, was arrested months after the sarin incident, convicted of murder and sentenced to die. So far, he's managed to avoid the gallows with appeals and testimony in new cases, when his later crop of followers wind up in court. They call themselves *Aleph* today."

"Which means?"

"Nothing, per se. It's the first letter of three alphabets— Arabic, Hebrew and Phoenician. Presumably, they view their cult as the beginning of all things."

"And you think this Supreme Light is another *Aum*?"

"Susumu Kodama preaches his Great Reckoning against sin and a corrupt society," Kayo said. "To most, it has no more reality than Armageddon or the final days of tribulation in the Bible."

"But you think he's up to something."

"Toi Takumi seemed to think so. Whatever the secret, he silenced himself forever to keep it."

They had left Toi handcuffed in the basement of Kayo's safe house, nothing they could do about the bleeding from his severed tongue. He might survive, or might not. At the moment, Bolan didn't care.

It bothered him, embarking on a tangent, leaving his primary mission to pursue what might be nothing, but he trusted the lieutenant's instincts well enough to stick with him awhile and check it out. If the Supreme Light were about to trigger an apocalypse in Tokyo, preventing that would take priority over his war against the Sumiyoshi-kai.

But only for the moment. He would check it out, do whatever he could to spare the city's innocents from harm if some kind of attack was planned, then he'd get back to business with Takumi's clan. Distractions were a part of life and part of every battle, but a warrior did his best to overcome them and survive.

"This guru is a con," Bolan observed. "You think he'll cop to planning some kind of attack on Tokyo?"

"I may be able to persuade him," Kayo said.

"Like with Toi?"

"I see his choice as evidence that he had something serious to hide. He is a true fanatic. If Kodama has some mercenary end in mind, as I suspect, greed makes him vulnerable. He gains nothing by self-sacrifice."

"Maybe you should have brought Toi's tongue along."

"I have a better plan. If he proves reticent, we take him back to speak with Toi."

"One-sided conversation?"

"Or an object lesson."

"How much farther?" Bolan asked.

"Another two blocks. Turn left at the light."

Asakusa, Tokyo

Susumu Kodama was not expecting visitors. The rapping at his door at that hour put him in mind of trouble, complications, headaches—all the things he did not need. He could refuse to answer, leave the caller standing on his doorstep until weariness set in and whoever it was departed, but it went against Kodama's grain to hide in his own home.

He checked the peephole. Through its fish-eye lens, he saw a bland face peering back at him: short hair, tired eyes, with worry lines between the straight black brows and deep parentheses around the mouth from frowning. An official, from the look of him, which at the present hour, meant police. But he had come alone, and that was something.

Kodama saw his mistake as soon as he opened the door. A *gaijin* had been lurking to the left, unseen, and stepped into the open now, staring beyond Kodama, past the foyer, as if seeking any others in the house. At the same time, the Japanese policeman pushed the cult leader backward, entering the house without a pretense of asking permission.

"Officer—"

"Lieutenant, if it matters."

"May I see your warrant?"

The lieutenant made a show of patting at his pockets. "I've forgotten it, it seems," he said. "You don't mind answering some questions, do you?"

"I answer nothing without first consulting my attorney. If you have no warrant, you must leave my property at once."

Kodama saw the punch coming but could not dodge in time. It staggered him, and while he might have kept his footing, one leg struck the low-slung coffee table, and he toppled over, flailing, tumbling to the carpet. Blood spray from his nostrils stained the deep white shag.

"We understand each other now, eh?" the lieutenant asked. Behind him, the *gaijin* had still said nothing.

"What I understand," Kodama spluttered, struggling up to hands and knees, "is that you have destroyed your pitiful career. I will sue for this brutality and take your last—"

The kick came out of nowhere, caught him in the ribs and flipped him over on his back. He lay there, gasping, grimacing in pain, completely at the mercy of these strangers in his home.

"Consider this a reckoning, though not, perhaps, a great one," the lieutenant said.

Kodama felt his stomach lurch, a new sensation, separate from the sharp pain of bruised or broken ribs. "Great reckoning" could not be a mere slip of the lieutenant's tongue. He knew something. Was it enough to hang Kodama if he kept his mouth shut through a beating, waiting for the chance to call his lawyer?

And what if the lieutenant and his *gaijin* friend allowed no opportunity for that?

"I'm injured," he complained, stalling.

"Not badly, yet."

"You can't do this, Lieutenant."

"Yet, it seems I am."

Time for another tack, Kodama thought, trying once more to rise. "I don't know what you want," he wheezed. "Perhaps if you explained…"

"The Great Reckoning," the lieutenant said, looming above him. "Your words, I believe, for some sort of apocalypse. You cannot save yourself by feigning ignorance."

"The sacred texts of Bishamon predict a reckoning for sinners. That is all I preach."

"And never gave a thought to making it come true?" the other stranger asked, the first time he had spoken.

"And who are you?" Kodama asked.

The self-proclaimed lieutenant answered, saying, "We are colleagues in a vain attempt to save your life. If your disciples carry out the plan, your fate is sealed. If you obstruct us…well, you may not hang, but you will die. I guarantee it."

"There is no plan. I tell you this in all sincerity."

"And I tell you that you have made a serious mistake." Stepping behind Kodama, the lieutenant handcuffed him, clamping the cuffs painfully tight. He steered the man toward the stairs, the *gaijin* following.

Downstairs, they had barely cleared the final threshold when a chunk flew off the doorjamb, splinters prickling

at Kodama's cheek. He recognized the bullet strike but
heard no gunshot, ducking instinctively. On either side
of him, his captors gripped his pinioned arms, rushing
him toward a car parked at the curb.

CHAPTER EIGHTEEN

Bolan missed the muzzle-flash, but knew that forward motion was their only hope. The car was only yards away, the only cover they could hope for without doubling back inside Kodama's building. That meant being trapped, and that was no alternative at all.

Clutching the guru's right arm with his left hand, Bolan freed the Steyr from its hiding place beneath his raincoat, thumbed off the safety, and held the weapon ready to return fire if he got the chance. A silencer served double duty as a flash suppressor, but he didn't need a visual to hear the second bullet strike Kodama, slapping flesh and fabric.

Bolan felt the warm blood on his left cheek, saw the guru start to slump away from him and kept the lurching captive more or less upright, still moving forward. It was just a graze below Kodama's shoulder, nothing major, but from personal experience he knew it had to have hurt like hell.

"Keep going!" Bolan snapped at him, and in another second they had reached the Honda, all three huddled in its shadow.

From the angle of the hit, the shooter had to be across the street. The only way to spot him was to offer him a target, and because they needed Toi's guru alive, Bolan decided it was his job to play decoy. The shooter wasn't bad, although he'd rushed his first, best chance to get the job done. Keep it quick and stay alert. There was a fifty-fifty chance Bolan could pull it off.

He pictured what he'd seen across the street when they'd arrived, remembering the urban landmarks, then stood, scanning the far side of the two-lane blacktop, waiting for it. When the flash came, it was small but obvious, and Bolan dropped back under cover as a bullet creased the Honda's trunk lid, whining on to strike the white apartment building facade behind him.

Do it now, he thought, before the shooter had a chance to think and relocate. Bolan rolled to his right, angling his AUG across the street, and fired a 3-round burst toward the lamppost where he had glimpsed the muzzle-flash. One of his bullets rang on metal over there, the other two lost somewhere in the night.

It was enough to make the shooter duck and dodge, however, looking for a safer place to stand his ground and fight. Across the street, he had a choice of shrubbery outside another block of apartments, or a panel truck parked at the curb. The truck was his best bet, no honest surprise when he chose it.

Bolan chased his target with another burst, trying to lead the runner, saw him stumble as he reached the van, but couldn't tell if that was from a hit or diving headlong out of sight. Whichever, he could not afford to leave the shooter where he was, still breathing, maybe fit to follow them, or at the very least fire on the Honda as they fled.

The Steyr wasn't silenced, and he knew the shots he'd fired were bound to raise alarms from the apartment dwellers all around him. Some were likely dialing 119—the Japanese version of 911—already, summoning police. Whatever Bolan planned to do, he had to do it now, regardless of the risk involved.

Translating thought to action, he was on his feet and

moving in another heartbeat, sprinting over pavement, veering to his left halfway across the street, to keep from making it too easy for his enemy. The shooter, if he wasn't badly wounded, would be crouching somewhere on the far side of the panel truck, prepared to fire on any target that appeared to left or right. On top of that, it was impossible to run across two lanes of asphalt silently, so he would be forewarned of death's approach.

Ten feet from the van, Bolan dropped prone and pressed his cheek against the pavement, scanning underneath the vehicle and catching shadowed motion in the light provided by a street lamp to his left. He fired a third short burst, his bullets grazing blacktop, and immediately heard a cry of pain.

No miss, this time.

He rose and ran around the van, still cautious, but aware of how the shock from bullets drilling flesh and bone could spoil even the finest shooter's aim. He found his target lying crumpled on the curb, one arm outflung, a silenced pistol out of reach where it had slithered when he fell. The shooter lay with pelvis shattered, bleeding out, but kept a stolid poker face.

"Who sent you?" Bolan asked him, guessing it would be a waste of breath.

"Kutabare, gaijin!" the wounded warrior rasped, and closed his eyes.

Bolan drilled him with a mercy round between the eyes, then frisked the body as it shivered into death, taking a wallet, leaving the assorted tools and weapons hidden underneath a stylish blazer. On the jog back to his car, he wondered who it was he'd killed, and what had led the shooter to them in the first place.

They were riddles that could still prove lethal, if he dropped his guard.

Nakano, Tokyo

THEY FOUND NO ambush waiting at the safe house, no
sign that the place had been disturbed while they were
gone. Kayo kept the handcuffs on Susumu Kodama as
they guided him downstairs for a reunion with his die-
hard acolyte, but from the staircase Bolan saw that they
had come too late.

Toi Takumi lay with a broad pool of blood surrounding his head, one cheek plastered to the basement floor
where it was clotting. He had thrashed around some
in the midst of dying, etching abstract patterns on the
gray concrete. The severed portion of his tongue lay
several inches from his open maw, as if he had regret-
ted his decision in those final moments and had tried
to take it back.

Too late.

Kodama sagged between them, muttering what had
to be a curse in Japanese. "What have you done to him?"
the guru asked.

"He did it to himself," Bolan replied. "That's loyalty
you're looking at. He died for you and your Great Reckoning. Are you prepared to do the same?"

"I'm wounded," the guru replied. "I need a doctor."

"Yeah. Good luck with that."

Bolan turned to Kayo and said, "He's all yours."

The Executioner heard a raspy sound from the baton,
extended with a flick of the lieutenant's wrist. Kayo's
first swing hit Susumu Kodama's bloodied arm and
wrung a cry of pain from his thin lips. The guru staggered, fell to one knee, raised his good arm to protect
his head and face.

"What is it that you want?" he squealed.

"Let's go with full disclosure," Bolan answered.

"I am a minister. I counsel and I share the truth as it's revealed to me."

"Cut to the chase," Bolan advised him. "This reckoning of yours."

"Not mine. Lord Bishamon demands a recompense for sin."

"And you make the arrangements, eh?" Kayo asked.

"I guide my flock."

"We're getting nowhere," Bolan said.

Kayo lifted the baton again. The guru cringed and bleated out, "It wasn't my idea!"

"If you blame Bishamon again—"

"My life is worthless if I tell you."

"How's it looking now?" Bolan inquired.

"I won't survive in prison."

"Think about surviving through tonight," Bolan suggested.

"You must protect me if I tell you everything."

"From what?" the Executioner queried.

"The colonel."

"Colonel? What colonel?" Kayo demanded.

"If I tell you, can you promise me protection?"

"I can promise you will never leave this room alive unless you speak," Kayo said.

Kodama thought about it for a second, seeing no way out, and finally replied, "Colonel Fulian Sun. You'll find him at the Chinese embassy."

Shiodome, Tokyo

SHOEI SATO TOOK THE news as he took everything, with no outward display of emotion. It might not have been accurate to say that he felt nothing. Who could tell, behind the stoic mask he wore in common with his two surviving comrades? At times like this, their faces might as well be carved from alabaster. What was happening inside, no one could say.

And they would never tell.

"How did he die?" Tamura Min inquired.

Tadashi Jo seemed nervous, sitting in his Cadillac, surrounded by the remnants of The Four, but he replied without a tremor in his voice. "Gunshots," he said. "First wounded, then a final kill shot."

"An execution," Nakai Ryo said.

"So it appears," Jo stated.

"While he pursued the task you set for him," Sato observed.

"He must have been careless."

If that stung any of them, they concealed it well. "You know this from your cop contact?" Tamura asked.

"Yes."

"What else was found?" Nakai queried.

"A pistol with a silencer, perhaps his own. Various items of equipment."

"No one else was killed?" Tamura pressed him.

"No one else was found," Jo said.

Sato came close to frowning but restrained himself. At one level, it seemed impossible that Koyuki Masuda or any of The Four could fall in battle without slaying any of his adversaries in the process, but he also knew that none of them were supermen. They only seemed that way to men without the training or the discipline to rival their achievements. It was easy, sometimes, to believe that reputation was a shield. In fact, while it intimidated enemies and gave Sato an edge, he was no more invincible than any other man.

"We shall pick up where he left off," Sato announced, knowing the others would agree with him.

"Sometime, but not tonight," Jo said. "Our godfather requires your presence to protect him while the present difficulty is resolved."

"We can't resolve it if we're guarding him," Nakai replied.

"Our godfather has decided he must leave the city. He is going to the house in Shizuoka, on Suruga Bay."

Sato felt his companions watching him, waiting to hear what he would say. Though bound by oath and honor to obey their leader's command, they would follow him, he sensed, if he broke protocol and told Tadashi Jo they had to first avenge their comrade. He was on the verge of saying it, could almost taste the words that would undo them all, but Sato stopped himself from speaking them. His ancestors, their history, all weighed against his friendship for a single man, whoever he might be.

Instead of challenging Jo, he replied, "When this is finished, we will hunt Koyuki's killers."

"Our godfather expects no less," Jo said. "But first, the family."

"The family," they said, as one.

"When is he leaving?" Sato asked.

"Now. As soon as we arrive to join the escort."

So be it, Sato thought. He had no special love for Tokyo, preferred the countryside in fact, but running from a fight did not sit well with him. He knew Tamura and Nakai had to feel the same, anxious to find Koyuki's killers and eliminate them—both as vengeance for a friend, and to remind all future adversaries that they paid their debts in blood.

"We'll follow you," Sato said, turning from Jo and heading toward their black Lexus LS 460 L sedan.

His two surviving brothers were beside him as he reached the car, and Sato asked, "Who wants to drive?"

Nakano, Tokyo

"YOU ARE A Chinese agent, then?" Kayo asked. "A communist?"

Despite his pain, Kodama smirked at that. "I care nothing for politics," he answered.

"What, then?"

"Colonel Sun is a facilitator. He provides support. His motives are irrelevant, as long as they serve Bishamon."

"We're back to that?" Bolan asked.

When Kodama turned to him, his face was scornful. "I don't care if you believe, *gaijin.* I've led a life of thievery and shame, until our Lord saw fit to save me from myself. Scoff all you like. I feel the same about your Jesus."

Bolan wondered if the guy was faking, even now, in this extremity, and didn't think so. They were dealing with a psychopath who'd left the rails of "normal" criminality and veered into a true believer's la-la land. What made him dangerous was zeal, combined with the resources of a ruthless government.

"So, what's the plan?" Bolan demanded. "Spell it out."

Kodama thought about it while his good hand clutched his wounded, aching arm, then said, "Why not? You are too late to stop it now. The Great Reckoning is upon you."

"Sounds impressive," Bolan goaded him.

"You mock, but I expect no less from a barbarian *gaijin.*" He nodded toward Kayo, said, "Your monkey understands, I think. Japan has reached the final depths of its corruption by the West, what you would call rock bottom. Since the Great War, we have been infested with outsiders, fouling everything they touch. Our so-called statesmen are a pack of whores. Our sacred culture dies a little more each day. Lord Bishamon showed me that I must act, before it is too late."

"And now you're acting," Bolan said.

"Before the day is out, you'll see. Thousands will die. The Yakuza's involvement and exposure will produce a mighty uprising against the state and all the hypocrites in charge."

Bolan was properly convinced: Kodama either was a whack-job, or he should be nominated for an acting award. Was it even possible to fake the gleam of pure fanaticism in his eyes?

"The plan," Kayo said. "Since we're too late, as you explain, what is the harm?"

"I must admit my dream was vague, at first. Beyond conviction that a mighty sacrifice must be presented to Lord Bishamon, I was adrift until the colonel recognized my need."

"A communist who has no gods decided to assist you?" Now Kayo's tone was scornful.

"Sun was moved by Bishamon, though he may never realize it. When the Lord places his hand upon a subject, choice is not a question any longer."

"Your Bishamon's no great fan of free will," Bolan observed.

"Where has it taken us so far, *gaijin*?" Kodama challenged him. "Your own Bible depicts what happens when a feeble god leaves humans to their own devices. First in Eden, then with Noah, next with Sodom and Gomorrah, finally with Christ himself, we see that humans *will not listen*. They will not *obey*, unless compelled to. Whether that compulsion comes from leaders in the flesh, or from Lord Bishamon on high, the end result is beneficial. Blessed peace will reign when all obstacles are removed."

"And how'd your colonel plan on doing that?" Bolan asked.

When the guru answered, it appeared that he was talking to himself, or to some spirit guide whom Bolan couldn't see. "What now? Am I allowed to tell these infidels? Of course, why not?"

He seemed to snap out of the trance, turning to Bolan with a beatific smile. "We use the tools provided by Lord Bishamon from nature, with technology supplied by man—in this case, by the Sumiyoshi-kai. Kazuo Takumi does not realize that he is aiding us, of course. That is a gift from his rebellious son, another tool of Bishamon."

"Explain," Kayo ordered.

"Shall I?" Still holding the smile, Kodama cocked his head to one side, as if listening. Whatever voices spoke to him, they seemed to give assent. "All right, then," he continued. "You may be familiar with *Bacillus anthracis*."

"Anthrax," Bolan said, feeling the small hairs prickle on his neck.

"In this case, *weaponized* anthrax. Your government, *gaijin*, abandoned its production long ago, or so we're told. The Russians waited longer, but have now supposedly destroyed their stockpiles. Thankfully, my friends in China are not so shortsighted. They destroy nothing that may have future use to them. That is, I think, the benefit of living in an ancient culture. It is easier to take the long view."

"You have anthrax," Kayo said, with a stunned expression on his face.

"From the supply provided, we have reproduced the spores in quantity. It's relatively simple. Dry the spores, mill them to the smallest size attainable. I will not bore you with the science—which, in truth, I barely understand myself. Dispersion was the final difficulty, but young Toi has solved that for us. Like a flight of angels, we shall soar above the city and dispense justice from Bishamon."

Stone crazy.

"You have aircraft?" Bolan asked him.

"I do not, but Kazuo Takumi does—or, rather, *did*. They have been pressed into the service of our Lord."

"You follow that?" Bolan asked the lieutenant.

"Takumi has helicopters. Three of them, I think," Kayo said.

Bolan turned back to the guru. "Where are they now?"

"Oh, no. I can't make it too easy for you, can I?"

"You want to take this?" Bolan asked Kayo.

"Gladly," the lieutenant said.

"The clock's running. I'll meet you upstairs."

Tsukiji, Tokyo

IT SEEMED ALMOST too easy to Kazuo Takumi, leaving his established life behind. He knew that it was only for a short time, while his enemies were hunted down and finally eradicated, but it still seemed to him that the act of fleeing Tokyo should feel more…what? Significant?

Running away was dangerous. It damaged his prestige, no matter how he tried to put a normal face on his evacuation of the city. Friends and foes alike would understand that he'd been driven from the capital by adversaries who'd outwitted him—so far, at least. Financial losses were inconsequential, when compared to the erosion of his hard-earned reputation.

Still, embarrassment was better than the grave.

He'd given up on Ando, now convinced his loyal retainer had to be dead, along with Koyuki Masuda. That was a double shock, losing one of his oldest friends and one of The Four within a single day. More proof that it was time for him to slip away and plan the next phase of his life-or-death campaign at a safe distance from the battlefield.

Tadashi Jo had brought in the remainder of The Four, as ordered. Takumi supposed the three survivors were not pleased about it, but he trusted them to honor their commitment to the Sumiyoshi-kai and to himself as their *oyabun*. With them beside him, and the other soldiers he was taking to his home away from home in Shizuoka Province, Takumi believed he would be safe enough for the time being.

Long enough, at least, to find out who was plaguing him and settle it.

He had reached out to Toi, but could not contact him. Three unanswered calls were all that he allowed his spiteful son. Whatever happened to Toi, the child had brought upon himself. If he was lost, Takumi would feel something, he supposed, but the long-standing rift between them had convinced him Toi would never be his heir. He had to think about Tadashi Jo now, and ask himself if there was someone better suited to command the family when he was gone.

Or did it even matter, after he was dead, what happened to the Sumiyoshi-kai?

That thought felt almost blasphemous. Takumi had invested half a century—his whole life, as it were—to the defense and service of his clan. He would continue that tradition until he drew his last breath, but beyond that...what?

No matter.

Everyone was waiting for him now. They had six cars downstairs, enough for everyone and all the weapons they'd brought out of hiding for the journey to Suruga

Bay. It seemed foolish to keep them waiting any longer, all of them at risk each moment that they spent in Tokyo from that point on.

"Let's go," he said.

CHAPTER NINETEEN

Nakano, Tokyo

Kayo got the answers, but it took a while. He came out of the basement looking weary, bloodstains on the sleeves of his white shirt. "There is a warehouse in Nerima," he said, on his way to the kitchen sink. "Near Toshimaen, the amusement park. Kodama rented it last month. It's large enough to serve the helicopters as a hangar."

"He has the anthrax there?"

"It's what he said," Kayo answered, while he washed his hands. "I don't think he was lying, at the end."

Bolan could hear the doomsday clock, already counting down, but still he asked, "You want to shift them out of here?"

Kayo grabbed a dishtowel, shook his head. "It does not matter now."

"How far from here to where we're going?"

"If we had a helicopter of our own, three miles," Kayo said. "Driving, closer to five."

"Did he give up a schedule?"

"No. The goal is sunrise, for its symbolism and the early traffic, markets opening and the produce deliveries. He was not sure how soon the helicopters would be ready."

That made sense. Kazuo Takumi's birds would be the corporate variety, not equipped for aerial application of anthrax. Some work would be required to modify them for delivery. If he could catch them on the ground...

He spent five precious minutes with his arsenal, preparing for the strike, loading the Milkor's cylinder with six incendiary rounds. Incinerating anthrax spores would do the job, but there was still a risk of personal exposure in the process, breathing in an ugly, agonizing death while they were wiping out the strain. He had no source for hazmat suits, offhand, but did have an idea.

"Do you keep any of those masks around?" he asked. "The ones I see so many people wearing on the street?"

"Perhaps," Kayo said. "I'll check." Tossing his towel on to the counter, the lieutenant left him for a moment and returned bearing a small box with a label Bolan couldn't read. The lieutenant opened it, revealing cheap surgical masks with elastic ear loops.

"Good to go, then," Bolan said, as he replaced his weapons in their duffel bags. "Unless you want to sit it out."

"After I've come this far?" Kayo asked, slipping on his jacket. "Before I hang, I still hope to accomplish something."

"When we wrap this up," Bolan said, "I can likely get you out of here."

"No, *Cooper-san*. I chose the path, and I will see it through."

There wasn't time for philosophical debates, and Bolan understood the Japanese concept of duty. It had been a major break for the lieutenant when he'd jumped the rails to join Bolan's crusade, but he had no intention of avoiding the responsibility for what he'd done. Whatever followed after—if there *was* an after—he seemed ready to accept it, even if that meant the gallows at the Tokyo Detention House.

Bolan hefted his duffel bags and left the kitchen, passing through the living room. Kayo followed him and locked the door behind them as they stepped into the night. Darkness concealed most of the city's rank pollution, but it couldn't mask the smell. Bolan found it incongruous that a society obsessed with cleanliness would foul its air so badly that the simple act of walking down a city street required a special breathing apparatus, but he had no time to dwell on it. An urgent cleanup job was waiting for him, and if Bolan showed up late, thousands would die.

No pressure, right. Just do or die, and make damn sure you got it right the first time.

He slid behind the Honda's wheel, Kayo in the shotgun seat, prepared to navigate. "Go south from here," the lieutenant said. "On Waseda Dori we turn west and follow that, perhaps three miles, until we reach Kan-Pachi Dori. Turn north, then, and it will take us to Nerima."

"Simple, right?"

In the dashboard light, Kayo smiled at Bolan, the first time since they had taken Toi Takumi. "Do not worry, *Cooper-san*," he said. "I won't lead you astray."

Nerima, Tokyo

"Toi should be here by now," said Shinzo Mori. "He's already half an hour late."

"*Nigegoshi*," Keizo Hata said, smirking.

"Cold feet, my ass," Mori replied. "I'll warm them for him with a blowtorch if he leaves us hanging here."

"Don't worry," Hata said. "They're still making adjustments to the final helicopter. Even if he doesn't show up, we can go ahead without him."

"And do what?" Mori demanded. "Send postcards to all the TV stations, telling them the Sumiyoshi-kai released anthrax? You know we need police to find him with his father's aircraft. It is his final contribution to the reckoning."

"And if he doesn't come, we cancel it?" Hata challenged. "I shall let you explain that to Master Kodama."

Mori did not like the sound of that. "You're right," he said reluctantly. "We still have time."

The techs were finishing their work on the third helicopter, spot welding the makeshift dispersal rig's dual nozzles to the Bell 206L's fuselage, below the tail. First they had taken out the rear seats and replaced them with a holding tank made from an oil drum, fitted with an air compressor that would force the tank to void its contents on command, at the touch of a newly installed toggle switch. From there, the pilot simply had to follow his assigned course over Tokyo, dispensing Lord Bishamon's judgment upon all the sinners below.

Assuming that the hookup functioned properly.

They had no opportunity to test the rigs, either in flight or on the ground before takeoff. There was a backup plan, of course, if any of the systems failed. In that case, Master Kodama's divine wind would become a classic *kamikaze* mission, each of the selected pilots pledged to sacrifice himself as needed, for the cause.

And they were dead, in any case, although they didn't know it yet.

Mori had been commanded not to tell the pilots that their master's plan called for the stolen helicopters to be shot down by police. The aircraft had to be downed and traced back to their owner, for the pantomime to be complete. Discovery of Toi Takumi's corpse would seal the deal, directing public outrage toward the Sumiyoshi-kai.

Assuming that the spoiled bastard finally showed up to play his part and did not leave them stranded.

It was not Mori's prerogative to question what Master Kodama had been thinking when he welcomed a Yakuza brat into the inner circle of Saikosai Raito. It would take a blind man and an idiot to overlook the risks involved. Still, Toi had seemed to be a true believer and had certainly been generous with his allowance, spending dirty money to achieve deliverance.

But now, where was he, as the deadline rapidly approached?

Mori tried calling Toi again, and once again, the call went straight to voice mail. Muttering a curse, he dropped the cell phone back into his pocket, wondering if he should call Master Kodama and alert him to the problem.

No.

The very last thing Mori needed was to come off sounding weak and indecisive. He'd been honored with appointment as the mission's supervisor, and he would not fail the master through faintheartedness. Whatever happened in the hours ahead, whether he lived or found his way to paradise ahead of schedule, Mori would stay the course.

His comrade was right. They *could* proceed without the spoiled brat, if he left them no alternative. The helicopters' registration numbers were enough to link them with Kazuo Takumi and the Sumiyoshi-kai. From there, it was a short step to indictments and a show trial, where the godfather's denials would be useless. Tokyo's survivors would demand revenge, and in their grief would turn to someone who had answers to their questions.

And their prayers.

Master Susumu Kodama's time was coming. Mori hoped that he would be there, basking in the bright reflected glory of their Lord.

Suginami, Tokyo

DESPITE THE HOUR, traffic on Kan-Pachi Dori kept Bolan from rushing toward his target as he would have done, with clear lanes all around. The semi rigs were out in force, delivering produce, seafood and other goods to the markets that would soon be open for the early trade from restaurants and groceries. Whole fleets of cars were also on the move, stacked high on tractor-trailer auto transporters.

Kayo seemed relaxed beside him, more at ease than he had been at any time since their first meeting, hectic hours earlier. From Bolan's view, it was as if the cop had shed some weight that smothered him—or was he simply giving up on any prospect of survival? That could be a risk for any soldier, slipping into fatalism that appeared to conquer fear, but which, in fact, encouraged reckless action that could doom a mission or a man.

Bolan wasn't about to push it, focused as he was— and as the lieutenant ought to be—on what was waiting for them in Nerima. He had no idea how many members of Kodama's cult would be on hand to guard or operate the helicopters they had stolen from the Sumiyoshi-kai. One pilot each, for sure, but would they need another crew member to operate the gear they'd rigged for spraying anthrax over Tokyo? Would there be techs on hand, still working on the apparatus—and if so, were they prepared to fight?

Some cults, he knew, were led by individuals content to bask in adoration, leading lives of luxury and sloth, without attempting to subvert society. Kodama had been cut from different cloth, possessed by visions of himself leading a revolution that would "cleanse" society while leaving him in charge. He clearly hadn't planned on dying in a basement, but he didn't matter now.

The question was: What would his people do without him?

Would they fold on learning that their guru had been taken off the board, or would they fight to the death to realize the fantasy he'd planted in their heads?

Bolan narrowed his focus to their mission of the moment: halt the anthrax flights, eliminating anyone who tried to stop them, and destroy the weaponized bacillus. Anything beyond that point, as far as the Supreme Light was concerned, was someone else's problem. He would gladly leave it in their hands and get back to the job that he was meant to do in Tokyo.

Right now, stopping the helicopters on the ground was paramount. If they took off, Bolan had no way to pursue them, much less bring them down. Metro PD had aircraft, but a dogfight over Tokyo could lead to tragedy. Even if all three choppers were shot down without dispersing any anthrax, it could be released after they fell to earth.

The Honda's dashboard clock told him the time, but couldn't clue him in as to the time remaining on their unknown deadline. If Kodama hadn't known exactly when the helicopters were supposed to fly, nobody did.

"You want the Steyr when we get there?" Bolan asked Kayo. "I've got nothing else to offer you except the .308, and I don't recommend it for the job we're taking on."

"No, thank you. I've been trained to do with less."

The .38 revolver, six shots going in, and maybe extra speed-loaders if Kayo had been feeling paranoid that morning. Bolan knew he had reloaded at the safe house, but it wasn't much to start with, even so.

Forget it. Let it go.

The job came first, and if Kayo felt that he could pull his weight with what he had on hand, so be it. Bolan wouldn't waste time worrying about him, unless the lieutenant did something to jeopardize their task.

In which case, he would cut the man loose, leave him to sink or swim.

Harsh rules, for a harsh world. The only world Mack Bolan knew.

Nerima, Tokyo

THE WAREHOUSE WAS not difficult to find. Susumu Kodama had provided accurate directions in his final moments, when the hope of rescue by his ancient god evaporated, and he realized that death was only moments in his future. He'd lacked the fortitude to craft a final lie, and now Kayo sat staring at the massive building with its peeling paint and rusting metal walls, wondering if his own death lay within.

Had Susumu Kodama felt betrayed, that moment when he realized that giving up the final secrets of his cult was not about to save his life?

It made no difference.

"No guards outside," Bolan said, "and I don't see any cameras."

"There wouldn't be," Kayo replied. "Kodama said he thought to renovate it for a meeting place, but he ran out of time."

"Prayer meetings after the apocalypse?"

"Remember, he expected to prevail. And he originally planned for the attack to fall later this year."

"What bumped it up?"

Kayo had to smile as he replied, "You did. Kazuo Takumi's troubles made him see that there would never be a better time. The bloodshed worked to his advantage, and he feared that if the godfather fell before the day of reckoning, Toi would be useless to him and might even leave the cult. He could not let unknown opponents finish off the mobster, without implicating him in the anthrax conspiracy. It might be years before Kodama could have found a way to blame another family for what he had in mind."

"That doesn't sound as crazy as he seemed," Bolan said.

"He was rational enough about the plan," Kayo granted, "but his motives were insane."

"Still are," Bolan replied. "And he's got people still on task. Let's get in there."

Kayo had no need to double-check his gun. It was fully loaded, six rounds in the cylinder, and he carried enough spare ammunition to kill twelve more men besides, if he made each shot count and never missed.

If he was still alive, after they met the enemy.

They'd parked a block south of the warehouse, walking toward it through a light, cool rain that felt like mist. Kayo knew that he had to look atrocious, like some kind of homeless scarecrow after all that he'd been through the past few hours, but he didn't care. Appearances were for superiors he wanted to impress, or the rare woman whom he hoped to charm. This night had been about cruel, bloody work in the pursuit of justice, and it was not finished yet. The side trip to Nerima was a detour, a distraction from the main event.

Kayo hoped that he would live to see the first job finished, but if not, the prospect of annihilation did not trouble him. He was exhausted by the life he'd led, more so than he had ever realized before Matt Cooper showed him that solutions could be simple if you threw away the rule book. Suddenly, Kayo realized that, while he worked for the police department, he'd been handcuffed from his first day on the streets. So many rules and regulations screened the criminals from rightful punishment that chasing them became a futile exercise, subverted by impressionable jurors and appellate courts.

It still felt alien to Kayo, raised as he had been in a society that valued order, devoid of America's do-it-yourself vigilante tradition, but he was getting used to operating as a force outside the law. Oddly, knowing that there could be no future in it had not dimmed the raw appeal of action.

When the end came, as it must, he would accept it as a true son of Japan.

Nearing the warehouse, still unchallenged by security, the lieutenant drew his .38, holding it down against his thigh. Its weight in his right hand was comforting.

Whatever happened next, he thought, was destiny.

THE FIRST DOOR Bolan tried was unlocked. Whatever else the members of Supreme Light planned for Tokyo, they hadn't given much thought to security.

Stepping inside, he left the Milkor on its shoulder sling and held the Steyr ready for whatever opposition they encountered. Bolan didn't know whether Kodama's acolytes were trained in combat or a bunch of nerds who couldn't fight their way out of a paper bag. In either case, the quickest way to throw them off their game was getting in the first punch, hard and fast.

He followed voices from the back door, down a little hallway, to the main warehouse. It was a huge place, drifting into slow decline, with cobwebs in the rafters, rusty walls inside as well as out. A forklift sat to one side of the entryway where Bolan stood, potential cover if he needed it, but he was focused on the three Bell helicopters gleaming under the fluorescent ceiling lights, a clutch of seven men gathered around the third aircraft in line.

No takeoffs yet. They'd made it for the kickoff.

"Want to warn them?" Bolan whispered to Kayo.

The lieutenant thought about it for a second, then called out, *"Taihoshichauzo! Mada tatte menomaede anata no te o hoji shimasu!"*

Something on the lines of *Freeze, you're busted*, Bolan thought.

And they did freeze, for roughly two, three heartbeats, then they scattered, four of them reaching for weapons as they ran. Bolan dropped one of them in midstride, not waiting to see if he pulled out a gun or a cell phone to warn other members outside the warehouse. His target hit the concrete floor and slithered through his own blood to a huddle halt.

Kayo bagged the next one, leading with his .38 and firing once, clipping the runner as he pulled some kind of semiauto pistol from beneath his windbreaker. The would-be shooter fell, his weapon soaring out in front of him and clattering across the warehouse floor.

Two down, and one of those remaining bolted for the first chopper in line, its door already open to receive him as he scrambled up into the pilot's seat. The farther warehouse doors were closed, preventing an airborne escape, but that reality eluded Bolan's target as his hands flew over the controls, flicking assorted toggle switches.

Bolan drilled him through the head and pitched him over into the copilot's seat, just as the chopper's rotor blades began to turn. Without a live hand on the throttle they could not accelerate, but still spun lazily, reminding Bolan of a sluggish children's ride.

The other cultists died trying to run away. One of them got a shot off, as a slug from the lieutenant's weapon drilled his chest, but it was lost somewhere among the vaulted warehouse rafters and its hanging light fixtures. No score.

When they had seven bodies sprawled on cold concrete, Bolan turned to Kayo. "Mask up," he advised, "and move back in the hallway."

Bolan slipped on his mask as he spoke, and crossed to stand behind the nearest helicopter. It was hard to miss the work that had been done, transforming the executive aircraft into a lethal crop duster. He saw the drum that would be full of anthrax spores, the pipes and nozzles rigged up to expel them, all in place. Both of the other helicopters had been rigged identically.

He and Kayo had reached them in time.

The Milkor's maximum effective range was four hundred yards. He didn't need the launcher's reflex sight from thirty feet, but Bolan used it anyway, taking no chances. Starting with the farthest chopper first, he slammed incendiary rounds into each aircraft's fuselage, exactly where the drums of anthrax nestled in their burlap cradles, and he blew them all to hell. The ruptured fuel tanks helped, ensuring that no stray spores managed to escape.

Bodies were roasting in a lake of liquid fire as Bolan turned away, trailing Kayo back along the hall and out into what passed for fresh air in Tokyo. From the outer threshold, he emptied the Milkor's remaining three rounds, whipping the warehouse firestorm to a fever pitch of heat.

Retreating toward the Honda, Bolan didn't know whether Kodama's zealots had a backup plan for the Great Reckoning or not, and it was none of his concern. Police could handle anything the cult dreamed up from this point on. He had another job to finish.

And Kazuo Takumi's clan was bound to make it difficult.

CHAPTER TWENTY

Shizuoka Prefecture

Kazuo Takumi normally enjoyed the drive from Tokyo to his retreat in Shizuoka. Counting all the highway's twists and turns, it totaled eighty miles or more. It was a scenic drive, once you escaped the urban sprawl of Tokyo, passing Mount Fuji and Lake Kawaguchi, then rolling along the coast to reach Suruga Bay. He liked to watch the scenery unfold, play tourist and forget about his business for a weekend or a holiday.

Not this time.

This time, he was running from a fight—something he'd never done before.

During the past two wars he had engaged in, Takumi had spilled no blood with his own two manicured hands, but he had stayed in Tokyo, at risk, to plot their tactics, call the shots. He had emerged victorious from one of those wars, while the other had been a bloody draw, maintaining what he'd held before the shooting started, gaining no new ground.

This time was different.

Takumi still had no idea who he was fighting, or the reason they were waging war against the Sumiyoshi-kai. It baffled him, and that was almost…frightening.

He checked his watch against the long familiar landscape. The Audemars Piguet Prestige Sports Collection

Royal Oak Offshore Chronograph confirmed that they were thirty minutes out of Tokyo and making decent time, approximately halfway to their destination. Nestled in the backseat of his limousine, surrounded by Tadashi Jo and The Three—he already had plans to make it Four again—the *oyabun* felt reasonably safe. Security, however, hinged upon identifying and destroying his still faceless enemies, before Yamaguchi-gumi or the Inagawa-kai began encroaching on his turf.

Those plans, he took for granted, were already in the works. Vultures were quick to smell a free meal, even when a wounded lion still had fight left in him yet.

"Music," Takumi said, to no one in particular. Jo used the limo's intercom to reach the driver, and a moment later, they were treated to the lilting tones of bamboo flutes. The *oyabun* did not recognize the tune, but found the music soothing to his nerves. Whether the limo's other passengers enjoyed or hated it was none of his concern.

Takumi had initially refused to wear a pistol on the drive from Tokyo, but finally, reluctantly, heeded Tadashi Jo's suggestion that it might be necessary and, in any case could do no harm. Unlike most of his troops, the clan leader had the necessary license and permit to carry firearms, renewable at three-year intervals under prevailing law. His chosen weapon was a Glock 25 chambered in .380 ACP, with fifteen rounds in its staggered box magazine. He carried no spare magazines, certain that if he could not do the job with what he had, after all of his soldiers failed, then he was meant to die.

He listened to the dueling flutes and tried to let their music carry him away. It worked sometimes, when he was troubled by some difficulty with his business or his arrogant, rebellious son, but this time there were nagging voices in his head, demanding his attention, asking questions.

Where was Kato Ando? Who had killed Koyuki Masuda? What was Toi involved with, that had cost the lives of two crack killers sent to find him? Thinking of his son's involvement with the damned Saikosai Raito cult brought heat into Takumi's cheeks. If he learned that Susumu Kodama had set his dogs on Kato and Koyuki, there would be no place in all Japan—no place on Earth—for the so-called guru to hide. He always paid his debts, and he was looking forward to that one.

But first, he had to keep himself alive.

No small trick, that, under the present circumstances. Running shamed him, even if the men around him did not see it, but Takumi placed the family above himself. He had no heir to take the reins if he was killed in battle. His survival was a duty to the Sumiyoshi-kai.

And he would crush the enemies arrayed against him, if it was the last thing that he ever did.

Marunouchi, Tokyo

"THE MONK KNOWS EVERYTHING," Kayo said.

"No one knows *every*thing," Bolan replied.

"Permit me to rephrase. The Monk knows everything of any value about crime in Tokyo."

"Is he a real monk?" Bolan asked.

"At some time in his past, perhaps. Who knows?"

"Maybe the Monk?"

Kayo laughed at that, but kept his eyes on the pedestrians around them. They were walking north in the stylish heart of Marunouchi, which, itself, was rather like the heart of Tokyo. Bounded by the Imperial Palace to the west and Tokyo Station to the east, Marunouchi was one of the capital's oldest business districts, nearly destroyed by an earthquake and fire in 1923, now home to hundreds of multinational corporations. The avenue was closed to normal vehicles, patrolled by cops on bicycles who gave the district's shoppers, diners and CEOs plenty of room.

The Monk met none of those criteria. Kayo had described him as a former law adviser to the Yamaguchi-gumi family, retired now, but remaining in the know. The Monk maintained a network of informers: Yakuzas and cops, dealers and users, pimps and hookers, gamblers and shylocks, lawyers and doctors, cab drivers— whoever could feed him intel on the city, regardless of rank or their stance in the eyes of the law.

They found him lounging at a table outside a small café. A folding white cane lay in plain view on the tabletop.

"He's blind," Bolan observed, stating the obvious.

"And still sees everything," Kayo said.

Let's hope so, Bolan thought, but kept it to himself.

They had lost track of Kazuo Takumi, not hard to imagine in the termite hill of Tokyo. The *oyabun* owned a string of penthouse condos, but he wasn't in residence at any of them, nor had he been seen at either of his two posh offices since Bolan started wreaking havoc in the man's backyard. If he had fled the city altogether, finding Takumi among Japan's 6,852 islands and 127 million people would be next to impossible. If he'd left the country, forget about it.

"Ah, Lieutenant," the Monk said before Kayo had a chance to speak. His choice of English was explained when he added, "You have a *gaijin* friend."

"You heard us talking," Kayo stated, as he sat.

"And I smelled you coming," the informant countered. "You still wear Issey Miyake cologne, although it needs to be refreshed this morning. Your companion smells like…gunpowder."

"It's been a hard night," Kayo said.

"So I hear. I'm sorry that you've come to this."

"We all do what we must."

"And now you seek Kazuo Takumi. To finish something?"

"If we can."

"He's left the city, I'm afraid," the Monk informed them.

"And you've lost him?"

"Please. When was the last time I lost anyone?"

"I can't remember."

"No one can." The Monk allowed himself the vestige of a smile, then said, "Kazuo Takumi has a house in Shizuoka. You know Suruga Bay."

"It is very large," Kayo said.

"You need not search it all. Takumi's property lies one mile inland from Oikawa Port, along the Ooi River, at the south end of Osakagawa Ryokuchi Park."

"I will find it."

"I have no doubt," the Monk replied. "But will you find your way back home?"

"I'm not sure where that is."

The Monk turned sightless eyes toward Bolan, seated opposite.

"Has the *gaijin* led you off your path, my friend?"

"I choose my own path," Kayo stated.

"Then pursue it to the end. Suruga Bay."

"You have been very helpful," the lieutenant said.

"I have done nothing but arrange a meeting. How it ends…" The shrug was barely visible.

Southbound on Naka-dori Avenue, Kayo said, "He thinks we're going to be killed."

"No reason you should go the extra mile," Bolan replied.

"I lied to him," Kayo said.

"How's that?"

"I did not choose the journey, *Cooper-san*. The path chose me."

Suruga Bay, Shizuoka Prefecture

SHOEI SATO WAS bored after the ride from Tokyo, annoyed by the warbling, chirping flute music that his godfather demanded as their traveling theme. It put him in mind of geisha houses—not bad, in itself—but those were places he went to relax and flush the world out of his head. The journey to Suruga Bay was not a pleasure jaunt, by any means, and so the music was incongruous. A mockery.

If he were honest with himself, Sato was shaken by Koyuki Masuda's death. It made the point he normally ignored: that all of them were ultimately vulnerable, and their days on Earth were numbered. No surprise, that, given all the lives he'd personally ended, but it was not something that he chose to dwell on, either.

So, forget it, Sato told himself, as he stepped from the limousine and stretched his stiffened muscles. Do the job, and then get on with seeking your revenge.

Wise counsel. And the job, he thought, might well be part of the revenge he craved.

Was it coincidence that, in the midst of these attacks upon his family, Kato Ando had disappeared and Masuda had been eliminated trying to discover what had happened to the godfather's attack dog? It was possible, of course—but so were UFOs, abominable snowmen and the monster said to lurk in Lake Ikeda, on Kyushu.

In his personal experience, Sato had found that true

coincidence was rare in dealings with the Sumiyoshi-kai. Losses were nearly always someone's fault, whether an enemy's or some pathetic idiot within the family who could not follow simple rules.

Tadashi Jo was barking orders at the other soldiers as they piled out of their cars, greeted by others who'd been summoned to the godfather's estate by phone, as they were leaving Tokyo. A rapid head count showed him thirty-seven gunmen prepared to fight and die, if necessary, for their clan leader. Sato assumed there were a few more in the house, and some scouring the grounds for prowlers. Call it fifty guns, then, plus himself, Tamura and Nakai, an army in themselves.

As far as weapons, there would be no shortage. Sato saw assault rifles and submachine guns, shotguns, every man wearing a pistol. From past visits, he knew there were heavy weapons in the house: at least two Minimis, the Belgian light machine guns made by Fabrique Nationale d'Herstal with a cyclic rate of fire exceeding 700 rounds per minute; and an M134 Minigun from the United States, a Gatling-style weapon with six barrels capable of spewing an extravagant two thousand rounds per minute.

Police would have a field day if they ever got around to raiding Kazuo Takumi's estate, but bribes had thus far kept any such inconvenient visits from occurring. What would happen if his enemies from Tokyo discovered where they'd gone and came to find them? Would the neighbors—one a middle-rank vice president of Nippon Steel, another highly placed with Mitsubishi—summon officers if trouble came and shooting started? Almost certainly. And would their wealth offset Kazuo Takumi's efforts to ensure that Shizuoka's prefectural police played deaf, dumb and blind?

That remained to be seen.

Tadashi Jo stood before him now, lips moving. Sato realized he had not heard a word of what the first lieutenant was saying.

Tamura saved him, answering, "We're ready. Leave us to it. If intruders come, we'll handle them."

"And quietly, if possible," Jo stressed. "We must avoid humiliation of our godfather."

Sato supposed he might have smiled at that, if he was not a stranger to emotion. But why bother, anyway, unless it was to irritate Jo? Their clan leader had already endured humiliation; every member of the Yakuza with half a brain knew that. An enemy he could not stop had ravaged Kazuo Takumi's business in the United States and now in Tokyo. His worthless son was missing in action, as always, and he'd been driven to hide in his summer home, far from the city.

What further humiliation could there be?

Only death.

And that, in his godfather's case, might even be a blessing.

Osakagawa Ryokuchi Park, Shizuoka Prefecture

DARKNESS HAD FALLEN on the park when Bolan pulled his Honda behind a line of trees and switched off the engine. Across the two-lane road immediately to his left, a low stone wall provided nothing in the way of real security before a wooded hillside rose and crested, hiding Kazuo Takumi's rural hideout from their view.

"I doubt that he'll have mines on public land," Bolan said. "But there could be cameras or something else. You never know."

"He shall not stop us," Kayo stated.

"Confidence is great," Bolan replied. "But keep your eyes open, regardless."

"Do not worry, *Cooper-san*."

"Still just the .38?"

"I may find something useful, once we're on the grounds."

"Your call," Bolan conceded. Stepping from the car, he flexed his shoulders, then got busy with his mobile arsenal.

The Steyr was going with him, absolutely, and the Milkor MGL. He wore the Glock already over black slacks and a turtleneck to match, adding a bandoleer of ammo for the rifle and another for the 40 mm launcher. To his belt, he clipped four RGD grenades and *tanto* blade in its scabbard.

Overkill? He hoped so, but the worst mistake that any soldier ever made was leaving gear behind on the assumption that he wouldn't need it. Bolan would prefer to lug an extra twenty pounds or so, rather than come up short on hardware in the midst of battle, when his life was on the line.

He'd heard it in a movie somewhere, sometime: Never let them say you died from lack of shooting back.

Amen.

Kayo had nothing to check except his six-gun, already reloaded. He was still wearing the suit he'd had on when they met, the jacket buttoned now to hide as much as possible of his white shirt. Not exactly Mr. Stealth, but there was nothing to be done about it now.

A car rolled past, and Bolan let it clear the next curve, passing out of sight before he crossed the blacktop with Kayo at his side. Scaling the hillside was a chore for his companion, slipping twice in his street shoes, needing a hand up from Bolan to keep from backsliding on down to the curb. They made the crest five minutes after starting out, and saw Kazuo Takumi's place roughly a quarter mile ahead of them, the house lit up, while darkness cloaked the grounds.

That could be good, or bad.

Without night-vision goggles—something his armorer hadn't had in stock when Bolan visited his shop—the night could be both friend and enemy. Bolan was skilled at working in the dark, less sure about Kayo, but the Sumiyoshi-kai had a home court advantage, playing on familiar ground. They might have booby traps in place, though Bolan wasn't sure they'd risk explosives, but if the *oyabun* was spooked enough to run, who knew?

He'd talked about it with Kayo on the drive from Tokyo, trusted the cop to use his head and keep his wits about him when the shooting started, as he had so far.

"From here on in, watch every step," Bolan advised.

Kayo nodded, and they started down the hill toward Kazuo Takumi's reckoning.

Chinese Embassy, Minato, Tokyo

COLONEL FULIAN SUN took the call at half past midnight, routed through the embassy switchboard to his private apartment. He had not been asleep when the phone rang, too restless on this night when such momentous and terrible things were supposed to happen. He recognized the caller's code name and his voice, remembered from the one and only time they'd met in person, joined by Susumu Kodama.

"You have news?" the colonel asked.

"Bad news," Captain Takahira Amago replied. "The worst, I'm afraid."

Sun kept his face deadpan, though there was no one

else to see him in his bedroom, and his voice was level as he said, "Explain, please."

"There will be no reckoning," the policeman said. "We have failed."

He sounded like a man grief-stricken, which would fit the profile of a true believer. Colonel Sun, for his part, felt dismay and an unpleasant churning in his stomach.

"That is not an explanation," he replied.

"The flight was interdicted. All three aircraft are destroyed, together with their cargo. Seven men are dead. Police are on the scene."

"And those responsible?" Sun asked.

"Still unidentified."

"The helicopters can be traced, as planned?"

"In time, no doubt. Whether the cargo can be recognized is something else. The fire…"

"I understand," the colonel stated.

Sun was not trained in the forensic sciences beyond the basic knowledge necessary to commit a simple crime and get away with it: blood spatter, fingerprints, transfer of hairs and fibers. He had no idea if fire eradicated every trace of anthrax spores, or if they could be recognized among the ashes, charges filed against the Sumiyoshi-kai for terrorist conspiracy. If that were possible, he still might salvage something from the wreckage of Susumu Kodama's plan. A scandal in the government, if nothing else.

"Was the son among those killed?" he asked.

"No. He's missing, with his father and Master Kodama."

"Are your officers pursuing them?" Sun asked.

"Not yet. A warrant will be issued for Kazuo Takumi when the aircraft are identified as his. Toi is not considered active in the family. Master Kodama should be overlooked, unless the dead are linked somehow to Saikosai Raito."

"And will they be?"

"I cannot say."

Sun swallowed bitter disappointment, mixed with worry. The police captain, once vital to his scheme, had now become a liability. Would he begin to reconsider his involvement as the net was cast for members of his cult? What would he say or do to save himself from prison?

"We should meet," Sun said. "You've been of great service, regardless of the outcome. I wish to reward you for your help in person."

"Of course!" The captain's voice revealed surprise and something close to pleasure, even in the midst of grief. "At your convenience, sir."

"I'll call tomorrow," Sun assured him, "and arrange for an appointment. Somewhere private."

"Yes. Until then."

Sun would do the job himself. He had not killed a man in years, but wet work was like falling off a log. Once learned and practiced, it was never quite forgotten.

Sun's next problem was Susumu Kodama. He was "missing," whatever that meant. Had he fled Tokyo to escape any fallout from his Great Reckoning? Had the unknown raiders who'd foiled the anthrax attack done away with Kodama, as well? Colonel Sun didn't know, but he had to find out, and the sooner the better. The cult leader at large was a threat that he could not afford to ignore. The lunatic might try to blackmail Sun, or be arrested on some other charge and spill his story of a grand conspiracy to curry favor with the law. Wherever he had gone, if he was still alive, Kodama had to be found and killed.

As for the Sumiyoshi-kai, if Toi Takumi was not implicated in the anthrax plot, his father might well escape prosecution. He could claim the aircraft had been stolen—which they were—and create a solid alibi. With friends like his, long grown accustomed to substantial bribes, Takumi might even strike a martyr's pose, lamenting groundless persecution. None of that helped Colonel Sun, or Beijing's plan to rack Japan with chaos.

Sun cursed the whole damned cast of characters involved in what had seemed a solid and straightforward plan. Part of the guilt was his, Sun knew, for trusting criminals and zealots, but such people were a spymaster's normal stock in trade.

Above all else, he had to preserve deniability.

He had to survive.

CHAPTER TWENTY-ONE

Shizuoka Prefecture

There was an eight-foot chain-link fence around Kazuo Takumi's property, with concertina razor wire coiled at the top, but it was not electrified. Bolan applied his Leatherman all-purpose tool and snipped the links, low down, and held it open while Kayo wriggled through, then followed, crudely fastening the flap behind him.

It would pass inspection long enough, he hoped, for them to reach Takumi's house and get the party started. Bolan had observed the ground for ten long minutes prior to making his approach: no dogs and no patrols along the fence so far. He saw no cameras, but couldn't swear there weren't some tiny fiber-optic eyes watching their entry to the property.

If so, they'd find out soon enough.

Takumi's grounds were sparsely wooded, not a forest like the one they'd tramped through on their hike in from the park, but darkness pooled among the trees, untouched by lights burning outside the house. Guards had been stationed on the patio, and Bolan knew others would be on watch at any entrance to the place.

The house was built in the style of a sixteenth-century Japanese country home, but with all the modern amenities and then some. Its centerpiece was a two-story grand pavilion with cantilevered verandas, wings extending to the north and east, with a separate guesthouse on stilts to the west. A tiered pagoda rose above a bonsai garden, while multiple satellite dishes sprouted from rooftops. Bolan saw no paper walls, which would have made their penetration easier, but guessed there might be some inside the house, for style's sake.

Either way, the house was built of wood, which guaranteed that it would burn.

They met no roving guards and triggered no alarms on their approach. The final thirty yards were open lawn, well kept, no cover once they made their final rush to reach the house. That meant downing the guards Bolan could see, and causing a diversion that would draw others away from the glass doors he planned to use for entry, on the south side of the sprawling residence. Kayo would go with him, as agreed, snatching the first piece from a fallen enemy that suited him, and then was free to go off hunting on his own, as he desired.

It wasn't much, in terms of strategy, but splitting up let them cover more ground, more quickly, than they could have as a team. It also doubled chances of escape, if anything went wrong inside.

Bolan scoped the two guards on the patio, framing each in turn with the Steyr AUG's integrated telescopic sight. He chose the taller of them as his first mark, stroked the rifle's trigger and sent four grams of copper-jacketed death hurtling downrange at 3,100 feet per second. It drilled the lookout's temple, tumbled on a ragged path while passing through his brain, and took out the opposite side of his skull in a burst of pink and scarlet.

Shifting slightly to his right, Bolan triggered another silenced round, clipping the second mobster's vocal cords before he could raise an alarm at the death of his friend.

He fell across the first gunner's twitching legs, clearing the way for Bolan and Kayo to advance.

"No stopping once we're on the grass," Bolan advised. "No turning back."

"Banzai!" Kayo whispered in reply, and smiled.

THE FIRST EXPLOSION made Kazuo Takumi jump and spill his *sake*, the warm liquor soaking through his slacks. He dropped the cup and scrambled to his feet, eyes wide, resembling those of a startled deer. The Three moved to surround him instantly, each man armed with an automatic weapon in addition to the ninja gear they carried with them everywhere.

Takumi did not need to ask what the explosion represented. He could work that out himself. His enemies had followed him from Tokyo somehow, and now they meant to finish what they'd started in the capital.

He cursed them silently and offered up a silent prayer, no feeling of hypocrisy at all, asking to learn the cause of all this persecution, at the very least, before he died.

Which, at the moment, seemed entirely possible.

Instinctively, Takumi drew his Glock 25, though no target was yet visible. He trusted The Three to a point, but their recent reduction from four had caused him to question their skill for the first time since he had employed them.

"Where is Tadashi?" Takumi demanded.

"Checking the guards," Nakai replied. "You should come with us now."

"Come where?"

"To find a safer place."

The clan leader wondered if there was a safer place. His country home did not contain a panic room, and it was just as well. He'd sampled some, when they became a craze with wealthy CEOs in Tokyo, and found them claustrophobic, with the smell of airline lavatories. Worst of all, once locked inside the box, a test run, he immediately felt more helpless than secure.

"We should get out of here," Tamura suggested.

"And go where?" Takumi challenged him.

"It doesn't matter. Back to Tokyo, or pick another city. Anyplace that isn't under fire."

"I'm staying," Sato said. "These are the bastards who killed Koyuki."

"You don't know that," Nakai replied.

"I feel it," Sato said.

"He's right," Takumi interjected. "We must stay and fight."

Running a second time, he knew, meant that he might have nothing to come home to, even if he managed to survive the night. Tamura and Nakai did not see fit to argue.

"Smoke," Sato said, sniffing at the air. Takumi took another moment to detect it, but the ninja was correct, as usual. The house—some part of it, at least—was already on fire.

"We need to get outside," Tamura said. "These houses burn like a tinderbox."

Takumi had never seen a tinderbox, but he understood the allusion. Wood and paper sliding doors guaranteed that fire would spread swiftly through any home built on traditional lines. Culture had triumphed over common sense in that regard, despite the lessons learned in World War II, when the American B29s rained hell on Tokyo, Kobe and other cities.

"To the bunker, then?" Nakai suggested.

The estate was not entirely indefensible, despite its classic style. One building stood apart, almost concealed by greenery, where Takumi could stand and fight.

His final stand, perhaps. And if it came to that, he meant to go out like a samurai.

KENICHI KAYO SAW the first round from Matt Cooper's 40 mm weapon strike a corner of the roof on the east wing of the mansion, erupting into instant flame that spread with startling speed. He guessed it was a thermobaric round, recalling a briefing he had received on military weapons likely to be used by criminals and terrorists. He did not understand exactly how they worked, nor did he care. The grim reality was frightening.

Halfway across the lawn, Cooper unleashed a second 40 mm round. This one punched through the *shōji* sliding door in front of them and detonated in the room beyond, a high-explosive blast this time instead of blooming fire. Kayo heard men screaming in the house and gripped his .38 so tightly that his knuckles ached as they approached the shattered door and plunged inside.

It felt strange, even in those circumstances, to barge in without first taking off his shoes. *Tatami* flooring underfoot felt alien through layers of leather as he stood with Cooper in the smoky wreckage of a game room, with its billiard table kneeling on one broken leg. Two Yakuza gunners were dying there, riddled with shrapnel from the blast, neither of them possessing fortitude enough to do it quietly.

Cooper ignored them, once he'd kicked their weapons out of reach. "We split up here," he said, according to their plan.

Kayo nodded. "*Hai.* Good luck."

"I'll see you on the other side."

An optimist, Kayo thought, not speaking of an afterlife. As for himself, turning away toward a connecting *shōji* door, he had already made his peace with death.

Shōji served dual functions in Japanese architecture. As sliding doors, they saved space wasted on Western swing doors, and their strategic placement also let rooms be expanded or closed off at need, either providing more room or allowing for a modicum of privacy. The privacy was out for Kazuo Takumi and his soldiers this night, Kayo thought. Before long, if they chose to stay inside the burning house, they'd be reduced to ash and cracked white bones.

As would Kayo, if he let himself be trapped.

He pushed the *shōji* door aside and stepped into a dining room. Its furnishings were minimal: a table with truncated legs, perhaps twelve inches off the floor, and chairs with none at all, though they had upright backs. It looked as if some prankster with a chainsaw had passed through and trimmed them down, taking the legs away with him.

There were no targets in the dining room. Kayo left it as he found it, with the table bare, and passed on through another *shōji* door to reach the kitchen. As he cleared the threshold, someone fired a submachine gun at him from behind an island in the middle of the spacious room, slugs ripping through the paper door and sizzling past into the dining room.

Kayo hit the floor and rolled, ending his move with shoulders pressed against the stainless-steel island that stood between him and his would-be slayer. Silence on the other side told him the gunner was waiting, possibly holding his breath, afraid to step out in the open.

Lure him out, then.

Drawing in a deep breath, the lieutenant released it in what he hoped was a convincing moan. For emphasis, he muttered curses with a feigned sob, trying to sound desperate.

Footsteps approached, circling the kitchen island to his left. Kayo gripped his .38 in both hands, waiting, and squeezed off the second that he had a target, firing one shot from a range of six or seven feet. His bullet drilled the Yakuza hardman beneath his chin and did not exit, though it may have bounced around inside his skull, shredding the brain. The soldier dropped, shivered and then lay still.

Kayo grabbed his weapon, recognized it as Minebea PM-9 used by the Japan Self-Defense Forces as standard equipment. He holstered his revolver, then checked the corpse for extra magazines and found three, one hundred rounds in all, minus those spent trying to kill him seconds earlier.

Better, Kayo thought, and went in search of other prey.

BOLAN HAD SWITCHED back to his Steyr when he left the lieutenant in the rec room, heading in the opposite direction through another sliding door. They gave Kazuo Takumi's home a fun house aspect, though he doubted whether any of its occupants were having fun right now.

The room he entered next was empty, but Bolan heard shooters moving nearby, catching distorted silhouettes in motion through the paper of adjoining sliding doors. Instead of waiting for his enemies to make the next move, Bolan dropped into a crouch and started plinking them through paper, trusting the suppressor on his AUG to add a measure of confusion to the mix.

At least three men were in the room immediately to his left, and Bolan took them down like targets in a midway shooting gallery, one round apiece, working from left to right. A couple of them cried out as they fell, the sounds alerting their collaborators in the room or corridor to Bolan's right. He saw those soldiers crouching, trying to make smaller targets of themselves, betrayed by lights that cast their shadows on the paper door.

Two more went down before his semiauto fire, and while he'd gone for kill shots, Bolan still used caution when he slid the nearest door aside, surveying the result. One of the two men in the corridor was still alive, but not for long, struggling to breathe with ruptured lungs. The other had already gone to his reward or punishment, if there was any to be had.

Thin walls could work both ways, he knew—and they also transmitted sound. Takumi's house had turned into an echo chamber, angry voices shouting questions and replies in Japanese, some simply cursing from the sound of it, none of their racket useful to the Executioner, except in finding hardmen to kill. He didn't know where he should look for Kazuo Takumi in the rambling house, now filling up with smoke, and realized the architecture gave his enemies escape hatches to the outside from almost every room.

He switched off to the Milkor one more time and fired an HE round through the nearest sliding door, angling from south to north. The grenade wouldn't detonate from slicing through paper, but a wooden wall or other solid obstacle would set it off. The blast, when it came, was at least sixty-odd feet downrange.

More shouts, mixed in with screams. Bolan slashed through the ruptured paper door without retracting it and went on with his hunt.

THE BUNKER WAS located in the Yakuza chief's decorative garden, built to blend in with the greenery. Entry was through a space behind a miniature Shinto shrine, concealed from inattentive passersby. The inner room was twenty feet by thirty, reinforced concrete above, below and on all sides. Air circulated through vents in the roof, concealed among ferns and flowers. Gun ports on all sides permitted grazing fire from its defenders, pillbox style. A periscope allowed perusal of the garden on three sides. The bunker's door was solid steel, three inches thick, rated as bulletproof and blast resistant.

Stepping into it, surrounded by The Three, Takumi knew how his ancestors had to have felt, crouching in caves and bunkers very much like this one, waiting for American marines to burn them out with flamethrowers or shred their flesh with satchel charges on a hundred different Pacific Islands in the final war of empire.

He felt trapped and sorry that they had not tried to flee after all, in one of the cars.

Too late now.

The sounds of battle from his nearby house were muffled in the bunker but still audible. Takumi pictured the destruction of his summer home and felt a fleeting sense of loss, but he refused to focus on it. Houses were available to anyone with money, and his cash reserves were deep. Not that they helped him here, below ground, waiting for the end.

"We should have brought Tadashi," he declared.

"There was no time to look for him," Nakai replied.

"He might come yet," Tamura added. "He knows where to go."

Takumi knew better. His first lieutenant would be dead soon, if he wasn't already. Even if he came, the clan leader doubted that The Three would crack the heavy door to let the man in.

They were protecting him, of course. Why did he feel as if he were their prisoner?

Nothing to do but wait, Takumi thought. One of his men, at least, should have been on the phone by now, summoning reinforcements. Even if they all forgot, or died before they had a chance to call out, he could trust his neighbors to alert police and firefighters. That meant investigation of the weapons carried by his men, a threat of prison for collecting them, but Takumi employed a firm of lawyers dedicated to defending him from any charge or lawsuit. At the very least, he could delay a trial for years, and if convicted, could postpone incarceration while he went through various appeals.

But there would be no trial and no appeals if he died in the bunker.

The Yakuza mobster sat down to hide the sudden tremor in his legs, hoping The Three would not sniff out his fear and turn against him, leaving him to face his enemies alone.

KAZUO TAKUMI'S FUN HOUSE was in flames. Bolan's incendiary round had lit the farthest point from where he planned to enter with Kayo, buying time, but once the fire caught hold there was no stopping it. Firefighters might save parts of it, if they arrived in time, but Bolan heard no sirens in the distance yet.

He'd cleared four rooms so far, leaving a trail of bodies in his wake, with no sign of the Yakuza boss or Tadashi Jo. Bolan was feeding the Steyr a fresh magazine when a screaming hardman crashed through the paper wall to his left, swinging a sword that he'd picked up somewhere along the way.

Bolan blocked the first swing with his rifle's fiberglass-reinforced polyamide stock, the blade missing his left hand by an inch or less, then lashed out with the Steyr's muzzle, clouting his adversary with the weapon's sound suppressor. The swordsman stutter-stepped away from Bolan, spitting curses the Executioner couldn't translate, and was winding up another swing when Bolan shot him in the chest at point-blank range. The Yakuza died on his feet, gaping at Bolan in surprise, as if he'd thought he was invincible.

Bolan moved on. Behind him, he could hear the flames now, racing through the house, devouring everything before them. Men were screaming back there, leaping for their lives from any exit they could find before the fire caught up with them and made escape impossible.

Apparently, their willingness to die for their godfather had limits, after all.

Good news for Bolan if they kept on running once they cleared the house.

Not good if they regrouped outside and waited for him to emerge.

He put that out of mind for now, with rooms still left to clear, but spared a thought for his companion, somewhere in the far wing of the house, wondering if Kayo was alive or dead. Bolan couldn't afford to dwell on that, however. They'd agreed on a meeting place if both of them got clear, but Bolan wasn't going anywhere until he'd satisfied himself that he had finished off the job he'd come to do.

Cut off the viper's head and leave it thrashing, bleeding out. Whatever happened to it after that was someone else's problem.

By the time he'd cleared eight chambers in the house of sliding doors, Bolan knew he was near the end of his selected wing. The central portion of the house was blazing like a bonfire, moments from implosion as its walls burned through like pages of a book. He didn't hear much screaming from the heart of the inferno anymore, a blessing for the mobsters who'd been trapped inside.

Was Kazuo Takumi one of those who'd been incinerated? Thinking so would make the rest of Bolan's mission simple, but he couldn't swallow that on faith alone. He had to *see* the man dead or, at the very least, convince himself that the godfather of the Sumiyoshi-kai had not escaped.

It was not finished yet.

CHAPTER TWENTY-TWO

"I should be out there with my men," Takumi said.

None of The Three disputed what he'd said. Shoei Sato was on the periscope, turning it slowly while he scanned the garden, seeking enemies. Tamura Min and Nakai Ryo crouched before two of the bunker's gun ports, peering through the slits with automatic weapons close at hand. Their silence, the impression of ignoring him, made the Yakuza boss angry.

"I said—"

"We heard you," Sato interrupted, without turning from the periscope's eyepiece. "With all respect, you must protect yourself in the best interest of the family."

With all respect, he'd said, and yet it did not sound respectful. Takumi imagined that The Three were judging him, condemning him for cowardice, although they would not voice their thoughts aloud.

"What do you see?" he asked them, all at once.

"Nothing," Tamura said.

"No one," Nakai echoed.

"The house is nearly gone," Sato stated, adding as an afterthought, "I'm sorry."

He did not *sound* sorry, but that was no surprise. Did any of The Three feel anything at all?

The house meant nothing, merely wood and paper. Takumi could always find or build another one, if he survived this night. He normally disdained all contact with police but now found himself hoping they were on their way to rescue him. Perhaps they would wipe out the enemies he had not managed to identify.

Unless...

A grim, unworthy thought occurred to him. What if his neighbors failed to call for help? Would they stand by in silence, hoping that Kazuo Takumi and his soldiers would be purged forever from their midst?

Another notion, more disturbing than the last. What if the same policemen he had paid so generously over many years decided that they'd had enough of him and dragged their feet before responding to his present crisis? They could always make up some excuse, why they were late arriving on the scene and found him dead.

Ridiculous.

Money bought loyalty, and the police would suffer from a failure to perform their duty properly, as well as losing all that future income from Kazuo Takumi's family. As for his proud, aristocratic neighbors, it was foolish to suppose they would allow a war to rage unchecked around their homes without calling for aid.

He rose, was on the verge of daring anyone to stop him as he left the bunker, when a powerful explosion echoed through the garden, stinging his eardrums. He could not feel the shock wave there inside his concrete womb, but pictured the destruction of his country home.

"The propane tank," Sato advised.

"I'm going out," Takumi said.

The Three exchanged cool glances, then Tamura answered, "That's a bad idea."

"You will not stop me," the Yakuza boss said, rising to his full height, wearing an expression of determination.

"No," Nakai agreed.

"All right, then. Bring your weapons."

"We won't stop you," Sato told him, "but we are not going with you, either."

"What?" Kazuo felt as if he had been slapped across the face.

"You brought us to defend you, Master," Sato explained. "We cannot do that if you make yourself a target."

"You owe me a duty!" Takumi insisted.

Sato nodded. "Yes. But if you go out there, you'll die, and what becomes of duty then?"

Takumi glared at each of them in turn, then went back to the camp chair he'd just left and sat again. It shamed him when he felt a surge of sweet relief.

BOLAN WAS ON his last room when the wild man came for him. Another shouting Yakuza hardman, but this one hadn't brought a sword to the gunfight. He had an FN Minimi, the standard model, fifteen pounds of bloody murder plus a fat box magazine containing two hundred rounds of 5.56 mm NATO ammunition on an M27 disintegrating-link belt. He came on firing short bursts, as if he knew what he was doing, cutting zigzag patterns through the paper walls, apparently without regard to who might be on the receiving end.

After the second burst, Bolan was on his belly. He couldn't tell if the shooter had seen him and missed on his first try, or if he was just spraying death all around in the hope that he might get lucky. Either way, he stood a chance of scoring if he kept it up.

So Bolan had to stop him. Fast.

He waited for a clear view of the shooter's upper body, legs still hidden by the tattered, sagging remnants of a sliding door he'd shot to hell. The Steyr's Swarovski 1.5x sight framed his opponent's chest and shoulders in its black ring reticle and Bolan squeezed off, going for a double-tap from twenty feet.

The slugs ripped through his target's sternum, separated by an inch or less. Dying, the gunner lurched backward, index finger locked around the light machine gun's trigger, firing all the way until he hit the floor and impact jarred the roaring weapon from his hands. As if on cue, a portion of the ceiling tumbled down on top of him in flames, with dark smoke swirling after it to mask the scene.

Bolan was out of time. The fire was catching up with him, and if he lingered in the house, he would be roasted with the others he'd heard screaming earlier. That wasn't how he planned to go, particularly with his mission uncompleted.

Sparing Kayo one last thought, somewhere between a silent requiem and prayer, he rose and backed off from the wall of fire, to reach the nearest exit. Like the rest, it was a sliding door that opened on the night. Flames had short-circuited the power on the grounds, but now offered illumination of their own to light the way.

Outside, surviving members of the Sumiyoshi-kai were running every which way, maybe looking for their godfather, trying to spot an enemy, or simply working up the nerve to flee and leave it all behind. Bolan would be outnumbered on the open ground, as he had been inside the house, but he would also make a better target there.

No way around it. If he meant to find Kazuo Takumi and Kayo—if he meant to live at all—he'd have to take the risk.

Another section of the ceiling fell as Bolan stepped outside into a scene from hell.

TADASHI JO WAS LOST. Not literally—he knew where he was and how he'd gotten there—but he was dazed, his thoughts spinning like truck tires bogged in mud. He stood on the south lawn and watched Kazuo Takumi's house burning while soldiers, many of them singed or wounded, milled about like chickens in a farmyard, obviously having no idea where they should go or what they should do next.

The worst part: he had no idea himself.

He had returned from his inspection of the troops to find his boss, when the shooting started, but the man had vanished with The Three. Jo cursed Takumi for abandoning him, and the so-called ninjas for usurping his authority to help the godfather escape. Now he was stranded, burdened with an automatic rifle he had yet to fire, no enemies before him, no coherent thoughts on what he should do next.

Jo had already counted cars and found none missing. If The Three had taken Takumi away somewhere, they had to have fled on foot. Where would they go in that case? Not to any of the neighbors, he decided. They were rich snobs who were forced to tolerate a gangster in their midst, because his wealth and influence matched theirs, but none of them would shelter Kazuo Takumi from killers in their homes.

Where, then?

He could not picture the escapees walking to the nearest town, when they might meet police at any point along the way. They might find someplace in the woods to hide and phone for help from Tokyo, more than an hour's drive away, but that, too, seemed unlikely.

Gunfire broke Jo's focus on the problem. Turning toward the sound, he saw three of his men firing at shadows cast by leaping firelight, wasting ammunition on ephemeral opponents. Moving toward them cautiously, aware that they might turn on him if startled, he began to call out from a distance.

"It's nothing! Hold your fire!"

It took another moment for the three to register his order and obey. Turning to face Jo, their expressions mirrored his disordered thoughts, making him hope that he seemed more composed.

"Have any of you seen the godfather?" Jo asked.

Two soldiers shook their heads. The third muttered, "No, sir."

"Then we must find him," Jo said. "Come with me to search the grounds."

The one who'd found his voice turned toward the burning ruin of the house and asked, "What if he's in there?"

Then I'm in charge, Jo thought, feeling a sudden surge of hope. But he replied, "In that case, we can't help him. But we must be sure."

"He could be anywhere," another of them said. "Was he not with The Four? I mean, The Three?"

"He was," Jo said—and then it hit him.

If Takumi and his escorts were alive, if they'd escaped the house before it started to collapse, there was someplace where they could hide without leaving the grounds. Jo cursed himself again, for having overlooked the obvious.

"This way!" he snapped, and started toward the decorative garden with its secret buried in the shadow of a shrine.

BOLAN WAS TWENTY YARDS from the house when four Yakuza gunners spotted him and tried to bring him down. They had enough firepower, but they weren't coordinated, didn't think it through. Sometimes the hasty, crazy firing worked, scoring a lucky hit, but this was not one of those times.

A drop and roll left Bolan facing them, the Steyr AUG tracking to find them, while the Milkor's weight was slung across his back. He worked the skirmish line from left to right, scoping the fattest of the shooters first and drilling him below the loose knot of his necktie with a single 5.56 mm round from fifty feet. The gunner dropped to his knees, wide-eyed, and toppled over on the grass, twitching the final seconds of his life away.

That caused the other three to hesitate and reconsider their position, but they didn't have much time. The second round from Bolan's AUG opened another mobster's gut and knocked him sprawling, clutching at himself and bellowing in pain.

Leaving him to it, Bolan caught the third hardman as he turned to run, a grave mistake under the circumstances. Round three clipped his spine below the rib cage, shattered, blasting fragments through his stomach and liver, severing his descending aorta. Death was seconds away as he belly flopped onto the lawn, useless legs splayed behind him, immobile.

That left one, and he was smarter than the others, sizing up his target while the Executioner was taking down his friends. The shooter almost got it right, but jerked his submachine gun's trigger at the last second, instead of squeezing it. The burst that should have shattered Bolan's skull missed him by inches, chopping fresh 9 mm divots in the lawn.

The guy had missed his chance and seemed to know it, as the Steyr swung to find him, but he wasn't giving up. He shouted something in a high-pitched voice and stood his ground, ready to fire another burst and get it right this time—until his weapon jammed. The sudden, stunned expression on his face would have been comical, if it were not the look of death.

Bolan fired one more time, center of mass, and finished it. His target lingered for a heartbeat, spitting blood and still defying gravity, before his knees buckled and he fell over backward, landing with his arms outflung, embracing—what?

Bolan was in no hurry to find out.

Springing to his feet, he moved on in his circuit of the country home that had become a funeral pyre. He didn't know how many men were trapped inside there, roasting, and he felt no sympathy for any of them but Kayo, hoping the lieutenant had been able to escape—or, at the very least, that he had met a quicker, more merciful death.

If Bolan found Kayo, they could go on with the hunt together. Otherwise, he'd finish it alone.

But either way, the search for Kazuo Takumi wasn't finished yet.

KENICHI KAYO HAD escaped the burning house, in fact, but not before a falling ceiling beam had struck him, nearly knocking him unconscious, opening a ragged wound across his scalp that bled into his eyes. His jacket had caught fire at the same time, searing his cheek and left arm as he struggled to remove it. He had nearly lost his submachine gun in the process, but retrieved it from the fire before he fled, crashed headlong through a wall of *washi* paper and collapsed outside.

The trick was getting up again.

He could have lain there while the house crumbled around him, buried him in burning rubble, or Takumi's soldiers found him lying helpless on the porch and executed him. Instead, Kayo struggled to his feet, cast about him for a target or a clue.

Where would he find the Yakuza boss in the chaos of the once immaculate estate?

Kayo did not see the godfather, but he *did* spot Tadashi Jo, retreating from the house with three companions, moving briskly toward the estate's large garden. Were they leaving? Did they plan to meet their *oyabun* somewhere beyond the firelight? Either way, Jo was a target worth the effort, if Kayo could not find the man in charge.

He followed them, checking his Minebea PM-9 to verify that it had not been damaged during his near miss with fiery death. It seemed all right, and he picked up his pace, closing the gap as Jo's party neared an ornate gateway leading to the garden. Shadows lay beyond it, and Kayo feared that he might lose sight of them there, unless he stopped them now.

He shot the soldier farthest from the clan's first lieutenant first, no qualms about a short burst of 9 mm rounds into the gangster's back. The SMG's vertical fore grip helped him steady it, although the recoil sent a shock of pain along his scorched and throbbing arm.

The other hardmen were turning when he shot the second soldier, not a clean job, bullets ripping through the target's groin, but it was good enough to put him down. Tadashi Jo and the next-to-last man standing both returned fire, muzzle-flashes blinking at Kayo while he tried to hold his weapon steady, using its iron sights to frame the younger man, stitching holes across his chest.

Kayo never knew which of them finished him. Perhaps Jo, maybe both of them together. He could no more count the bullets striking him than he could trace them back to a specific weapon. As he fell, Kayo squeezed the trigger of the submachine gun he had taken from a dead man, emptying the Minebea's magazine in one half-second burst. Before he hit the sod, he saw Jo's soldier slump and crumple, while the second in command of Sumiyoshi-kai reached down to clutch a wounded leg.

It was the best that he could do.

Kayo flashed back to his meeting with the Monk, the blind man speaking of his chosen path, telling him, *Pursue it to the end.* He'd found the end now, felt the warm blood pulsing out from wounds below his rib cage, and was pleasantly surprised to feel no pain of any magnitude.

That's shock, he thought, and welcomed it.

A shadow loomed above Kayoi, blocking out the firelight from the crumbling house. Tadashi Jo coming to finish him?

Already done.

Kayo tried to reach his revolver, but his hand would not respond. The figure knelt beside him, pressing fingertips against his neck, and then Kayo felt nothing at all.

NO PULSE. KENICHI KAYO'S eyes were open, but whatever they might see, if anything, it was invisible to Bolan. Had some ancient mystery been solved, or was it simply darkness everlasting?

He had seen Kayo's last stand from a distance, ran to help him, but arrived too late. The cop had taken two Yakuza gunners with him, but Tadashi Jo, wounded, had limped and staggered through a gateway leading to Kazuo Takumi's garden, vanishing in shadows there. Bolan went after him, leaving the lieutenant where he lay.

Bolan already knew the garden sprawled over an acre, maybe more. He'd seen that much on Google Earth, but hadn't noted any feature that would serve Tadashi Jo as a sanctuary. If the fugitive just wanted darkness to prepare an ambush, he had come to the right place, but he was hurt now, and it would be difficult for him to scale the garden's wall, if he was planning on escape.

Bolan followed the garden path in front of him, proceeding cautiously and silently. After a few yards, he picked up the sound of someone moving in the dark ahead, dragging one foot and whimpering. He liked the sound of that and followed, picking up his pace.

Another minute, and the faint moonlight above showed him Tadashi Jo, no longer hobbling, standing dead still on the path, using his rifle as a cane and speaking softly. Talking to the shrubbery? Bolan could not translate his words, but from his tone, it seemed Jo was expecting a response.

And when it came, it was a muzzle-flash, low down, around knee level, winking twice. The bullets struck Jo with a killer one-two punch and dropped him facedown on the pathway's paving stones.

Bolan moved to his left, merged with the greenery and started edging forward. As he neared the spot where he had seen the muzzle-flashes, he made out a low rise in the ground and recognized a bunker, cunningly concealed by grass and ferns. He couldn't see the entrance, and he didn't need to. At the moment, he was more concerned about the gun ports.

He could think of only one good reason for a bunker on Kazuo Takumi's rural property: to hide the *oyabun* if things went terribly, irrevocably wrong. Whether Takumi was alone in there, Bolan could not have said and didn't care.

The bunker's occupants could fire out through their gun ports, which meant Bolan could fire *in*.

He slipped the Milkor off its shoulder sling and broke the cylinder, replacing its spent rounds with more incendiary loads. The 40 mm XM1060 thermobaric rounds were little versions of the hellish fuel-air bombs, more energetic than conventional condensed explosives. Each round used oxygen from the surrounding air to generate an intense, high-temperature explosion, featuring a longer blast wave than a normal HE round.

How much air could there be inside a bunker?

Bolan was about to answer that.

He'd marked the gun port, memorized its placement, knowing that there had to be others. They would only help him, if he placed his first round properly, drawing more oxygen inside to fuel the roiling flames.

Using the weapon's reflex sight, he aimed, held steady and squeezed off. The Milkor made its standard popping sound, and then all hell broke loose. There was a flash, low down, and then the fire seemed to be sucked inside the bunker, blossoming within while startled voices screamed. Along the sloped side of the bunker, tongues of flame licked out from two more gun ports.

Bolan waited, reasonably sure he'd never know who was inside the pillbox, frying, then a door he hadn't seen flew open and a smoking figure spilled onto the grass outside. Waiting for more people to follow, Bolan gave it twenty seconds, then decided no one else was coming.

Switching off, he drew the Glock and moved to stand above the supine figure. It was Kazuo Takumi, his clothes in smoky tatters, with the left side of his face heat-shriveled, glistening. His breath came out in little panting gasps, lungs seared, a wound no medic could have healed.

"Gaijin," he gasped.

"That's me," Bolan acknowledged.

"Why...have you...destroyed me?"

"Not just you. Your family."

Takumi forced a smile at that. "You cannot...stop... the Sumiyoshi-kai."

"I meant your other family," Bolan replied. "Your son's dead. Killed himself, trying to help a psycho-cult spray anthrax over Tokyo."

He saw the knife go in, could almost feel it twist. Takumi's good eye leaked a drop of sorrow. "Toi?"

"You leave nothing behind except bad memories. They'll be forgotten soon."

"But...why?"

Bolan considered how to answer, then discovered there was no one left to hear him. With a final wheeze, Kazuo Takumi had checked out.

Now it was Bolan's turn. He glanced back toward the embers that had been a stylish home, saw half a dozen hardmen staring at the ruins, and he left them to it. Fading back into the night, he focused on a job that still demanded his attention.

EPILOGUE

Marunouchi, Tokyo

It was a fine day in the capital. The air was relatively clear for Tokyo, and Colonel Fulian Sun had picked a café on Hibiya Dori, near the Imperial Garden Theater, for his lunchtime meeting with Captain Takahira Amago of the Metropolitan Police.

Amago had called twice before Sun answered, at his office in the Chinese embassy. The colonel had been tempted to ignore him, but the man knew things. If arrested, he could link Sun to Saikosai Raito, to Susumu Kodama and the anthrax plot. Sun had diplomatic immunity, of course, but he could still be exposed and expelled from Japan as *persona non grata*. That, in turn, would mean denials from Beijing, blame shifted onto Sun alone, an exercise in fervent hand-washing.

And it would mean a firing squad.

His masters, if accused of plotting terrorism, would be honor-bound to sacrifice a scapegoat. And who better than a rogue agent who'd overstepped his bounds— or, better, yet, who'd gone insane? Sun would confess, of course; that was inevitable. In his final statement, he would thoroughly exonerate his various superiors and shoulder all the blame himself.

It was the least that he could do, to keep the remnants of his family alive.

But it would only come to that if Amago broke down and spilled his guts. That was a gross American expression, but in this case, Sun regarded it appropriate.

He hoped the captain might, quite literally, spill his guts, an act of expiation to his homeland through seppuku, capped by a confession to his role in the conspiracy, with no mention of Sun, China or anyone outside Japan.

And if Amago chose some other path…well, there were ways for suicide to be arranged.

"YOU'RE LATE," THE colonel said, as Captain Amago approached his sidewalk table. Even now, with all their plans in ruins, Sun still radiated smug superiority.

"It's busy at headquarters, as you might imagine, Colonel."

"Well, you're here now. What exactly do you want?"

No mention of Amago's rank or any other gesture of respect, however small. Amago felt his cheeks warming, anger the first emotion he had felt besides pure dread, since learning that their plan had failed.

"Master Kodama has been found," he said. "With Toi Takumi, in a safe house used by the police department. It appears that a lieutenant kidnapped and interrogated both of them, then caught Kazuo Takumi's helicopters on the ground, destroying them before they carried out their mission."

"One man did all that?" Sun asked him, sounding skeptical.

"We're looking into that, of course. So far, we have identified no cohorts."

"You're lucky, then. The trail ends with Kodama and Toi Takumi."

"For now, but when investigators focus on Saikosai Raito—"

"There is something to consider," Sun said, interrupting him. "If you are troubled by the prospect of investigation and exposure, you may wish to—"

When the colonel's head exploded, Amago first thought he was hallucinating, but the spray of blood that flecked his face seemed real enough. He raised a hand to wipe it off, but only smeared it as the nearly headless corpse of Fulian Sun sagged in its chair and slithered toward the pavement. The remaining portion of Sun's mouth sneered at Amago, mocking him even in grisly death.

Sniper, he thought, but there had been no sound of gunfire.

Silencer.

Amago sat, waiting his turn to die, then realized that if another shot were coming, it should already have struck him down. He bolted to his feet, then, knowing he could not let himself be found with a decapitated Chinese spy.

And as he turned to run, a squad car pulled in to the curb. Three officers got out, led by a major Amago recognized, from the National Police Agency's Organized Crime Department. The new arrivals stared at Amago and at his leaking lunch companion, sizing up the situation in an instant.

"So," the major said, "it seems the information we received was accurate."

"What information?" Amago demanded.

The reply ignored his question. "Captain, you will come with us. I'm placing you under arrest."

* * * * *

COMING SOON FROM

GOLD EAGLE®

Available August 4, 2015

THE EXECUTIONER® #441
MURDER ISLAND – *Don Pendleton*

On an uncharted island, a psychotic hunter stalks the ultimate prey: man. His newest targets are an international arms dealer—a criminal who was in CIA custody when his plane was shot down—and Mack Bolan, the Executioner.

STONY MAN® #138
WAR TACTIC – *Don Pendleton*

Tensions between China and the Philippines are on the rise, and a series of pirate attacks on Filipino ports and vessels only makes things worse. Phoenix Force discovers that the pirates are armed with American weapons, while Able Team must hunt down the mastermind behind the attacks.

OUTLANDERS® #74
ANGEL OF DOOM – *James Axler*

The Cerberus fighters must battle Charun and Vanth, alien gods intent on opening a portal to bring their kind to earth. If the alien forces succeed, an invasion from a barbaric dimension will lay siege to Europe…and beyond.

COMING SOON FROM

GOLD EAGLE®

Available September 1, 2015

GOLD EAGLE EXECUTIONER®
SYRIAN RESCUE – *Don Pendleton*

Tasked with rescuing UN diplomats lost in the Syrian desert, Mack Bolan is in a deadly race against time—and against fighters willing to make the ultimate sacrifice.

GOLD EAGLE SUPERBOLAN®
LETHAL RISK – *Don Pendleton*

A search-and-rescue mission to recover a high-ranking defector in China leads Mack Bolan to a government-sanctioned organ-harvesting facility.

GOLD EAGLE DEATHLANDS®
CHILD OF SLAUGHTER – *James Axler*

When Doc is kidnapped by a band of marauders in what was once Nebraska, Ryan and the companions join forces with a beautiful but deadly woman with an agenda of her own...

GOLD EAGLE ROGUE ANGEL™
THE MORTALITY PRINCIPLE – *Alex Archer*

In Prague researching the legend of the Golem, archaeologist Annja Creed uncovers a string of murders that seems linked to the creature. And Annja is the next target...

CNMGE0815

The truck lurched forward along the side of the hill, and for a heart-stopping moment Bolan thought it was going to roll. Then he got it straightened and drove down to the road again. He hit the gas, heading straight toward the larger truck.

Seeing the oncoming vehicle, the bigger vehicle honked its horn, but Bolan didn't stop. When the two trucks were a hundred yards apart, he opened the door and dived onto the ground, rolling hard with the impact.

At that speed, the big truck couldn't turn aside fast enough. The front crashed into the smaller truck on the passenger side, crumpling the hood and engine compartment and sending the Italian truck flying through the air.

The large cargo truck hit its brakes after the impact, shuddering to a stop. Bolan didn't wait around to find out what they were doing. The moment he stopped rolling, he got up and bolted back to the truck, ignoring the steady stabs of pain from his left leg every time it hit the ground. He reached the vehicle, which Liao had thoughtfully backed up for him. Diving into the back, he banged his knee painfully on the machine gun on the floor as he yelled, "Go, go, go!"

Liao hit it and the truck sped away. "They'll never catch us now!" he shouted, pounding the roof with his fist. "We did it!"

"We aren't in Mongolia yet!" Bolan slumped against the tailgate, breathing heavily. His leg twitched, and he noticed his phone was vibrating.

He dug it out and answered. "We're—"

Akira Tokaido's voice screamed in his ear. "Missile! Evacuate the vehicle—they've locked-on an antitank missile!"

"Stop now! Right now!" Bolan yelled to Liao as he shoved the phone into his pocket and grabbed the machine gun with his other hand.

The truck skidded to a halt, and as the other man turned to him, Bolan yelled, "Incoming missile. Get out now!"

Liao scrabbled at the door handle and got it open as Bolan hit the ground on the other side of the rear door. He made sure Liao was scrambling away from the truck before running himself.

As he did, he saw the bright flash of a missile launch about a kilometer away, and shouted, "Hit the dirt!" as he dived to the ground.

Two seconds later the world exploded.

Don't miss
LETHAL RISK by Don Pendleton,
available September 2015 wherever
Gold Eagle® books and ebooks are sold.